# The Raven Thief

## Also by Gigi Pandian

# The Raven Thief

*A Secret Staircase Mystery*

Gigi Pandian

**MINOTAUR BOOKS**
**NEW YORK**

First published in the United States by Minotaur Books, an imprint of St. Martin's Publishing Group

THE RAVEN THIEF. Copyright © 2023 by Gigi Pandian. All rights reserved. Printed in the United States of America. For information, address St. Martin's Publishing Group, 120 Broadway, New York, NY 10271.

www.minotaurbooks.com

Designed by Gabriel Guma

The Library of Congress Cataloging-in-Publication Data is available upon request.

ISBN 978-1-250-80501-0 (hardcover)
ISBN 978-1-250-80502-7 (ebook)

Our books may be purchased in bulk for promotional, educational, or business use. Please contact your local bookseller or the Macmillan Corporate and Premium Sales Department at 1-800-221-7945, extension 5442, or by email at MacmillanSpecialMarkets@macmillan.com.

First Edition: 2023

10  9  8  7  6  5  4  3  2  1

*For Pa*

# The Raven Thief

# Chapter 1

**H**igh in her hidden turret, concealed by oak trees on the steep hillside and disguised by its improbability on top of a supposedly normal house, the conversation was not going the direction Tempest had hoped.

"Don't do it." She held out her hand. "I'm serious. You'll regret it."

Her companion didn't drop the item he held tightly. For three seconds, he didn't move at all. Then, he had the audacity to smile as he moved his hand closer to his lips.

"I warned you." Tempest looked away, shifting her gaze to the window slit of the secret tower. She didn't want to see him suffer.

But . . . she was curious by nature, much to her detriment. She turned back in time to see him gasp. He didn't cough—he'd been a stage performer long enough to know how to suppress a cough—yet his hands flew to his neck and he gasped for air.

"Back in a sec." Tempest ran down the first of her two secret staircases. It was crude and narrow, with steps more like a slanted ladder than real stairs. If Tempest hadn't climbed those steps thousands of times, she would have carefully backed out. Instead, with her hands on the smooth larch wood handrails, she was nearly flying as she skidded downward. Once she reached the second and proper secret staircase, lights clicked on every few steps as she passed hidden sensors. Three seconds later she reached the kitchen, where she found sweet coconut-milk rice pudding in the fridge.

Not pausing to make sure she'd closed the fridge door behind her, she lifted the wing of the dragon sconce in the hallway and the hidden door slid open once more. She bounded up the stairs two at a time.

Sanjay's face was bright red when she reached him, out of breath. He scooped a heaping spoonful of the rice pudding into his mouth and gave a contented sigh. "I thought you didn't want me to have Ash's donuts so you could have them all to yourself."

"Is that what you think of me?" She couldn't tell if his shrug of a reply was directed at her or was an expression of his relief. Rice and sugar were much better antidotes to spice-induced suffering than water. She also didn't want to admit to herself the not insubstantial grain of truth in his assumption.

"You weren't kidding that these donuts weren't regular pastries. Who puts chili peppers in dessert? These death donuts are all yours."

Tempest took a bite of one of her grandfather's heavenly snacks. This batch of vada donuts—one of Grandpa Ash's unique treats he'd created after retiring—was exquisite. A perfect balance of heat and sweet.

The hidden turret above Tempest's bedroom was only accessible through the two sets of secret staircases. Many people knew about the existence of the first secret staircase that led to her bedroom, even if they didn't know how to activate it.

The octagonal secret room at the very top of the house was one Tempest didn't reveal to many people.

From the yard, the turret looked like an ornamental spire on a quirky house built by Secret Staircase Construction as an experiment, as Tempest's parents tried out their ideas on themselves before bringing their unique brand of renovation to the homes of other people. In reality, the turret hid a cozy spot for Tempest to think while unencumbered by the world below. After moving back into her childhood bedroom last summer after her world had collapsed, it was a welcome retreat. No matter how dire the immediate circumstances, how much heartbreak and destruction surrounded her, and how frustrating it was to have moved back home into her childhood bedroom after losing her own house, the sight of her very own magical secret staircases appearing before her eyes never failed to lift her spirits.

"In spite of your attempt to kill me," Sanjay said, "I'm glad we have this time to ourselves." He took a step toward her. A lock from his artfully disheveled black hair swept across his forehead, causing Tempest's stomach to do a little flip-flop.

*Damn.* Why, again, had she thought bringing him up here was a good idea?

Sanjay gave her a shy smile. Tempest groaned. Sanjay was many things, but shy was not one of them.

Ever.

She crossed her arms and glared at him. "What are you hiding from me?"

He blinked rapidly, but quickly recovered. "You mean this?" He grinned as a bouquet of posies materialized in his previously empty hand, as if from thin air.

*Not bad*, Tempest admitted to herself. He was dressed not in the tuxedo and bowler hat he wore when he performed on stage as The Hindi Houdini, but in a black short-sleeved T-shirt and chinos. The flowers literally couldn't have been up his sleeve.

She accepted the bouquet. "Nice cover. You're avoiding telling me something." She looked for more signs that he was hiding something but instead found herself getting distracted by his slightly parted lips and large brown eyes. They'd dated once, years ago, when their lives made it impossible to spend much time together. But now that they were both in Northern California within a few miles of each other . . .

*Focus, Tempest.*

"You're not planning on asking me to be your assistant again, are you?" She'd been the one to command far larger audiences than he ever had. Until the night it all fell apart.

"What? Of course not." He cleared his throat.

She raised an eyebrow at him.

"It's impossible to say no to Lavinia," he blurted out.

Of all the things she'd imagined he might say, that wasn't one of them. Tempest's dad's company had recently finished renovating a section of Lavinia Kingsley's house. Secret Staircase Construction didn't do normal home renovations. They specialized in bringing real-life magic into people's homes through touches like handcrafted sliding bookcases that opened when you pulled a favorite book from the shelf, hand-carved grotesques with hidden levers leading to secret rooms, and now that Tempest was working for her dad, personalized magical stories accompanied every nook.

Fifty-five-year-old Lavinia Kingsley, who ran popular local café Veggie Magic, had kicked out her cheating husband a few months ago. Her soon-to-be ex-husband, Corbin, had once used their large, luxurious hillside basement as an office for his writing. Now that he no longer lived there, Lavinia's directive to Tempest's dad was to turn the space from Corbin's writing cave into a combination of a meeting space for her book club, home office, and reading nook. There was enough space for all three.

"It's your fault I'm in this impossible situation," Sanjay huffed. "I only went to Lavinia's café in the first place to help you trap that homicidal maniac. By then it was too late. I was hooked by her pie."

It was a fair critique. But Tempest wasn't feeling especially generous today. Or for the past several months, if she was honest about it. Not since her life plan had been yanked out from under her. She'd taken steps to put it back together, but it still felt like a jigsaw puzzle with not quite enough pieces slotted into place to see what picture would be revealed. Six months ago, Tempest would never have imagined she'd have gone from a headlining illusionist in Las Vegas to the storyteller who brought magical elements to Secret Staircase Construction and who was secretly looking into a family murder she'd only recently learned wasn't an accident. But sabotage and family curses will do that to a well-planned life.

"She's not easy to say no to," Tempest admitted. The struggles of the renovation were fresh in her mind. "What did she convince you to do?"

"Perform at her housewarming party."

"That's great." Tempest gave him a smile. A genuine one. She knew he didn't usually accept small jobs, since he was successful enough these days to have large audiences and paychecks, but gigs for friends kept him grounded.

"Try the opposite of great," Sanjay insisted.

"It's good for you to accept requests from friends. I can't imagine she'd want you to do a dangerous act. Besides, she can't recreate the Ganges River in her backyard." Sanjay had once escaped from a coffin tossed into the Ganges River in India. It wasn't even one of his most dramatic stunts.

"She doesn't want just any type of performance. She wants a *fake séance*. I'm supposed to help christen in her new, post-Corbin life with a séance that will banish his spirit from the property."

Tempest's smile disappeared. "But he's not dead."

"You think I didn't point that out? She insisted it was symbolic. I didn't mean to say yes."

"Then tell her no."

"You agreed it's impossible to say no to that woman."

"We both know nothing good happens when you agree to do a fake séance."

"Why do I have to be so damn good at them?" Sanjay was entirely serious. The man had a healthy ego. "You know they're a waste of my talents. You're the one who included a séance table in the new layout."

Tempest scowled at him. "Don't blame this on me. It's not a 'séance table.' It's simply a round table. My design included that table for her book club meetings."

"Your dad built the table with hidden drawers and secret hiding nooks. She told me about them so I could use them to create illusions for the séance."

"Of course he did. We're 'Secret Staircase Construction.' We don't do minimalism. What does she want you to do?"

He shrugged. "She left the details to me but wanted something cathartic to feel like she's banishing Corbin Colt from her life. What kind of name is that anyway? He sounds like an '80s action movie hero."

"It might be a pen name. 'Corbin' means 'raven.' He plays that up in his supernatural thrillers."

"He's a writer? Never heard of him."

"We were born a couple of decades too late. He had some

bestsellers more than thirty years ago, but hasn't been popular for a long time. He's a handsome guy now, but he still uses a thirty-year-old author photo on his book jackets. According to Lavinia, that's why he's started having affairs."

"Because he still uses an old photo?"

Tempest rolled her eyes. "Because he's washed up. He's grasping at fame that he had ages ago and can't recreate. He recently turned sixty, which apparently was the catalyst."

Sanjay snorted. "It wasn't the catalyst."

"Until thirty seconds ago, you didn't even know who he was, besides being Lavinia's almost-ex-husband."

"Doesn't matter. If he's insecure enough to need to start cheating because he celebrated a particular birthday, one that isn't even that old, he was most certainly having affairs before now."

"Wisdom from your mentalism act?"

Sanjay nodded. "I wish I could forget everything I learned about people when I was performing those shows."

Sanjay was charming enough to be a natural with mentalism, pretending to be a mind reader. Except he hated it. Some of the things he intuited about people, even in the context of a fanciful magic show, disturbed him. He was successful enough these days that he didn't have to perform mentalism acts. Or séances, for that matter. But he wasn't kidding. It really was impossible to say no to Lavinia Kingsley.

"Since you know the space so well," Sanjay continued, "that's why I was hoping—"

Tempest's phone rang. She was fairly certain he'd been about to ask her to be his assistant, but he was saved from her comeback by the name that flashed across the screen. Lavinia Kingsley.

Sanjay's eyes grew wide. "I'm not here. Whatever you say, I'm not with you."

"Hi, Lav—" Tempest began, but she couldn't even finish the name before Lavinia spoke over her.

"My new basement was burglarized."

"*What?*" Hidden Creek could sometimes feel stiflingly small, but burglaries and robberies were uncommon.

"He wrecked everything."

"*He?* You saw who—?"

"It was Corbin." Lavinia's wrath came through as clearly as if she'd been in the turret with Tempest and Sanjay. "I'm going to kill him."

# Chapter 2

How bad is it?" Tempest stepped through the carved wooden archway leading to the newly remodeled basement that Lavinia herself had named "Lavinia's Lair." Tempest's dad, Darius, had carved four skeleton keys into the cedar, signifying the four members of Lavinia's book club, the Detection Keys. Tempest ran her fingers over the smooth wood of the most ornate key, with a skull and crossbones on top, before following Lavinia inside.

Sanjay had begged off, saying he had to practice for an upcoming show. It was true, yet Tempest suspected he would have made time if he wasn't afraid of seeing Lavinia and agreeing to even more than he already had.

"Corbin didn't damage anything your team built," said Lavinia. "I thought he did at first, because my papers were strewn about. Sorry you had to come out here needlessly. Turns out he did something far worse."

Tempest felt her skin prickle. "What?"

"I'll show you."

Like much of Hidden Creek, Lavinia's house stood on a steep hillside. A half-hidden basement was mostly underground, leaving room for windows and a door on only one wall. As newlyweds nearly thirty years ago, Lavinia and Corbin had converted the unused space into Corbin's home office for writing. Lavinia could have moved into a new house to get a fresh start, but she loved her home and its views of the wild hillside.

The basement wasn't accessible from the house above. Like the nearby detached garage, it could only be reached by an external door. Inside, the underground space had previously been two dark rooms with high ceilings but only a sliver of natural light from two small windows. Tempest took a moment to appreciate the space she and the Secret Staircase Construction team had converted from a dim basement office into a bright and airy getaway. They'd expanded the windows, knocked down an oddly placed interior wall that hadn't been load-bearing, and added a new partition to separate an entry hallway and half bathroom.

It had been up to Tempest to interview Lavinia to figure out what stories to tell through the physical details. Then the rest of the team figured out structural issues and constructed the pieces. They had only just wrapped up the build.

Three distinct sections now filled the open-plan space: a cozy spot for book club gatherings, a reading nook, and a home office for Lavinia to work on business related to her café, Veggie Magic. It no longer resembled the dark and moody space where Corbin attempted to write a worthy follow-up to *The Raven*, his big hit debut novel that Tempest had always considered a rip-off of Poe. The book followed a man seeking the truth about his wife's unsolved murder. She'd been found with the feathers of a large black bird surrounding her. As the story progresses, the grieving widower begins to suspect that he himself transforms into a raven when he blacks out. But that setup wasn't the hook that turned the book into a bestseller. The ending twist was a good one, Tempest had to admit. But tucked away in his basement office, surrounded by many of the creepy ravens gifted to him by readers, Corbin was never able to write a worthy successor.

Now the first thing anyone entering the underground lair would see when they emerged from the entry hallway was a cozy pub, which they'd named the "Oxford Comma." It was designed to look as if you'd stumbled across a narrow cobblestone lane in Oxford, England, as a nod to Dorothy Sayers's Lord Peter Whimsey and Harriet Vane novels, Edmund Crispin's *The Moving Toyshop*, and other Golden Age mystery novels set in Oxford that Lavinia loved. A merry-go-round horse stood next to the Oxford Comma's antique door, both of which Tempest had found at a salvage yard, and two stone gargoyles looked down from above. The faux pub's walls didn't reach the ceiling, but instead were capped to look like ramparts from the walls of an Oxford college.

To unlock the door, you had to feed a special treat to the merry-go-round horse—a coin from the basket dangling from his mouth. The horse's jaw pivoted, so if you looked closely, you could activate the lever without a coin. Inside, this was the section of Lavinia's Lair where the book club would meet around the round table with secret compartments—the table Sanjay would be using for his séance in a couple of days.

Tempest had made the initial sketch proposals based on the intersection of Lavinia's favorite classic mysteries and what Lavinia wanted to get functionally out of the space, all the while keeping in mind that the result needed to be not just practical—but magical. To simulate the magic of a cozy pub, there was space on the wall for the projection of a flickering fireplace that could be turned on by a remote control.

Stepping out of the Oxford Comma and looking to the right, you'd find a reading nook through a bamboo forest, which captured details from the Japanese *honkaku* and *shin honkaku* mystery novels Lavinia loved. To reach the nook, you had to walk through a short passageway that looked like a limestone cave from Seishi Yokomizo's *The Village of Eight Graves* and a mini bamboo forest with hidden glass apothecary jars labeled with the names of various metals, a nod to Soji Shimada's *The Tokyo Zodiac Murders*. The short path ended at a comfy armchair of purple fabric next to a side table large enough for a reading lamp, mug, and a few books below. This was Lavinia's personal reading nook.

Beyond the bamboo forest and limestone cave was a reproduction of a dahabeya riverboat, inspired by Agatha Christie's *Death on the Nile,* though much smaller than the one that would have transported Poirot down the Nile on that perilous journey. In this version, only one decorative sail emerged from the wooden riverboat, and instead of multiple rooms, only the infamous lounge had been recreated. An antique wooden desk was the biggest piece of furniture in the room, where Lavinia worked from home when she wasn't at Veggie Magic. A computer was discretely hidden by a rolltop desk.

A river surrounded the boat, though the water was an illusion, only a painting on the floor. You could walk across the river, since it wasn't either water or a trench, but that wouldn't get you inside the boat. The riverboat was five feet above the floor. Under it was the only storage space beyond the visible bookshelves in the pub. To get inside the raised riverboat, unless you felt like getting a workout by hoisting yourself up the high base, you needed to know the secret to getting the gangplank stairway to descend.

Lavinia stepped on a spot on the painted river that looked like a simple stone but in reality was a lever. What looked like a wooden crate on the edge of the boat unfolded into a stairway, and the two of them walked up the steps to the home-office riverboat.

"He took my old Remington typewriter." Lavinia jabbed her finger at the steamer trunk that served as a coffee table. "The one with a katakana keyboard my mother gave me."

"Why does he want a Japanese typewriter?"

"It's a novelty that isn't worth much." Lavinia balled her hands into fists before relaxing them. "A true Japanese typewriter is incredibly complex. Katakana typewriters are simpler. The keys mirror Western letters on a standard keyboard. It was a gift from my mother, since it's a linguistic combination of Japan and the West, like me. Corbin only wanted it because I love it."

Lavinia Kingsley had long ago gotten used to the confusion her name caused people. Named after a beloved relative of her father, she'd been born in Japan to a Japanese mother and British father who'd been studying Japanese literature. Her father had passed away several years ago at age ninety, and her eighty-seven-year-old mother had been fine on her own until she had a bad fall. Refusing to move into assisted living, Kumiko moved in with her daughter. Temporarily, Kumiko insisted. Needing a wheelchair annoyed her to no end because it made people question her competence even further, never considering that she might hold a PhD or speak an assortment of languages fluently. Lavinia had gotten her love of classic mysteries from her mother, who had a PhD in Japanese and comparative literature. Kumiko was a scholar of the *honkaku* style of classic Japanese detective fiction—roughly the equivalent of a Western whodunit with a fair-play puzzle plot—among other literary topics.

It was Kumiko who discovered Lavinia's husband's infidelities. Even though Corbin had known her for nearly three decades, he continued to underestimate her.

"Why would he take a Japanese typewriter but not mess with anything else?" Tempest scanned the room. *What was it that felt off?*

"He knows how much that piece of metal means to me. It's not worth much, if anything. I wouldn't put it past him to have tossed it into a dumpster on his way home. My mom gave it to me when I first got a job as a bookseller. It's one of the few things I owned from my life before Corbin Colt. I've had it since I worked at the bookstore where I met him. That's why he wanted it. To take my life away from me." Lavinia paused and took a deep breath. When she spoke again, the anger was gone. "I really thought damage had been done to the construction at first. I'm sorry I called you before thinking."

"I could look around just in case one of the crew moved it while finishing the riverboat—"

"It was him. He stole it."

The more Lavinia spoke, the more it seemed like she was trying to convince herself. She was clearly distressed. Was she thinking rationally?

"I haven't changed the locks in this section of the house," Lavinia continued. "Only the main house I live in. Besides your crew, he's the only one with a key. With so many workers coming and going, and the fact that it's not accessible from the main house, I thought I'd wait until the work was done. I know, I know. Your team finished up a few days ago. I've been so busy planning for the housewarming party that I didn't do it. I was foolish not to do so. And now he's got it. Only . . ."

"Only *what?*"

Lavinia hesitated before speaking. "I've got a security camera for the front door of the house. Just one. It's wide-angle, so it picks up the image of anyone who comes into the basement as well. It's not on all the time but turns on when it detects motion. I looked. I didn't see Corbin."

"So, it wasn't him?"

"It wasn't anyone. *Nobody* left here with that typewriter. But the thing is . . ." She trailed off.

Tempest waited a few moments. Patience was never one of her strong suits. She walked over to the windows. They looked like they were large enough for a person to fit through, but she knew no one could. The windows only opened a few inches, to let in fresh air and a breeze. She cracked the window next to the riverboat. A bird on a nearby branch took offense and cawed.

Lavinia nearly jumped out of her skin. "*That's* what has me annoyed." She pulled the window shut. "Annoyed at myself, really. For letting the thought even enter my mind."

"What thought?"

"The only thing that triggered the video during the right time frame was a raven."

# Chapter 3

A raven," Tempest repeated.

Lavinia's face darkened. "I know Corbin's supernatural thrillers aren't real. But these last few months have messed with my sense of reality. That's why I needed this space."

A bird cawed from outside. Somewhere nearby. Tempest looked out the window, but no birds were in sight. She drummed her fingertips on the glass before spinning around. "What if Corbin isn't *quite* that big a jerk?"

Lavinia scoffed.

"He could have simply hidden it," Tempest said.

"I thought of that. I looked around. Didn't find anything. I need to take care of some paperwork, but feel free to look for yourself. I thought there might be hidden nooks I hadn't found yet, but I spoke to your father about it. He said I knew about everything you'd all built."

"He's at another job site today, otherwise I'm sure he would have come over as well."

"That's what he said. I'm glad you had time to stop by with how much the business is booming."

It was going so well that Tempest hadn't had time to catch

her breath to plan all the other things she was supposed to be doing in her life. She was at the beginning stages of building her own house (so she wouldn't be living in her childhood bedroom forever), was planning a farewell stage show her manager had arranged to be televised, and was still trying to find out what had really happened on two of the worst nights of her life.

Tempest began her search for the missing typewriter there on the riverboat. The steamer trunk coffee table was more than it seemed. It was their version of a "smuggler's nook" on the boat—a place to hide things. There wasn't room to build it below the faux boat without giving up too much storage space beneath it, so instead the steamer trunk coffee table was more than it seemed. When you first opened the lid of the trunk, you'd see what you believed was the bottom of an empty trunk. That was an optical illusion. The black velvet base was false. Tempest lifted it up. The *real* bottom of the trunk was empty as well.

"That was the first place I looked." Lavinia took the false bottom from Tempest's hands and put it back in place.

Tempest moved on to the Oxford high-street pub. She fed the merry-go-round horse a coin. A faint *click* sounded as the Oxford Comma pub's door unlocked. Lavinia had already searched for the typewriter, so it couldn't be hidden anywhere obvious. But Secret Staircase Construction's architecture was anything but obvious. Around the central table, the two walls framing the door were lined with high bookcases. The oak shelves, built by her dad, were filled with a combination of books and bookish knickknacks, from pen-filled mugs with cute sayings like "happiness is pie and a good book" to candles with labels that noted the scent as "old books."

The books on the shelves were old, but not like what Tempest thought of as "movie-set library" old. These weren't leather-bound tomes with matching spines. Most were decades-old paperbacks with spines so cracked it was a miracle they held together at all. The only shelf containing books that looked remotely uniform showed a cluster of bright spines; modern reprints of classic crime fiction reissued by the British Library. Tempest stepped onto a chair to look on top of the bookcases. Empty. She jumped down.

There was no way Secret Staircase Construction would renovate a space devoted to scenes from books and *not* include a sliding bookcase. (Though, ironically, they rarely built secret staircases. Most of their work inside homes wasn't that invasive.) Tempest tugged on a hardback edition of John Dickson Carr's *The Dead Sleep Lightly*. Moving the book freed a pin held in place by the weight of the novel. With the bookcase unlocked, Tempest slid it to the side. It only moved two feet, and the opening didn't lead anywhere since there was nowhere to go. Instead, a shallow cutout left space for two cushions that could make a comfy reading nook if Lavinia or any of her guests were ever inclined to read in a nook like the cozy hand-built forts of their childhoods instead of in a proper armchair.

Tempest lifted the cushions. There was nothing there. It was hardly big enough for a hiding spot anyway.

The back wall held a built-in kitchenette with an electric kettle, a small porcelain sink, a beer-keg tap that wasn't yet hooked up, and open shelving with accoutrements for tea and coffee. There was no fridge, but a glass jar of cookies rested on the butcher-block countertop next to the kettle.

Tempest's silver charm bracelet caught a beam of light. The charm bracelet meant even more to Tempest now than it had five years ago when her mom had given it to her as a twenty-first-birthday gift—right before Emma Raj vanished, never to be seen again.

Tempest's adult life had begun with the tragedy, and it continued to loom over her whole family. How could she truly be free without knowing what had really happened?

Each charm of the birthday gift bracelet represented Tempest and her mom's shared love of magic. A clue hidden in the bracelet's charms had gotten Tempest one step closer to figuring out what had happened to her mom when she vanished. But Tempest hadn't made nearly as much progress solving the mystery as she'd hoped. Cold cases were difficult, more difficult for an amateur, and even more difficult when the official verdict was death by suicide.

"I told you I searched," Lavinia said as Tempest emerged from the pub. Lavinia was seated at her desk in the riverboat, typing on a laptop. The windows of the riverboat were open spaces, not filled with glass like the sole window of the pub, so they could talk to each other as clearly as if they'd been standing eight feet apart in a living room. Tempest kicked down the doorstop of the pub's door to hold it open.

Instead of stepping onto the gangplank stairway to join Lavinia back on the riverboat, Tempest opened the storage room beneath. The space was just under five feet high, so she couldn't stand, but a light illuminated the empty space. It wasn't *completely* empty. A mirror rested against the wall. The four-foot square mirror was originally purchased with the idea of reflecting more light into the basement, but when they decided to enlarge the windows (since they had to knock down part of the wall to fix dry rot anyway), the mirror was no longer needed. But Lavinia liked the one they'd sourced, so she'd kept it. Tempest tilted it forward. Nothing was behind it. Not even dust. She squatted and pivoted on the balls of her feet as she looked around the tiny room. Closing her eyes, she thought about where a typewriter could be hidden. The storage space smelled of freshly cut and treated wood.

She bumped her head as she backed out of the storage space—and nearly bumped into someone outside the door.

"Don't sneak up on an old woman," the wheelchair's owner said, but the hint of a mischievous smile hovered on her lips as she turned her head to speak.

Since Lavinia's mother, Kumiko Kingsley, was temporarily in need of the wheelchair, one of Lavinia's requests for the Secret Staircase team was that everything be accessible. They'd succeeded with everything in the basement except for the riverboat gangplank, which would have needed to stretch out across most of the room to have a reasonable incline. Kumiko insisted she'd be walking again soon and that Lavinia didn't want her prying in her home office anyway, so they went with an unfolding staircase for the riverboat.

"How's Ashok?" Kumiko asked.

Tempest smiled. "Didn't you see him two days ago when he brought lunch to the crew?" Kumiko and Tempest's grandfather had gotten to be friends since she'd moved in with Lavinia.

"Two days is a long time. And where's my daughter?"

Tempest shifted her gaze to the riverboat desk. "Lavinia was here a minute ago."

"You're taking the Case of the Missing Typewriter?"

Tempest winced. "I wouldn't put it exactly like that."

She pointed a bony finger at Tempest. "Don't deny it. I know you solved that girl's murder when the police had the wrong fellow."

Tempest wished she could forget that on her first job for Secret Staircase Construction, her stage double had been found dead inside a wall that had been sealed for nearly a century.

"Did she tell you I gave it to her?" Kumiko continued. "The typewriter. Not a dead body. I bought it shortly after I met her father at university in Osaka."

Like her daughter, Kumiko defied stereotypes. Tempest loved her for it. Kumiko and her English husband had taught at several universities across the world before settling in Northern California, where Lavinia spent the later years of her childhood.

Kumiko made a habit of playing along with people's assumptions until she could speak up and send them off with their tail between their legs. "No English," she had been known to feign, with a supplicating gesture, when someone had assumed so first. It was an amusing proposition since she'd been a lecturer at Oxford for a time.

Kumiko looked up at Tempest. "You didn't answer my question about your grandfather."

"He's been missing Morag since she's been away." Tempest didn't *think* Kumiko's flirtation with her grandfather was anything more than bonding over good food and the shared experience of being Asian foreigners in the U.K. in the 1970s. Still, it wouldn't hurt to remind Kumiko that Grannie Mor would be back from Scotland next week.

Lavinia appeared around the corner of the hallway entrance, carrying a banker's box. She dropped it in front of the merry-go-round horse. It landed with a thud.

"The last of Corbin's papers I found around the house." Lavinia wiped her hands together, as if washing off invisible dirt. "I'm going to burn them after the séance and read a few lines of his terrible prose as I toss the pages into a bonfire. That'll rid the last of his spirit from this place." She gave a satisfied nod.

Tempest looked past the box, into the open door of the pub. An old paperback novel rested in the center of the table. Anthony Berkeley's *The Poisoned Chocolates Case*. A stolen typewriter was such a small thing. . . . Would Corbin have used his key simply to steal the old typewriter, or was something more going on? It's not like Corbin would have put poison in the coffee or tea. . . . Would he?

"You'd better replace the coffee and tea." Tempest pointed toward the kitchenette. "And those cookies."

Lavinia gave a nervous laugh. "You think the typewriter theft is a diversion from his real motive? No. No! He wouldn't do that. Corbin is capable of many things, but not hurting me. Not like that."

Kumiko was already on her way to the kitchenette. She scooped up the containers. "I'll have them tested."

"You know someone who can test for poison, Ma?" Lavinia gaped at her mother.

Kumiko gave them an enigmatic smile. "You don't get to be eighty-seven without meeting a few people who know things. If you'll excuse me, Tempest, I'm off to test my daughter's cookies for poison."

"Here's the number of a locksmith who should be able to change these locks today." Tempest texted Lavinia the number, then slipped out of Lavinia's Lair. She paused underneath the carved wooden archway that represented the Detection Keys. Whatever was going on with Corbin Colt, it wasn't going to end well.

# Chapter 4

The next morning, Tempest twisted a key in the grinning gargoyle's mouth to open the red door of the tree house.

Purists probably wouldn't approve of calling it a "tree house." Only the decks of the house were attached to trees. The covered deck that now served as a dining room was the original tree house, built when Tempest was a young child. As Secret Staircase Construction grew, Tempest's parents, Darius and Emma, experimented on their own land, and the playhouse became a proper two-story cottage in between two old-growth trees, which Tempest's grandparents now lived in.

The ground-level front door opened into a staircase leading up to the cozy one-bedroom house. Tempest closed the door and climbed the stairs. Keeping her grandfather company while her grandmother was away at an artist's retreat with her friends seemed like a nicer alternative than eating a bowl of cold cereal above her kitchen sink.

The lines around her grandfather's eyes crinkled with happiness at the sight of Tempest at the threshold of his kitchen. "Have you eaten?" He pointed to a platter of scones.

It was slightly before eight o'clock in the morning. She'd already showered and fed her fifteen-pound lop-eared rabbit, Abra. She'd never meant to keep Abracadabra in the first place. He was a gift from a friend, a bit of a joke since she was a magician. Tempest had never used live animals in her act, and didn't think of herself as a pet person, but the curmudgeonly bunny had won her heart when he bit a terribly annoying woman Sanjay was dating. Tempest learned then what a wonderful judge of character Abra was. She hadn't been able to part with the intelligent bunny.

Since getting into the groove of working with her dad, Tempest had been waking up at dawn. Today her dad had already left with Gideon to get supplies for the building project Secret Staircase Construction hosted each semester to mentor high school students. It wasn't a formal internship or apprenticeship for academic credit, but since Darius had grown up in foster care before being formally adopted as a teenager, he was keenly aware of how much positive support from a parental figure could do. Though Tempest was his only biological child, he was a father figure to so many others. He was sure to build time into job planning so he could be back at the Secret Staircase workshop two afternoons a week to teach kids who wanted to learn how to construct a simple building. Each semester a different group of kids built a structure of their choice, as long as it was small enough to fit through the barn doors to be hauled away to its new home afterward.

Darius and Gideon didn't need Tempest to buy the lumber that day. She could have slept in. Yet she didn't. She hadn't been sleeping well for months. Now that she knew there was more to her mom's disappearance and her aunt's supposedly accidental death, she woke up most days with her heart thudding as her mind processed the snippets of truth she now knew about the Raj family curse.

Her grandfather donned a fedora on his bald brown head as they stepped onto the deck for cardamom scones topped with blackberry jam along with mugs of jaggery coffee. The winter air was crisp, but they still ate outside. Only the fiercest weather would bring Ash inside to the kitchen's breakfast nook. Tempest wasn't sure which he loved more: the fresh air or the opportunity to wear one of the hats from his vast collection.

"Dangerous coat for a proper meal." Ash tilted his head toward the white peacoat Tempest had found while thrifting with her former, and perhaps once-again, best friend Ivy.

"I haven't spilled jam or coffee on it yet." Tempest breathed in the uniquely sweet scent of the jaggery coffee and warmed her hands on the ceramic mug. "You don't have to eat a full second breakfast just to keep me company."

"I haven't eaten yet. I was talking with your gran. A storm is approaching Colonsay. They've had to shift from painting at the seaside to working from photographs inside."

"They can't be surprised. Who thought it was a good idea to have a retreat on an island in the Scottish Hebrides in winter?"

Ash chuckled. "My theory is the 'artist's retreat' is mostly an excuse to catch up with her university girlfriends, since half of the group are from her uni days. One of them had to sweet-talk the cottage proprietors to open in the winter. Now that you're safe at home instead of tempting the family curse in Las Vegas, she felt she could go. Rentals in more temperate locations were already booked up."

This was exactly why Tempest couldn't tell her family she was investigating real crimes being blamed on the 'family curse.' Her family wanted to keep her safe. It was under-standable after the tragedies the Raj family had suffered for generations. But she couldn't live in a cage. She'd disproven the family curse. *The eldest child dies by magic.* The *real* curse was a killer who'd taken advantage of a dangerous stunt that had ended in a couple of tragedies to create a full-blown curse by killing Aunt Elspeth and then silencing Emma Raj when she got close to the truth about what had happened to her sister.

Ash sniffed the air and jumped up, disappearing into the kitchen. He was already slow-cooking something for lunch. Most of his cooking was a fusion of South Indian, Scot-tish, and California cuisine—reflecting his own life—which meant a wide variety of delicious meals. One of the perks of working for Secret Staircase Construction was that Ashok Raj made home-cooked lunches for the crew on most work-days. He was a self-proclaimed *dabbawalla*, the name for the messengers who transported hot meals as part of the com-plex lunch-delivery system in Mumbai, in which stainless-steel tiffin lunchboxes filled with home-cooked meals were picked up by bicycle deliverymen who would stack the tif-fins and deliver them across the city. In addition to giving him joy, feeding people during retirement helped him stay in shape and connect with people. He always brought extra cookies on his bike rides across town, which he'd end up sharing with people he met along the way—usually after he learned their life stories.

Ash was born in South India and had moved to Scotland as a teenager to get a fresh start after a family tragedy, at-tending the University of Edinburgh. That's where he met Morag—Tempest's Grannie Mor. And now they'd been mar-ried for fifty-six years. Ash's mother tongue was Tamil, but like so many people in India, he'd also learned English from a young age. His accent was still mostly South Indian, with a smidge of Scottish and a sprinkling of Californian.

A text message from Kumiko popped up on Tempest's phone before her grandfather returned: *No poison.*

That was quick. Tempest wondered if Kumiko had a Rolodex of business cards like her grandfather's. After departing from Lavinia's Lair empty-handed the previous afternoon, Tempest felt even more foolish for making the poison comment.

She was lost in thought when her grandfather scooped her mug from her hands to top it off. When he returned the warm and steaming mug, she told him about the case of the missing typewriter. "I was so sure it was just a bad joke," she concluded, "and that I'd find it hidden beneath the false bottom of the smuggler's nook."

"He's not a good man, Tempest. I'm sure he stole it for spite." He ran a finger around the rim of his own mug. "Could you get me an invitation to Lavinia's séance?"

Tempest observed her grandfather for a few seconds while she sipped her coffee. His round cheeks and large brown eyes gave him a cherubic countenance, so it was easy for him to look innocent. Yet he was clearly keeping something from her.

"You," she said slowly, "hate séances."

He gave her a charming smile. "I want to support Sanjay."

"He'd rather you not be there. He'd rather *nobody* be there."

"Humor an old man." Ash chuckled and squeezed the back of her hand.

She narrowed her eyes. He didn't want to go to see Kumiko, did he? "What aren't you telling me?"

"What are you talking about? You have the most suspicious mind, Tempest." He didn't look her in the eye as he took her half-empty mug back to the kitchen.

She was about to go after him when her grandfather spoke again. This time, it wasn't to her. "Ah! Have you eaten?"

"Darius heard my stomach rumbling and said I should come up."

Tempest recognized the newcomer's voice. Gideon Torres. He appeared a second later. He hovered on the threshold of the deck for a moment as he spotted Tempest, but hunger won out. He went straight for the remaining scones. One was already in his hand before he sat down and greeted her.

She smiled at the sight of Gideon, Secret Staircase Construction's part-time stonemason and stone carver. Sitting across the table from the handsome (if somewhat quirky and old-fashioned) man who'd helped her solve a murder gave her an added boost beyond the caffeine she'd ingested.

"Don't skip the blackberry jam." She pointed at the nearly empty porcelain bowl. "It's heavenly."

Gideon gave a moan of pleasure after smearing the last of the jam onto the scone and taking a bite.

At twenty-five, Gideon was a year younger than Tempest. Like her, he was still figuring out his life. He'd recently told his parents he wasn't actually studying to apply to architecture graduate school and was instead content to work part-time for Secret Staircase Construction while working on becoming an artist, with stone as his medium. He was a multicultural mash-up like her, with a French mom and Filipino dad, both of whom were professionals who were finding it challenging to let their son follow his own path.

Maybe they were right to be concerned. His face was gaunt and dark circles under his eyes dominated his face.

"Sometimes I think I'd starve to death," Gideon said after swallowing the last of the first scone, "if it wasn't for your grandfather and my mom."

Ash chuckled as he dropped off a mug of coffee in front of Gideon. "Let me make some more—"

"No, no," Gideon insisted. "What's left here is perfect."

"It's only scraps—"

"I'm sure. Please don't worry."

Ash shook his head and retreated into the kitchen.

"You look like you haven't slept," Tempest commented.

"I didn't realize I'd been up all night until I heard my phone ringing in the house. It was your dad telling me I was late. He likes to be at the lumber yard when it opens." Gideon eyed the last scone but opted to pace himself. Instead, he wound his long fingers around the mug of jaggery coffee.

"New sculpture?"

"It's almost done." He beamed with a contented smile that made him look like he had everything he could ever need in the world, in spite of the fact that his lips were so dry a new crack split open as he grinned.

"Let me get you a glass of water." Tempest stepped into the kitchen, where her grandfather was doing dishes.

A haphazard pile of stainless-steel lunch containers had been drying on the dish rack. To make room for the new dishes, Ash was now stacking and locking the tiffins in their neatly assembled forms that made them easy to transport by bicycle. On a single corner of the kitchen counter, they looked completely different than the sprawling mess that had taken up the whole dish rack.

*That was it.* She knew she'd missed something yesterday.

"Gotta go." Tempest hastily filled a glass of water for Gideon, sloshing half its contents onto the table as she set it down, then lifted Grandpa Ash's hat and kissed his bald head. She ran down the tree house steps and out the door.

# Chapter 5

When the door to Lavinia's Lair swung open, it wasn't Lavinia herself who greeted Tempest.

"Well, well, well . . . Lavinia forgot to mention we'd have a famous guest joining our book club discussion today." With a critical eye, the woman looked Tempest up and down, from the thick bun Tempest had pulled onto the top of her head down to the ruby-red sneakers she was wearing with a simple fitted T-shirt and jeans.

The woman herself was dressed more like she was ready for an evening out at the theater, not a breakfast book club meeting, in red slacks a red silk scarf and a sleeveless black blouse. In low heels, she was as tall as Tempest at five feet ten. The only incongruous element of her appearance was a nearly undetectable patch of dog hair on the blouse. Her voice was gruff yet polished, reminiscent of the transatlantic accent actors in mid-century Hollywood movies used that sounded like something in between American and British.

"I didn't mean to crash your meeting," Tempest said, "but if you don't mind a five-minute interruption, I might be able to find Lavinia's missing typewriter."

"You can?" Lavinia appeared in the doorway, looking elfin

in both size and demeanor compared to the reproachful member of her book club.

"*This* is who you called for help yesterday?" The stranger resumed her inspection of Tempest.

"Tempest," said Lavinia, "this is Sylvie Sinclair, one of the members of the Detection Keys book club."

As she stood on the threshold of the space she'd worked hard to create, Tempest was even more certain she was right about where she'd find the missing typewriter. "I really am sorry to interrupt, but I know where the typewriter is."

Lavinia frowned. "You remembered another hiding spot you built that you forgot to tell me about?"

"No. But if my theory is right, we missed one we all know about."

Lavinia stepped aside and Tempest hurried down the sloped entryway leading into the main room of Lavinia's Lair.

"Tempest!" Ivy called from underneath the gargoyles above the Oxford Comma's door. She swept her strawberry hair out of her face, revealing dark circles under her eyes. "Lavinia didn't tell me she'd invited you—"

"She didn't."

Tempest and Ivy had made progress these last few months in renewing their abandoned friendship, but Tempest wasn't exactly sure how far they'd gotten. Ivy was busy with two jobs plus school—working at Secret Staircase Construction part-time while she pursued her dream of becoming a librarian. Which meant that she was also working part-time at the Locked Room Library in San Francisco and taking online classes to finish the bachelor's degree she'd abandoned, so she could apply for a master's degree program in library and information science. And Tempest had been just as busy helping her dad get the business back in shape, preparing for her grand farewell stage show, and secretly looking into what had happened to her aunt and mom.

"The more the merrier." Another woman joined Ivy in the Oxford Comma's doorway, underneath the gargoyles. Her hair was dyed lavender, with black showing at the roots. A portion of a tattoo showed on her neck but was mostly covered by a sweater. Her inquisitive expression contrasted Sylvie's jaded one.

"I'm Ellery." The lavender-haired woman raised her coffee mug and gave Tempest a warm smile. "Cheers."

"Ellery," Lavinia said, "this is Tempest Raj, whose dad's company built this place. Tempest, this is Ellery Rios. She rounds out our four-member book club. Now, where did you want to look for a clue to where he's taken my stolen type-writer?"

"I'm not looking for a clue. Unfortunately, I don't think it was stolen at all."

"Why is that unfortunate if it wasn't stolen?" Ellery peered at Tempest from behind her oversize mug.

"I'll show you." Tempest walked underneath the gargoyles, into the book club meeting room she'd helped create, and sat down at the far end of the round table. The table was set with four coasters with mugs resting on three of them, and strewn around the tabletop were four paperback copies of *The Poisoned Chocolates Case*, with different covers and various states of spine crackling.

Tempest reached under the table and unlocked the hidden compartment meant to hold pens and paper. Sure enough, she pulled out two metal pieces that had once formed the frame of a typewriter.

Lavinia's face fell as Tempest held up the broken pieces.

"Neither of us was looking in *tiny* hiding places when we searched." Tempest popped open two more hidden compartments in the table. A dozen keys from the typewriter fell into Tempest's hand. She placed them on the table.

"I'm going to kill him." Lavinia's voice shook. So did her hands. "Thank you, Tempest."

"At least he didn't smash the pieces." Sylvie picked up a single key with her manicured hand.

"I can't believe he'd do this to me." Lavinia stifled a sob as she rummaged for her cell phone. Once she had it in her hand, she darted from the room.

"My, my." Sylvie cast a chiding glance at Tempest. "Maybe you should have thought it through before showing her what he'd done."

"I'd better check on her." Ivy ran after Lavinia. Sylvie shrugged and followed suit, leaving Tempest alone with Ellery.

Tempest counted the typewriter keys on the table. "Sorry to have wrecked your discussion."

Ellery shrugged. "Let me help. Can you show me where we can find the rest of the pieces?"

"Let's try the rest of the panels around the table first."

Ellery smiled as another secret panel popped open at her touch. "I would have killed for something like this when I was a kid. I'm the youngest of five, so all I got was hand-me-down toys and clothes, whatever my older siblings had liked."

"What did they like?"

"Sadly, dolls and race cars more than books."

"With your name, it's your fate to love books."

Ellery's lips turned up into a mischievous smile. "I really was named after Ellery Queen. But the 1970s TV show, not the books or authors. My mom was a huge fan, and they were already out of family names by the time they got to me."

"My parents almost didn't make it to the hospital when I was born because of a huge storm."

"A tempest."

The story about the storm was true, as far as Tempest knew, but it wasn't the whole story. When her mom and aunt had performed as the Selkie Sisters on the stage in Edinburgh, their most baffling and famous illusion was called "The Tempest."

Ivy returned five minutes later. By that time, Tempest and Ellery had found most of the pieces that made up Lavinia's beloved typewriter. There were still a couple of missing keys, but they had their answer.

Ivy joined them in the Oxford Comma. "Sylvie is making Lavinia some tea in the main house. We managed to stop her from calling Corbin to yell at him about something she had no proof of. Their divorce isn't final yet, so that wouldn't do anyone any good."

Ellery picked up one of the books from the table and slid it into her bag. "Next week instead?"

Ivy nodded. "I'll message the group later today."

The three walked out together. Ivy waved goodbye to Ellery as the lavender-haired woman got into her old clunker of a car at the bottom of the driveway, while Tempest stood under the archway of carved keys, eyeing a large crow watching them from a nearby barren tree branch. Or was it a raven? How did one even tell the difference?

"Are ravens and crows the same bird?" Tempest murmured aloud.

"I don't think so." Ivy joined Tempest underneath the archway. "Ravens are bigger. And spookier."

"Obviously."

"I'm not sure if Lavinia's typewriter is salvageable." Ivy zipped up her pink vest against the chill in the air. "Do you think I should offer to weld it back together as a piece of artwork?"

"Probably best to wait until she tries to fix it." Tempest gave an uneasy glance at the raven that was intently watching them.

The raven on the branch above them cawed, and when another bird's caw answered from a distance, he stretched his wings and took flight. Tempest and Ivy both watched as he disappeared into the trees.

"Okay, that's just creepy." Ivy zipped the collar of her vest even higher, until it covered half her face.

"What would have been creepy is if a murder of crows had joined him on the branch above us." Tempest wrapped her white coat more tightly around her as the wind picked up.

Ivy's auburn bob blew around her face. "An 'unkindness' of ravens. That's what a group of ravens is called. I looked it up the last time I saw one hanging around Lavinia's house."

"For some reason that's even more sinister than a 'murder' of crows." The empty branch swayed above them. "Please change the subject."

"How about some gossip?"

"A good choice, as long as it has nothing to do with me." Tempest stuck out her tongue at her friend.

Even though she and Ivy had officially moved beyond the rift that had come between them a decade ago, they weren't quite where they'd been before Aunt Elspeth had died in a supposed stage accident in Scotland. Grieving, Tempest had gone to stay with her grandparents in Edinburgh and ended up finishing school there, not realizing that Ivy had her own major life problems and had felt abandoned. Now, in Ivy's presence, Tempest felt the same ease she had when they were childhood best friends, but she knew not to take it for granted.

"I was thinking of the book club," Ivy said.

"I knew it." Tempest forgot all about friendship insecurities and the creepy raven watching their conversation from its nearby branch. "I didn't think it was only the broken typewriter that made that group seem like an odd mix of personalities. It's a strange group of friends."

"I'm not sure I'd call any of us friends. Haven't you ever joined a club? No, I don't suppose you have. That's not your style. We enjoy each other's company for our twice-monthly book club, but I don't see them any other time. Saturday mornings were the only time that worked for everyone on a regular basis. Ellery refuses to read anything too scary—so Gothic horror is out, even though it has a great deal of overlap with mystery. She's a caregiver for her widower dad, who's a handful, so she says day-to-day life is frightful enough. And Sylvie won't let us hear the end of it if the author doesn't have a PhD-level grasp of grammar."

"You hang out with that woman by choice?"

The edges of Ivy's lips ticked up into a smile, and this time when she spoke, she lowered her voice. "Like I said, we wouldn't be friends if it weren't for the books. But truly, Sylvie isn't that bad once you get to know her. And it's a treat when she brings her dog along to meetings. She can't comprehend why I don't admire the deep characterization of her beloved Dorothy Sayers novels, and that I find fault with her favorite books when examining them as fair-play puzzle plots. But I'm quite clear about how that's my preference, not something that determines the merit of a novel. Aaaand, now I'm just babbling."

"The bigger issue is that's not even proper gossip. You're far too nice a person, Ivy Youngblood. I want the gossip."

Now it was Ivy's turn to stick out her tongue at Tempest. "Patience, my tempestuous friend. My gossip is about our fearless leader. Lavinia loves books, but she *hates* the ones written by her almost-ex-husband."

"She already told me that when I interviewed her to come up with the plans for the lair."

"Did she admit she hated his books *long before* she kicked him out?"

Tempest blinked at her. Now, *that* was interesting.

"She told us we had to keep it a secret," Ivy continued, "so you've got to do the same. Even though I doubt Lavinia would care what the press thinks now. But when they were married, it would have been bad press to share that she hated her own husband's books. Since we talk about books all the time, she couldn't get around the subject. She said it proved how what they had was true love. Corbin is such a gorgeous guy that when his debut novel hit it big, a ton of people were fawning over him. Lavinia wasn't one of them. At the bookstore where she worked, she got him away from a crowd of people who wanted him to stay longer than the three hours he'd already stayed for a book signing. During their escape, she admitted she didn't like his book enough to finish reading it. They've been together ever since—well, until a few months ago."

"So much changed a few months ago," Tempest murmured.

"Still no sign of Moriarty?" Ivy was always the best at reading her thoughts.

"Moriarty? Cute. A good name for a nemesis."

"Since you don't know who he really is, I figure we need something to call him."

"I'd rather not think of him at all. It's too disturbing that that the police haven't found him and he's still out there." As she spoke the ominous words, she half expected the creepy raven to return. She shook herself. Why was she so jumpy?

Tempest stopped herself from saying out loud what she was thinking. That she was more worried than she wanted to admit to Ivy. Tempest Raj had a good self-esteem. Not quite Sanjay's level, but pretty damn close. She'd grown up being tall, brown, and that kid who liked to perform magic tricks, so she was good at not caring what other people thought of her. She knew she was smart, talented, hardworking, and fierce. So when someone else had nearly outsmarted her and had escaped from the police, it threw her. It worried her that she hadn't had any contact from a man she believed was capable of anything. Ivy was right. Moriarty was the perfect name for him.

# Chapter 6

A ntisocial much?" Tempest walked up to Victor Castillo, the newest member of the Secret Staircase Construction team, who was hiding in a corner of the garden behind both a pint glass and an especially bushy beard. His black beard had grown from neatly trimmed to full-on mountain man in the few months since Tempest had known him.

It was the day after Tempest had found the missing typewriter, and Lavinia's housewarming party was in full swing. The outdoor gardens had been overhauled as part of the renovation. Secret Staircase Construction had built custom trellises and repaired an old stone fountain, but for plants and paving they'd subcontracted with a local landscaper they'd worked with before.

Victor observed Tempest from over the rim of the glass. "Most days you amaze me with the brilliant ideas that can come out of your brain, especially for someone so young, that it wounds me you won't take my advice and become an engineer. And then you go and say something that reminds me how young you are."

"Humans." Tempest shrugged. "We're complex."

After the events of the last six months, Tempest was wary of letting someone else get close to her and her family. She had been the one to find Victor in the first place, but only to consult on her own home-building project, which was taking place on a section of hillside near a natural grotto. She hadn't been thrilled with the idea of hiring a new permanent team member, but her dad had pointed out their gaping deficiencies. If they wanted to do more than build their standard projects covered by her dad's carpentry skills, Ivy's tenacious labor, and Gideon's sculptural add-ons, they needed an engineer.

A structural engineer who was burned out at his corporate job in San Francisco where he'd been caught by the trappings of a high salary, Victor quit on his fiftieth birthday. He wanted to work part-time so he could build his own dream house and enjoy life, neither of which he'd had time to do. His life goals were a perfect fit for what Darius needed. By working part-time for Secret Staircase Construction, Victor could work far less and mostly at his home office. They also set him up with a drafting table and laptop table in a corner of the Fiddler's Folly workshop. And, of course, there was the big enticement of the home-cooked lunches Ash made for the entire Secret Staircase Construction team.

Tempest spotted her dad and Gideon huddled together underneath a Japanese persimmon tree nearby. It had lost its leaves for the winter and its branches were now filled only with the orange-colored fruit.

"I wouldn't go over there if I were you," Victor said.

Tempest raised an eyebrow.

"They're discussing permits." Victor shook his head. "I joined your dad's company to get away from bureaucracy. Not run toward it. Trust me. If you have the option to avoid getting involved in that side of the business, even if it means you run away kicking and screaming, take it."

"Noted." Tempest slipped away in the opposite direction from Gideon and her dad.

Tempest knew nothing about permits. The only thing she knew about structural design was what worked on a temporary set. Her contribution to Secret Staircase Construction was bringing back the magic that had vanished when her mom did. She was elevating her dad's business beyond being a small construction firm good at installing sliding bookcases and advising where to add a secret door.

Her strength as a stage magician had always been the stories she told. There were other performers who could have done what she did physically (though at a curvy five foot ten she was one of the larger performers doing acrobatics), who could have staged similar grand illusions if they'd had the crew Tempest had assembled (they were a talented group and she was disappointed they hadn't stood by her when the show was sabotaged), and who could have rivaled her sleight of hand (she knew she was pretty good, but many magicians were far better at close-up magic).

What Tempest Raj created as her character "The Tempest" wasn't simply baffling illusions on a theater stage. What The Tempest created was *a story*. One the audience couldn't look away from, because they were captivated by the story and astonished by where it went. Tempest created the type of magic that made you forget all your problems and feel like a kid again. That's exactly what she was doing now on a different stage. Lavinia's Lair was the latest example.

The party attendees had gotten a tour of Lavinia's Lair, but the party itself was an afternoon garden party taking place outside. It was a nice January day, but Lavinia had also planned ahead and rented a few heat lamps in case the weather turned cold.

Ellery and Sylvie from Lavinia's book club were sitting on a bench talking with Kumiko. Their animated body language made Tempest wonder if they weren't talking about books but about something far more serious. Tempest grabbed a drink from a caterer and hung back behind a hedge. In spite of her better judgment, after a few sips of whatever fruity concoction she was sipping, Tempest found herself walking toward the book club gathering.

"Join us, Tempest," Ellery said when she spotted her. The clouds above shifted, and sunlight fell across the group and made Ellery's lavender hair look a brighter shade of violet.

"Yes," said Sylvie. "Do join us. You can help settle the question we're discussing. Ellery and I hold opposing opinions."

"I asked this supposedly well-read pair whether they believe the *shin honkaku* and *honkaku* mysteries of Japan are fundamentally the same," Kumiko said, "only distinguished by the period of time in which they were written. The Golden Age of detective fiction in the English-speaking world is bracketed by the two world wars, even though the traditional fairplay mystery stretches far beyond those boundaries. Where do these styles of Japanese mysteries fit?"

"Professor Kingsley is keeping her opinion a secret," Sylvie added.

"Technically, that's Professor Kazumi-Kingsley." Kumiko's face crinkled into a smile. "I was Professor Kazumi-Kingsley for more than forty years. But I've lived so many places and been known by so many different iterations of my name that anything is fine now. Except 'ma'am.' I hate 'ma'am.'"

"Was that your literary focus?" asked Tempest. "When we were adding gargoyles to the façade of the Oxford Comma, you told me a little bit about your time in Oxford, including joining the rowing club—"

"You're misdirecting the conversation to have time to think." Ellery raised her glass to Tempest.

Tempest raised an eyebrow. "Something can be two things at once." She was indeed considering the question and wishing she'd had more time to read all the books that called to her.

"I wish I could have taken one of your courses," Sylvie said to Kumiko before turning to Tempest. "Did you know she lectured at one of Oxford's colleges for nearly a decade? Both she and her husband did."

"I was in the Oriental Studies program," Kumiko said, "when much Japanese literature, especially detective fiction, hadn't yet been translated into English. We read books in Japanese."

"But you gave lectures in English," Sylvie said. "Learning from distinguished educators and authors is so much more satisfying than the sound bites of storytelling that pass as entertainment these days. No offense, Tempest."

Tempest hadn't been about to take offense, but okay.

She left them to their discussion. The rest of the afternoon garden party was a success, even though the bouncy castle broke. Lavinia had rented the inflated toy for the half-dozen kids, but it deflated before the first kid had jumped on it. To avert disaster, Tempest's grandfather stepped in with an impromptu magic show for the kids. Lavinia had asked Tempest to do it, but Sanjay needed her help setting up the séance. Even though he hated the idea of stooping to do performance-art séances, since he'd agreed, he'd gone all out for Lavinia.

The party was scheduled to end before sunset, at which

point a small group of eight would move to the book club table in the Oxford Comma pub for the séance.

"You wanna hear something weird?" Sanjay asked as he instructed Tempest where to help him hang an invisible wire. "Corbin Colt wasn't the one who smashed up Lavinia's typewriter. He was in New York meeting with his publisher."

"How do you know that?"

He blinked at her as if she'd grown a second head. "Social media."

"You follow Corbin?"

"I had to research him to get details right so I can properly banish his spirit in this séance. And no, I can't believe those words came out of my mouth, either." He sighed. "Let's just get this over with. Then I'm never doing this again."

"Don't worry," said Tempest. "Another hour and you never have to think about Corbin Colt again."

# Chapter 7

The gargoyles are installed!" Ash grinned as he pointed at the stone creatures. "And the roundabout horse is in place. Lavinia's Lair is even better than the last time I brought the crew lunch here." He rocked back and forth on his heels and chuckled as he patted the wooden mane of the horse. "Could I get a proper tour? I missed the earlier one while I was entertaining the kids."

"Of course." Lavinia looped her arm through Ash's elbow. "But it's a few minutes until sunset, so you can't linger too long to praise your granddaughter and son-in-law's handiwork."

The small group inside Lavinia's Lair for the séance were Lavinia, her mom Kumiko, Sanjay, Tempest, her grandfather Ashok, book club members Sylvie and Ellery (Ivy had to study, so she'd gone home after making a brief appearance earlier), and a surprising last member: the newest member of their team, Victor. *Why was he here?* It wasn't as if the whole Secret Staircase crew had been invited to the séance part of the party. Ivy had been invited because she was in Lavinia's book club, though she'd declined. Tempest was there because Sanjay said he needed an assistant. It wasn't strictly true. He could have easily pulled it off on his own. She suspected he wanted moral support. Tempest knew she was overthinking things. She was nervous because strange things always transpired at Sanjay's faux séances.

Lavinia began the tour with the bamboo-forest reading nook. The potted stalks of bamboo didn't provide a complete visual barrier but still gave the impression of stepping from one realm into another. By the time you stepped through the faux limestone cave and past the mysterious apothecary jars to reach the purple armchair, there was no way you wouldn't be ready to sink into a novel from one of the bookcases nearby.

A secret panel on the floor parted the bamboo for a shortcut to the riverboat. It saved ten steps, at most. But that wasn't the point. The sliding potted plants had made Lavinia's face light up like she was a kid again the first time she saw it, and each subsequent time Tempest witnessed resulted in the same sense of childhood glee.

Today, it was Ellery who squealed with delight. "I already saw this at our last book club meeting, but it really is my favorite part. The most magical. As soon as I've saved up enough, you and I will talk, Tempest."

Stepping through the parted bamboo to the riverbank of the Nile, Sylvie pointed at the storage-room door underneath. "And that's the *least* magical spot here. I'd have thought you'd have covered that eyesore under the riverboat with blue skirting to look like the river." She sighed. "We might as well have a look since Ashok asked for a full tour."

"Have faith, Sylvie," said Lavinia. "A local mural artist is coming in. She'll be here before our next book club meeting. You won't have to look at my boring storage space ever again."

Ash ducked his head and led the way into the space. Kumiko followed in her wheelchair with her daughter close behind, followed by Victor and Ellery. Tempest smiled fondly at the bamboo before stooping to enter the storage space just in time to see her grandfather spot the banker's box of Corbin's old manuscript papers. Ash flipped open the lid.

"Grandpa," Tempest snapped. He wasn't usually so nosy. At least not with possessions. Only with life stories. He'd know more about someone after thirty minutes than Tempest would after a year.

"It's fine." Lavinia laughed as Ash moved on to poking his head around the mirror resting against the wall.

"*Ouch!*" Sylvie exclaimed as she bumped her head on her way inside. "I'm too young to be this stooped and too old to kneel on a concrete floor. I'm going up to the riverboat. Anyone else coming?" She stomped on the gangplank's secret rock lever to lower the steps.

Tempest held her breath. Luckily the Secret Staircase Construction team members were great at what they did, so the forceful stomp didn't break the rock lever. The steps descended. Ellery was the first one to climb onto the boat.

It was Sylvie who hesitated. "I didn't remember it was steps. I'm sorry you can't join us, Kumiko."

*Huh.* Sylvie might be prickly, but Tempest shouldn't have rushed to judge her.

"Don't worry about me." Kumiko turned her wheelchair toward the pub. "I'll be waiting at the séance table."

Sylvie stomped up the stairway gangplank and joined the others in the riverboat. Tempest lingered at the railing. Here, she felt like she was on a real boat, embarking on an adventure. She followed the others inside in time to see Lavinia showing Ash one of Tempest's favorite details in the raised riverboat: the smuggler's nook. When they peeked inside, both compartments were as empty as they had been two days before when they'd been looking for the missing type-writer.

Tempest felt pride at what they'd accomplished here. It was no longer a vast, unkempt study of a frustrated writer, but a magical reading nook, inspiring home office, and cozy book club meeting space for a woman getting a second chance at life.

They ended the tour in the book club meeting space where the séance would take place. Stepping past the merry-go-round horse and under the leering gargoyles, they entered the Oxford Comma pub, which looked more like a haunted manor this evening. The overhead lights had been dimmed and props added: a skull, candles, and old hardback books that did look like they'd come from a movie set. Plus the invisible wires nobody was supposed to see.

"My granddaughter tells me you'll be having a bonfire later tonight as well," Ash said.

"Not exactly," Lavinia explained. "That box you found is filled with Corbin's old manuscript notes he didn't take with him. I'm going to burn them."

"He left a whole box?" Ash asked.

She shrugged. "That's the notebooks he forgot. He wrote a lot. Not that he shared any of it with me."

"You haven't read his notes?" Ash prodded once more.

She shook her head. "I'll read a few lines as I toss his scribbles into the fire, but that's it. Fresh start. Remember?" She smiled. But not at Ash.

Tempest followed Lavinia's gaze. Maybe Victor's presence wasn't so surprising. From the way Lavinia was smiling now, and their body language earlier, Tempest suspected romance was in the air.

"The sun is going down," said Sanjay. "It's time to begin."

Tempest wasn't sure how he could tell. They'd hung black-out curtains over the two outer windows of the basement.

"Everyone, you can leave your cell phones in this bag," Sanjay continued in his commanding stage voice. "And those of you who still have drinks, you can leave them on the kitchenette countertop."

"You want us to relinquish our phones?" Sylvie blinked at him, incredulous. "You're serious?"

"I told you we're doing this right," said Lavinia. Tempest wondered if it had more to do with not wanting anyone to post photos of the event. Lavinia wanted catharsis, not ridicule.

In the end, everyone complied without too much protest. Ash was chuckling as he placed his into the black silk bag. "He's a wonderful performer," he murmured. "Just wonderful."

"Everyone!" Sanjay clapped his hands once. The bag was now nowhere to be seen. "Please take a seat."

He flipped up the tails of his tux and seated himself at the end of the table closest to the kitchenette, facing the pub's open door. Seven chairs were set around the table, with one open spot for Kumiko's wheelchair. Lavinia and Kumiko sat to Sanjay's left and right. Tempest was next to Lavinia, followed by Ellery, Ashok, Sylvie, and Victor.

The three caterers who'd seen to the needs of the fifty guests were outside. Two were cleaning up and one was stationed at a table underneath the archway outside the front door to Lavinia's Lair. She had a selection of drinks and snacks they could partake of after the séance.

Sanjay stood for a brief moment and used a copper candle snuffer to extinguish the burning wicks of the candelabra on the kitchenette countertop. The only light now came from a solitary candle placed in front of Sanjay. It cast a faint glow of light across the table, their breath making the light flicker and cast jarring shadows.

"Please, join hands."

At the sound of his commanding voice, their hands grasped those of their seating companions to their left and right.

"Corbin Colt, *the Raven*, has a weak spirit." The flickering light of the candle danced across his face as he spoke. "His spirit is mostly already gone from this space. Yet to banish it completely, we must call it forth before we can renounce him."

Sanjay rolled his head back and forth. With his chin lowered, he focused his gaze on the candle.

"The daylight garden party has done its work cleansing Lavinia's new home—yes, it is indeed a new home—and now this night will finish the job."

Their eyes adjusted to the dim, flickering light. The people around the table gasped one by one as they noticed the shadows that looked like claws hovering on the walls. Tempest shook her head and chuckled silently. *Of course.* Though it wasn't one of the things she'd helped him set up, he'd done that on purpose. There must have been claw-like cutouts hidden where the light would cast.

"Is that the resonant memory of Corbin?" he asked the darkness.

The candle went out.

Several people at the table gasped.

Tempest hadn't caught whatever motion Sanjay must have done to extinguish the candle, but she knew it was a controlled move. Maybe he'd timed it, knowing exactly when the remaining wick would burn out. Or maybe it wasn't even a real candle, though she could have sworn it was.

Sanjay could have replaced it with sleight of hand without any of them noticing, even her.

"Is that the Raven's presence?" Sanjay asked. "Yes! I felt his wing on my cheek."

A movement from above cut through the air. It wasn't a simple breeze. The two far-off windows were closed. This was the effect of the wire and gauze Tempest had helped Sanjay hang earlier.

"Can you feel his wings?" Sanjay whispered. "Can you all feel his presence?"

Ellery gasped. "I felt its breath on my cheek!"

Ash chuckled softly. Victor snorted.

"Corbin Colt," Sanjay continued, ignoring the naysayers. "No—*the Raven*. You've taken the shape of the raven, since your corporeal form cannot find footing here any longer. This space no longer holds the memories of your third-rate books, Lavinia?"

Tempest's hand was in hers, and she felt her give a start at the sound of her name.

"Lavinia," Sanjay repeated, "is there anything you'd like to say to the Raven who is now in our presence?"

"This," she said, "is my space now. You are dead to me."

The air shifted once more, as if an even larger bird was inside the room with them. A master performer, Sanjay led their minds expertly. Every new sound made a shiver run up Tempest's spine. The caw of a raven. The creak of a floorboard. The hissing of a ghostly whisper.

And then . . . something that wasn't a sound. Not exactly. It was more like a physical force, yet that wasn't quite right, either. Tempest didn't feel a physical sensation, yet she felt it every bit as strongly as if she'd been struck.

*The sensation of death.*

And it was close to her.

*Thud.*

Sanjay gave a strangled gasp. Tempest shivered. This wasn't part of the act. Something was wrong.

A soft, glowing light flickered on and off in an unstable cadence, like in those sadistic rooms at fun houses that always gave Tempest a headache. It took her a moment to realize it was the light cast from the faux fireplace.

The projection of the flickering fake fire stopped two seconds later. But it didn't matter. They'd all seen it.

In the center of the séance table—a table surrounded by eight people who hadn't broken hands—lay Corbin Colt's unmoving body, the handle of a bloody knife sticking out of his chest and the black feathers of a raven scattered around him.

# Chapter 8

S creams sounded from all sides of the table. Lavinia's were the worst of all, but several others were screaming in fear or shock, and at least two people were shouting to find a light.

The lights came back on six seconds later, rescuing them from the terrifying darkness. Even though it felt like so much longer, Tempest had learned to keep precise time on stage. No matter what external stresses were thrust upon her—and there were a lot of them in a physically demanding live show—she kept her calm and kept perfect time. Only six seconds had passed.

Sanjay stood with a toppled chair at his side. The light was steady this time. But Sanjay wasn't. His chest heaved as he took shallow, anxious breaths.

"This isn't happening," he whispered, echoing her own thoughts. "This can't be happening."

Tempest's grandfather, who'd been a medical doctor for forty years before retiring, leapt up and leaned forward over Corbin's body. Did he think it possible that Corbin was still alive with that knife sticking out of his chest?

Tempest's own reaction ping-ponged between disbelief

and fear. This was Sanjay's show. It had to be part of the performance. Even the handle of the knife had the look of a prop. *But it wasn't.* She knew Sanjay well enough to tell from his reaction. Besides, he'd never play such a cruel joke. It wasn't his style. In a Hindi Houdini show, you knew the exact level of macabre you were signing up for. This wasn't it.

When the truth sunk in that this wasn't part of a performance, fear crept in. Corbin Colt was very dead by the hand of a person who could be so cold and calculating as to stage a dead body for them all to see. His face was no longer handsome, but gruesomely terrifying. His features were frozen in an anguished expression. Was that a sticky substance around his lips and cheeks? What on earth . . . ?

Ash felt for a pulse and inspected the wound, but tried not to disturb the knife. Sanjay stood as still as a statue except for a heaving chest as he stared at the body. Tempest was certain now that they were looking at a body, not a patient in need of medical attention. Victor held Lavinia back as she tried to lean forward to help the man she'd once loved but now despised.

"That man ruins everything," Kumiko muttered, her gaze fixed on Corbin's pale face.

Ellery backed away, murmuring, "Blood. So much blood." She stumbled, and Victor moved to help her, letting go of Lavinia in the process.

Freed of his grip, Lavinia leaned over the table with Ash, but he assured her he could do more good if she didn't interfere. Ash was shaking his head. He must have known at this point there was no saving his patient. He took a deep breath and tilted his head upward.

Tempest followed his gaze. How had Corbin's body landed on the table? They'd heard a thud in the center of the table, but who—or what—had lifted or dropped him there? Shaking herself out of her stupor, Tempest stepped away from the group and studied the ceiling. Aside from the nearly invisible wire Sanjay had hung for the séance, nothing was visibly out of place.

"What are you doing?" Ellery asked.

The lights went out yet again.

"Not funny, Houdini," Sylvie seethed.

"That wasn't me!" Sanjay cried.

*Smack.* As the sound of a hand hitting a wall echoed in the room, the lights came back on. Kumiko's hand was raised on the wall's light switch. "Where are our phones, Houdini? Someone needs to call the police. Because someone else is playing a very nasty game. One of you killed my ex-son-in-law."

☠☠☠

None of them stayed inside the Oxford Comma pub with the dead man. While waiting for the police to arrive, Victor comforted Lavinia in the bamboo forest, Tempest sat with Sanjay and her grandfather in the riverboat lounge, Ellery and Sylvie huddled together next to the merry-go-round horse, and Kumiko blocked the open doorway to the hallway exit in her wheelchair, staying on the line with the 9-1-1 operator.

"There was nothing I could do," Ash moaned. "He was already dead."

"We know," Sanjay assured him.

"The caterers!" Lavinia cried. She rushed from the bamboo forest toward the exit, which her mother was blocking. "We should at least ask the caterers if they saw anyone else around."

"You're police now?" Kumiko didn't budge. "Nobody should leave this room until they arrive."

"I think she means," said Sanjay, "that the killer could have run away, and now they're getting farther away."

"We all know that's not what happened," Kumiko said, then muted her phone so the 9–1–1 dispatcher wouldn't hear what she said next. "This wasn't an outsider. It was one of us."

For the next seven seconds, the only sound in the room was the breathing of its stressed-out occupants.

Then, the sound of the outer door opening and footfalls coming down the hallway, obscured from view. The police, it turns out, arrive quite quickly when a murderer is at large.

Shaken from inaction by the sound, Ellery was the first to speak. "I've gotta admit," she murmured, "the police do act quickly when a murderer is in the room."

"This isn't one of those murder-mystery novels you all love to read," Victor spat out quickly and quietly, before the police rounded the corner into Lavinia's Lair. "There's no reason to think one of us killed him."

"Yet there is," said the newcomer. A man Tempest didn't recognize, dressed in a charcoal-gray suit and flanked by two uniformed police officers, strode into the room. His small, dark eyes swept over the room, taking it all in with a single motion.

Tempest's breath caught. She knew it was her imagination in overdrive after what they'd just seen, but she couldn't help thinking his observant black eyes looked like those of a raven.

"We spoke with the caterers who've been right outside the whole time," the man said. "Nobody has come in or out since you started this party. Whatever happened, it happened in this room." He looked from one face to the next. "I'm Detective Rinehart. I'm going to find out what's going on here. Now, take me to this body."

Sanjay groaned. "I swear I'm never performing another séance again."

☠☠☠

After giving statements, Tempest and Sanjay sat in the front seats of her unmoving jeep. A streetlamp a few yards away gave them enough light to see by.

The police had questioned them each individually. Searched them and took their fingerprints as well. The séance participants were told they were being questioned as witnesses but also cautioned that they could have legal counsel present. Nobody did.

When someone had sabotaged Tempest's show the previous summer, framing her and wrecking her career, Tempest had come to appreciate the legal advice to not say anything, but this was different. Someone in that room had to have seen something. There were eight of them, and like Kumiko had said, one of them had to be a killer. What other explanation was there?

"He's really dead," Sanjay whispered. "I was hoping . . ."

"I know." Tempest squeezed her eyes shut, but it was a bad choice. All she saw in her mind's eye was Corbin Colt's dead body. She felt ill.

Sanjay groaned. "Why did someone do this to me?"

Tempest opened her eyes and raised an eyebrow.

"What?" he asked. "That was an overly complicated place to leave a dead body. Someone went to a lot of trouble to stage him in the middle of my séance. They didn't have to do that."

"Please at least tell me the raven feathers were your doing."

He twirled his bowler hat in his tense fingers. There wasn't much room in the front seats of the jeep, but he managed if deftly. "Would it make you feel better if I did?"

"You didn't—?"

"Sorry. Couldn't resist." He stopped spinning the hat and grinned at her. But the smile didn't reach his eyes. He was more shaken than he wanted to admit. "Yeah, the feathers were me. But not the body. How the hell did he get onto the séance table? That detective seems competent, albeit with a bloated ego. He was looking for mechanisms that could have lifted a body onto the table. Rhinestone told me—"

"Rinehart."

"What?"

"The detective's name. It's Rinehart. Did you think that he looked . . . ? Never mind."

"What?"

"His eyes . . ." Tempest felt foolish even saying the words. "Did his eyes strike you as birdlike?"

"Absolutely," Sanjay replied without missing a beat. "I'm so glad that wasn't just me. I can see the headlines now. *RAVEN DETECTIVE CATCHES THE RAVEN'S KILLER.* That's probably why I was so distracted I forgot his name. It's too creepy to think about. Let's move on."

"Right. You were saying Rinehart and his team are looking for hardware that could have moved a body. I'm glad he's being rigorous, but there aren't any mechanisms in that room. I helped build it. I'd have noticed if anything was different. Getting the body onto the séance table isn't the only impossibility. There are two impossibilities for him to solve."

"Two? We've got the fact that there's no way for Corbin to have landed on that séance table—unless he was really a raven."

"Which he's obviously not, in spite of what your outrageous séance script suggested."

"You wound me, Tempest. That performance needed to be

over the top. Nobody was supposed to take it seriously. That was the point. But that's still only one impossible problem."

"We've also got the fact that his body must have been hidden somewhere in Lavinia's Lair," said Tempest. "But *we know it wasn't*. We toured the space right before the séance. Everywhere except for the bathroom. . . ." Sanjay cleared his throat. "I used the facilities right before we got started. No body."

"Oh."

Sanjay spun his bowler hat in his hands once more. "Someone must have been using one of your dad's secret panels for evil instead of good."

Tempest shook her head. "There aren't any big ones in this space. No place big enough to hide a body. Only the smuggler's nook in the riverboat, which we looked inside right before the séance. It's not like he was dismembered and then put back together. This isn't a stage show. There aren't any secret passageways, either. The emergency exits are the windows, which is why there are those big mallets next to them. There was no way for Corbin Colt's body to get into Lavinia's Lair after we were inside, yet we know for a fact that it wasn't there."

"He had to be somewhere," Sanjay insisted. "He was clearly tied up and gagged before being killed."

Her earlier observation clicked. "The sticky substance around his lips. Duct-tape residue."

Sanjay nodded. "Some kind of tape."

"You don't have to constrain someone if they're dead. . . . Corbin was alive but bound before the séance. It makes more sense now why my grandfather wanted to see if he could save him. He hadn't been dead long."

"As part of staging the body, the tape around his mouth was sloppily removed."

"But why stage him at all?" Tempest whispered as she looked out into the darkness through the car's front window, suddenly feeling very cold.

"Oh no," Sanjay murmured.

"You figured it out?"

"I think I did the *opposite* of figuring it out. I think we have a third impossibility. I didn't understand what Rinehart was telling me . . . but that's what he must have meant. It also explains why we were all searched. He had the nerve to keep asking if I was sure I didn't have any retractable prop knives in my magic kit—*magic kit!* Can you believe he called it that? Like a child's toy I bought off the shelf."

"Focus, Sanjay. What are you trying to tell me?"

"It's a real problem, how much our chosen profession is maligned. We bring people joy. Why are there so many haters?"

"Sanjay."

He cleared his throat. "Fine. I think I know why the detective was asking me about whether I had any retractable knives in my 'magic kit.'"

Tempest groaned. She thought back to Corbin's body. "That's why the handle looked so flimsy. *It was a fake knife.*"

"But how did a fake knife kill him?" Sanjay asked.

"That's the question."

"One of our *three* impossible questions."

Tempest pulled her coat more tightly around her. "Why isn't Ash done being questioned yet?"

"He told us not to wait for him."

"I know, but—"

"Your grandfather is a talker. I bet he's giving them a dozen theories. And I bet I can solve at least the problem of the fake knife before we make it back to your house. That's the one that feels like a child's trick." Sanjay popped his bowler hat onto his head and made a move to open the passenger-side door. "Meet you back at your house. By then, I'll have worked out multiple ways it could have been done."

"Oh, I've already solved that part of the mystery."

Sanjay's hand froze before he could open the door. "You have?"

"Well, part of it. You answered it yourself when you said *that's why we were all searched*. The fake knife was never what killed him. There's a *different* murder weapon out there. Somewhere. That's what the police were looking for."

"But *why?*" He swore. "Does everyone think magicians have 'magic kits' with fake knives? Were they trying to frame me?"

Tempest rolled her eyes. "Stop trying to make this all about you."

He blinked at her. "It was my séance."

"At Lavinia's house. His body was staged for all eight of us. The murderer wanted us to see the scene as they intended. *But why?* Why did we need to see that the Raven had been killed with a knife?"

Sanjay shivered. "Please stop calling him that."

Tempest hadn't even realized she'd done so. The whole scene had been staged so dramatically. A large knife handle as the first thing they'd all notice. The black feathers scattered all around his body. But the feathers were Sanjay's doing.

"Wait," she said. "Do you think the killer knew you'd use black feathers in your séance? They fit in so well with the rest of the scene the killer created."

"Lavinia was the one who suggested them. Oh! And she threatened to kill him just a couple of days ago."

"Who *hasn't* said that about an ex at one point or another?"

Sanjay didn't reply for three seconds, as a range of emotions flashed across his face. His large brown eyes held a trace of sadness, and his voice was subdued when he spoke. "I've *never* thought or said anything of the sort about you."

"Dating someone briefly doesn't bring enough passion to say that." Tempest regretted the words as soon as they were out of her mouth. It was an emotional self-defense mechanism. She meant it to be flippant, but it wasn't the time for a flippant comment—and more importantly, it wasn't true. The spark between them could have grown into something far greater if the timing hadn't been all wrong the first time around. It was a cruel thing to say, but she didn't know how to apologize without making it a big, awkward deal.

Sanjay's only reply was to open the car door and slam it behind him.

# Chapter 9

A *fourth* impossibility?" Sanjay stared at her. "And it's even more impossible than the others? You can't be serious."

He and Tempest were the first to arrive back at Fiddler's Folly. They'd agreed to meet at the tree house, and even after Tempest had royally stuck her ruby-red sneaker in her mouth and hadn't figured out how to apologize without making things weird between them, Sanjay still showed up. Tempest had thought it likely that he would. He was an emotional guy who reacted strongly in the moment, but he was trustworthy and loyal—often to a fault. If there was ever a friend in need, he was incapable of saying no.

They were currently seated in the curved banquette of the kitchen's cozy breakfast nook. It was too chilly outside to be on the dining-room deck, plus it felt so exposed after the violence they'd witnessed earlier that evening.

Tempest had wanted to wait for her grandfather so she could put his bike in the back of her jeep and drive them both home, but he'd insisted she go home to both fill in her father about what had happened and eat the leftovers in his kitchen. There were indeed plenty of leftovers in the tree house fridge, but Tempest's dad was nowhere to be found. His car wasn't in the driveway and he wasn't in the main house, his workshop, or even visiting Abra's hutch. Tempest sent her dad a text message, then she and Sanjay climbed the steps of the tree house of Fiddler's Folly.

Tempest's family home was far from the ancestral estate that the name "Fiddler's Folly" might imply. Her dad had no known family aside from Tempest and his in-laws, and her mom had run away from Scotland and the Selkie Sisters stage show she performed with her sister. The couple named it "Fiddler's Folly" after the instrument Emma Raj had loved and as a tongue-in-cheek reference to European follies, those ornamental buildings that served no purpose at all. The tree house and half-built fort on the hillside property had once qualified as follies, but no longer, now that Tempest's grandparents lived in the tree house and Tempest was turning the half-built Secret Fort into a separate home for herself. The main house had always been functional, albeit a quarter its current size when her parents had moved here twenty-six years ago and began experimenting with unique home renovations. The barn workshop was constructed after Secret Staircase Construction grew in size and they needed a proper workshop.

"I'm surprised you didn't spot the latest development first," Tempest said to Sanjay. "You're the one glued to your phone."

"Some of us are trying to focus on working out the first three impossibilities."

She handed him her phone with a headline pulled up. "How does the press even find things out so quickly?"

"There's gotta be a leak. I knew I didn't like Rhinestone."

"Rinehart."

Sanjay ignored her correction and accepted her phone and read the article on the screen aloud:

## AS THE CROW FLIES: THE SHOCKING IMPOSSIBLE MURDER OF AUTHOR CORBIN COLT

*Supernatural-thriller writer Corbin Colt, known for his breakout hit* The Raven, *was found dead of unknown causes at the home of his ex-wife, mere moments after appearing on his new partner's livestreamed video.*

Sanjay looked up before scrolling further. "An internet celebrity played a recorded video she claimed to be live? So what?"

"Keep reading. It couldn't have been recorded ahead of time."

*Colt was seen on Happy Hour with Hazel, filmed live in Forest-ville, Calif., at 5:15 p.m. A 9–1–1 call was placed from 55 miles away in Hidden Creek at 5:33 p.m. Police arrived seven minutes later.*

*Happy Hour with Hazel is a livestreamed show. Thirty-five-year-old influencer Hazel Bello interacts with her fans during her livestreams and responded to many live fan comments between 5:02 p.m. and 5:14 p.m. before Colt appeared at 5:15.*

*Forestville is at least a 60-minute drive from Hidden Creek—more than 90 minutes with that evening's traffic. But as the crow flies? The distance is less and the travel time much shorter.*

*Our source reports that the feathers of a raven were found surrounding the body. Had Colt, a student of the supernatural, found a way to fly like the Raven, or to teleport like a character from his lesser-known work* The Flying Dead?

Sanjay looked up again. "*The Flying Dead?* Is that a joke?"

Tempest rolled her eyes. "Didn't you look him up?"

"I did, but he wrote a book a year over thirty years. I didn't read about all of them. I don't need to. I think I've solved this already."

"You have?"

"Not the impossibilities. But the killer. I'm betting on Kumiko."

"You're a riot."

"I don't think she needs that wheelchair."

Tempest blinked at him. "I know surgery has come a long way in recent years. But she's not that good an actor when she does her fake act of not speaking English to mess with condescending jerks."

Sanjay shook his head. "It's *her shoes.*"

Tempest thought back on Kumiko's attire. She'd been dressed in a navy-blue wrap dress. What shoes had she been wearing? Slip-on flats. Maybe. "Okay. I give up. What about her shoes? You think she slipped off her shoes and stabbed him with her feet?"

"The bottoms of her shoes were scuffed." He gave a dramatic pause. "Proving she's faking it. She doesn't need that wheelchair at all."

Tempest groaned. Sanjay could be incredibly brilliant, but he also had gaping blind spots, exacerbated by the fact that he was well aware of his intelligence. "All that means is that she didn't buy new shoes after she had her bad fall. Of course her shoes have scuffs."

Sanjay frowned, then leapt up. "Someone else is here."

Tempest's dad appeared in the doorway and gave Tempest a hug, lifting her off her feet as he did so.

Tempest had gotten her height and ease of gaining muscle mass from her dad, who towered over her and whose arms

Sanjay had not inaccurately described as wider than the tires of either of their pickup trucks.

An imposing figure who'd shaved his head for as long as Tempest could remember, Darius Mendez turned heads wherever he went. Sometimes it was out of fear of his light-brown skin and large size, but more often than not it was interest of a romantic nature. He certainly had presence. Though you might not expect it from his size, he was the gentlest person Tempest knew. Tempest's mom had been the petite one, but never as gentle as her dad.

"You all right?" he asked as he set her down. "Dad's not with you?"

"Detective Rinehart wanted him to go to the police station to answer some more questions, since he examined Corbin Colt's body."

"Rinehart?"

"New guy. I think he's who they hired after Blackburn retired. I offered to stay with Grandpa Ash, but he wanted me to come home so you wouldn't worry. Why are you scowling? Ash has examined dead bodies before. Being a medical doctor for four decades prepared him—"

"That's not what I'm worried about."

Tempest gasped. "Is his health worse than he's let on?" Her grandfather was eighty years old and incredibly fit from all the bicycling he did. Having a purpose—cooking for people—also kept him young.

Darius kissed her forehead. "His health is fine. I don't like the fact that Rinehart wanted him to go to the police station."

"The detective promised to drive him home personally," Sanjay said. "That's the only thing that made Tempest agree to come back here with me. Ash thought you'd want to know what was going on."

He turned to Tempest. "Tell me everything."

"I'll make coffee," Sanjay said as he fiddled with a moka pot. "Not as good as Ash's, but it'll be caffeinated."

Darius ran his hand across his face. "Corbin Colt is really dead?"

"As a doornail," said Sanjay. "Which is a terrible expression, but there you go."

Tempest watched her papa. "You usually see my texts more quickly."

He didn't answer immediately. Was that guilt on his clean-shaven face? And was the scent she detected aftershave? Wait. Could her dad be *dating* someone? Part of her hoped he was. Apart from a couple of single dates he'd agreed to but then felt too uncomfortable to pursue further, he'd been alone since her mom vanished more than five years before. They knew she was dead, even though they couldn't bring themselves to say it out loud. Still, if he was ready to date, that would take some getting used to.

"I should have pulled off the road to look at that damn phone when it beeped," Darius said. "I went for a drive. I didn't like that a séance was happening, since nothing good happens when Sanjay holds one—"

"I know," Sanjay growled, spilling coffee grounds onto the counter. "You don't have to rub it in."

"Here's what happened," Tempest began, then went over everything she remembered, with Sanjay adding comments periodically.

"You really need to stop agreeing to do séances," Darius said to Sanjay once they were done telling him what had happened.

"Don't I know it. But Lavinia is impossible to say no to! I would have said no to anyone else."

Tempest doubted that was the case, but held her tongue.

Which was rather difficult. They'd each finished a second espresso and she was jittery.

Sanjay clutched his bowler hat. "I'm never doing this again. Especially now that I see she used me to kill Corbin. That has to be the solution."

"Lavinia isn't guilty." The words were out of Tempest's mouth before she realized she was saying them.

"When people tell you who they are," said Sanjay, "you should believe them."

"That adage doesn't apply here. She said she was going to kill him when she was angry that he'd wrecked a beloved, irreplaceable keepsake. People say they're going to kill someone all the time. It doesn't mean—"

"She hated him," Sanjay said, "enough that she needed to renovate her house and hold a séance to banish him."

Darius's jaw pulsed as he watched the two of them, but he didn't speak.

"If he'd ended up dead in any other situation," Sanjay continued, "Lavinia would have been blamed—she was vocal about hating him. But if he's found dead in not one but *four* impossible ways? And with multiple magicians as her fake alibi? A jury will surely let her off. That much confusion means reasonable doubt."

"You and I," said Tempest, "are the two people at that table who can be absolutely certain she didn't slip her hands out of ours. There was no faking that. I'd swear to it. It wasn't her."

"She could have paid someone."

"Unless that person is one of the fake spirits you conjured, I don't see how. Nobody broke the circle."

"I hate to think it's Lavinia," Darius said quietly. "But it makes sense. She was in really bad shape emotionally when she came to me about renovating the house."

"You two have known each other a long time," Tempest said.

He nodded. "Veggie Magic is a Hidden Creek institution. It's been here since we moved here right before you were born. Lavinia and Corbin had just moved here and it was just getting off the ground. But . . ."

"But what?" Sanjay asked.

"If she didn't do it, and if she can prove that to the police . . ." Darius paused and pushed open the sliding kitchen door to the deck. He walked to the smooth wooden railing and squeezed.

Tempest followed him outside. A cold breeze sent her hair swirling like tendrils of smoke.

When her papa spoke again, his voice was barely above a whisper. "If Lavinia didn't do it, it means your grandfather is in a lot of trouble."

"Because he's being interviewed at the police station? I told you, Papa. Grandpa Ash tried to give him medical attention. He wanted to make sure Corbin was dead, not just badly injured. Rinehart wanted to get his opinion."

Darius shook his head slowly, his jaw tightening with each shake. "There's more going on with Dad being questioned than you two realize, Tempest."

"It was inevitable," said Sanjay, "that Tempest became a great stage performer. Now I see she gets her sense of the dramatic from *both* sides of the family. I'm dying of suspense. What are you so conflicted about telling Tempest?"

"Corbin Colt had a restraining order against your grandfather."

# Chapter 10

**D**arius insisted on calling a lawyer for Ash. There was no way her grandfather should be speaking to the police without an attorney present if he was a real suspect.

Vanessa Zamora, Ivy's sister Dahlia's wife, was a criminal defense attorney. Calling her wasn't necessary. Ash had known of his right to an attorney and had called Vanessa himself. She was already there.

"You knew about a restraining order against my grandfather." Tempest paced across the floorboards of the tree house deck, fuming. "And you didn't think to tell me? When did this even happen?"

Darius reached out to squeeze Tempest's shoulder, but she pulled away. "Corbin had done something offensive—no surprise there—and Ash couldn't let it go. Lost his temper and shouted at him."

"What am I missing?" Sanjay asked. "That's not enough for a restraining order."

Darius ran his hand across his face. "The problem was . . . he let himself into Corbin's house to yell at him."

Sanjay blinked at Darius. "He broke in?"

"What did Corbin do?" Tempest asked. "Grandpa Ash is the least unreasonable person I know."

"Except that he bakes off-the-charts spice into his donuts," Sanjay muttered under his breath. "That's hardly reasonable."

Darius stretched his neck from side to side but took a moment before answering. "Around the first anniversary of your mom vanishing, the media was looking for anyone who would talk to them."

"I remember." Tempest felt her pulse jump. That first anniversary had been a terrible time, nearly as bad as when her mom had vanished. By the time a year was nearly up, they'd accepted that Emma Raj was dead. The most likely thing to have happened was suicide. That's where all the evidence had pointed. Only that had been a lie. Tempest now knew her mom hadn't taken her own life. Nor had her aunt Elspeth died in a stage accident in Edinburgh.

"Corbin Colt," her father said, "was one of the people eager to talk with the press. He told them how close he and your mom had been."

"But they weren't."

"Ash was furious. Emma was the type of person who was friendly with everyone, but to imply he was good friends with her so he could get back in the spotlight through our tragedy? It was too much for Dad."

"I'm surprised a judge granted the restraining order against a grieving father for the momentary lapse in judgment of going onto Corbin's property to yell at him."

Sanjay looked up from his phone. "According to the internet, Ashok Raj physically assaulted Corbin Colt."

"How did I not know this?" Tempest could barely breathe. She spun around in three pirouettes, nearly crashing into the deck's dining table. It was the only thing she could do to ease the feeling of frustration filling her body and soul.

"Because it never happened," her papa said when Tempest stopped spinning and came to a squeaking stop inches in front of him. "Not exactly. You'd already left for Vegas by then, and you'd gotten good at not looking at the abundance of internet rumors. I didn't want to pull you back into it, especially since Ash wasn't arrested. Because he didn't *exactly* physically assault Corbin Colt. He simply threatened him. That was enough for Corbin to stumble backward and twist his ankle—even though no reputable doctor could find anything wrong with his foot. Corbin tried to get Ash arrested for assault, but the officer who arrived knew your grandfather from seeing him around town on his bike, so he understood what had really happened: a grieving father shouted at a jerk. End of story. But Corbin couldn't let it go, so he presented enough evidence for a restraining order. None of us wanted to worry you."

"You didn't want to worry me? I would have stopped him from examining the body if I'd known he could have been accused of the crime."

"You'd never have been able to stop him," said Sanjay.

Tempest was so angry she'd forgotten he was there. "You don't think I could have—"

"As the outside observer to the family, I can see some things more clearly than you two can." Sanjay adjusted the cuffs of his tuxedo, flicking off an invisible speck of lint. "Ashok was a doctor for, what was it, forty years? Right. There's no way he'd turn his back on a man with a stab wound who was right in front of him. It's more possible to imagine the four impossibilities than to imagine Ash doing nothing when he thought he could help."

"He was clearly dead," said Tempest, causing her dad to wince.

"Lots of people can seem dead when they're not," Sanjay pointed out. "Haven't you read about those bells placed in coffins during times of the plague? It's pretty easy to be wrong about near-death and death."

"That coffin story is apocryphal," said Tempest, unsure if it was, but Sanjay had a large enough ego already. "But I take your point. I just wish he'd get home already."

Darius's phone rang. He picked up before it could ring a second time. He spoke a few disjointed words, but Tempest couldn't hear the other end of the conversation. She could only see the sheen of sweat forming on her papa's face. He clicked off, but it took a moment before he could meet Tempest's gaze.

"There was nothing Vanessa could do. They're holding your grandfather overnight. He's the main suspect."

# Chapter 11

I can't sit here and do nothing." Tempest paced the few feet of floor space in the tower above her bedroom.

"You're doing a great job wearing out the floorboards. But you nearly stepped on Abra."

She scowled at Sanjay. She'd never step on her beloved lop-eared bunny. He was safely munching hay on a bunny bed she'd made from a wicker basket.

It was two o'clock in the morning. This used to be her standard bedtime, when she'd leave the theater by around midnight and either have a late dinner or a long bath to wind down before bed. She missed the clawfoot tub from the house she'd lost in Las Vegas, and her luxurious mattress, but not much else from that bloated house she thought she was supposed to want. She was going to bed before midnight these days, to be up at dawn. Not that she could imagine going to sleep any time soon tonight.

"I shouldn't have broken my social media moratorium," Tempest said. "It's not like there's any useful information there. Just noise." Social media was lighting up with wild theories about how Corbin could be in two places at once.

"I like the theory that he had a twin," Sanjay said. "Totally unrealistic, since it's way too big a secret to keep in this day and age, but it's at least plausible."

"Unlike the idea that he transformed into a raven like his character, which people are saying."

"They don't actually believe that. Those ones are jokes." Sanjay tugged on his collar. "I think. The ones that make me nervous are the ones that say The Hindi Houdini summoned both him and evil spirits during the séance. I'm *truly* never doing a séance again. I don't care what you have to do to stop me. Just do it."

"Did you see there are also reputable news sources questioning whether he's really dead?"

"Yeah, that it's a publicity stunt in collaboration with you."

Tempest froze. "With *me?*"

"You wanted more publicity for your upcoming farewell stage show that's being filmed, and he wanted to drum up interest in his latest book that was probably going to be a flop. The sound bites say things like, *Two has-beens who are trying to make a comeback,* and *Is this the latest stunt gone wrong from illusionist Tempest Raj?*"

Tempest groaned. It was worse than she thought and reminded her yet again why she'd quit social media when she was embroiled in a scandal the previous summer. "They're right that it has to be a trick. He wasn't really a man who could transform himself into a raven."

"Have you read *The Raven?*" Sanjay asked.

"When I was a teenager, why?"

"How close is his murder to what happened in that book?"

Tempest considered the question. "The plot is that a man whose wife was murdered during a theft slowly begins to question reality as he seeks out the truth about her death.

It's suspenseful because the reader wonders if he's actually losing his mind."

"What about the murder itself?"

"You're not going to like this."

"I already hate it."

"A large black feather was found at the side of his wife's dead body. The feather of a raven."

Sanjay groaned. "Why didn't you tell me this before the séance?"

"First, you didn't even tell me you were using feathers. Second, we never thought there would be a murder."

"Proceed." Sanjay's face was flushed and his voice was clipped.

"You could read all of this on a gazillion pages online."

"I'd rather hear it from you." He gave her a charming smile that made her want to both punch him and kiss him.

"The main character thinks of the killer as 'the Raven' since the feather is his only clue. As he follows one false lead to the next, and the people he interviews tell him strange things, he begins to wonder if he's transforming into a raven himself. The astute reader is misdirected into thinking they've figured out the twist and that the man himself is his wife's killer. But in a twist that makes the book supernatural suspense instead of horror, and that made the book a big hit, the killer turns out to be his sister. In her bloody confession, his sister says her brother's wife didn't want to join their raven clan, so she had to die. The ending is left open-ended as to whether he and his sister are truly supernatural entities who can transform themselves into ravens."

"I hate stories without a real resolution." Sanjay flipped a coin absentmindedly between his fingers.

"That's why our stage shows, and those classic mysteries

at the Locked Room Library where Ivy works, are better than Corbin Colt's novels." Tempest winced. "Is it awful of me to say that? It's true, but it feels awful to say that now."

"Did you ever meet him?"

"A couple of times when I was around twelve or thirteen. It was at Veggie Magic, when we were both there at the same time and Lavinia introduced us."

She'd been at an age when she was starting to be interested in boys, and she remembered how handsome she thought Corbin Colt was with his jet-black hair, sharp jaw, and brooding expression. Not a squeaky-clean hero like the teen-idol musicians her friends had on their walls, but like the villain in a movie who had second thoughts and whose face betrayed his moral indecision.

Corbin Colt's early supernatural thrillers had been huge, but by the time Tempest met him he wasn't much of a literary celebrity. *The Raven* had made him not exactly a household name, but certainly known by the reading public for a time. If comparing him to Golden Age of detective fiction writers, he wasn't as famous as Agatha Christie or as obscure as Christianna Brand, but was revered like Ellery Queen by fans of his genre.

"So you don't know him well enough," Sanjay said, "to shed any light on things from that direction."

"I'm not trying to. I'm just concerned by all the misdirection from these impossibilities. Confusion that points to my grandfather."

"You saw the crime-scene team arrive before we left to give our statements. I'm sure they're doing their forensic thing."

"Which is what I'm worried about. Only my grandfather had blood on him."

"There's bound to be physical evidence elsewhere, like where the body was hidden."

"How?" Tempest asked. "How is there going to be any physical evidence when there's no physical space where his body *could have been* before he dropped onto the table?"

"That's what you were looking for above the séance table when Ash was examining him, wasn't it?"

"You spotted that? Thurston and Kellar's floating-lady illusion doesn't fit. Help me think of other magicians who had an apparatus that could drop a body into our laps."

The Golden Age of Magic brought illusions like levitations, disembodied spirits, and sawing women in half. Tricks for levitations would apply here. Some of those acts were simple and some complex, but all grand illusions needed equipment, and in most cases, a theater. Successful magic that astonishes takes far more effort than the observer thinks could possibly go into a trick, which is why it's able to be baffling. A combination of psychology, showmanship, clever props, and practice. So much practice.

"If we do find a magic trick behind it," said Sanjay, "doesn't that point even more toward Ash?"

"Or one of us."

"You're really creeping me out, Tempest. You're totally your character The Tempest right now, with destruction following in your wake."

That had been her tagline that her mentor, Nicodemus, had come up with long ago. She'd thought it overly dramatic when they first brainstormed it. But the public loved it when she said the only words spoken during her stage show: *I'm The Tempest. Destruction follows in my wake.*

"I should turn my wrath toward that home-wrecker girlfriend of his. She has to be in on the trick with her livestream."

"I don't know. . . ." Sanjay scrolled through more news on his phone. "Her livestreams aren't recorded, so it's just eyewitness statements. We don't really know anything yet."

"Except for what we experienced ourselves in Lavinia's Lair. We need to get back inside."

"The crime scene will probably be locked up until I'm back."

"Back? Oh, right." Tempest felt her stomach drop. She didn't think of herself as a needy person, but having Sanjay around was rather like being wrapped up in a sexy security blanket. She was more disappointed than she wanted to admit that he wouldn't be at her side as she figured out how to help her grandfather. "You've got those shows. When do you need to—?"

"I should already be packing. My flight is before dawn." Sanjay dropped his hat onto his head and moved toward the door. "I really should stop letting other people book my flights."

☠ ☠ ☠

After Sanjay departed at half past two in the morning, Tempest was left alone with her rabbit, the posters on the octagonal walls surrounding her, and her thoughts. She preferred the former two.

One of the eight walls was the doorway leading to the narrow secret staircase, another was a window, and the remaining six held framed magic posters. Her mom's favorite magician, Harry Houdini; her own favorite, Adelaide Herrmann; her mentor, Nicodemus the Necromancer; a Hindi Houdini poster of Sanjay's; one of her mom and aunt's Selkie Sisters posters; and one from her own show, *The Tempest and the Sea*, with an illustrated version of herself showing her long black hair swirling in the water and turning into dark waves. Most of the posters contained magical elements to conjure a sense of mysterious delight, like whispering devils and swirling ghosts. All except for the Harry Houdini poster, with a straightforward message that said it all: the handcuff king could escape any confinement.

Emma Raj had always said that Tempest was like Harry Houdini, because like Houdini, Tempest was a key that could open any lock. Opening locks applied literally in Houdini's case, as he was the handcuff king who could break out of any locked room or shackles, but Emma Raj also liked to think of it as also applying to Houdini's underdog origins. Hungarian immigrant Erik Weisz had worked hard for years before gaining any recognition, and changed his name to honor the father of modern stage magic, Jean-Eugéne Robert-Houdin. Emma Raj's tall, brazen, ethnically ambiguous daughter hadn't always fit in, but Emma made sure Tempest knew she could make her way any place in the world where she wished to be.

Tempest sometimes thought she was born a century too late for the style of magical entertainment she loved. But that, of course, was wishful thinking. A woman of color, who was also taller than many men, had to maneuver enough hurdles as a magician in the twenty-first century. The challenges of a hundred years ago would have been far greater.

Tempest had her own unique challenges, like everyone did. Her family had never wanted her to be a performer because of the Raj family curse. *The eldest child dies by magic.* Tempest had found out part of the truth, enough to know there was no supernatural curse. But she still didn't know the truth of her aunt's supposed stage accident or what had become of her mom.

It was five years ago that her mom was presumed to have died by suicide in the bay. That was when Tempest dropped out of college. She wasn't able to find out what had happened to her mom—none of them were—so she poured her grief into writing a stage show that told the story of her mom and aunt—both incredible women who'd died far too soon.

Years before Tempest was born, Emma and her sister Elspeth's Selkie Sisters act had enchanted audiences in Edinburgh, Scotland, before a rift sent Emma to California, where she met Tempest's dad. Elspeth stayed in Edinburgh and became a solo performer, performing magic at a theater in Old Town, Edinburgh. Ten years ago, a tragic stage accident had claimed her life.

Was it an accident—or was it the Raj family curse?

It turned out it was murder.

Tempest now knew that five years ago, Emma Raj was about to reveal who had killed her sister Elspeth. Before she could do so, she vanished on the stage of the Whispering Creek Theater, in front of a crowd of people.

Emma's plan had been to reveal the killer in her show. Was it because the police wouldn't believe her? Tempest didn't know the answer to that question. What she did know was that Emma didn't want Tempest to pursue the matter. She'd feared for her daughter's life. Because of the family curse: *The eldest child dies by magic.*

Was it really a curse, or a risky illusion and some bad luck, followed by an opportunistic killer? Magical stunts in nineteenth-century India could be dangerous. After two of Grandpa Ash's relatives died, both the eldest in their families, the legend began to grow. When Ash's own older brother died while performing a dangerous stunt, teenage Ash left the family's already-crumbling magic dynasty for Scotland, where he was accepted to medical school.

Like with her own family tragedy, Corbin Colt's murder was both mysterious and curious. How *and* why? Just like they were with her own mom's and aunt's unsolved murders, the two questions were linked.

Emma and Elspeth Raj's deaths were cold cases, so as much as it pained Tempest to admit it, they had to wait. It was the murder her grandfather was implicated in that needed her full attention. She'd already lost too many people she loved. She wasn't going to lose him, too.

Tempest squeezed her eyes shut as she thought back to Corbin Colt's dead body materializing out of thin air on that table, with a fake knife sticking out of his chest and raven feathers scattered around him, when he'd been seen alive minutes before more than fifty miles away. Even though she knew the feathers were from Sanjay and everything else had to be a trick, her rational mind faltered.

She wished Sanjay could have stayed, but she knew he had to get ready for his flight that was departing in a few hours. She'd already made plans to see Ivy in the morning, but the new day couldn't come quickly enough.

*Four impossibilities.* How was the impossible trick accomplished?

# Chapter 12

"C"an you move that creepy raven?" Tempest asked Ivy.

"Valdemar?" Ivy eyed the stuffed bird sitting high on a bookcase.

"If that stuffed animal starts squawking, I'll drive back over the bridge, no matter how bad traffic is right now."

"His sensor is only triggered if you get too close to him. We put him out of the way so his caws wouldn't disturb the patrons. The ones who want to see him will seek him out." Ivy pushed Tempest in the opposite direction. "Let's go into the train-car meeting room."

It was shortly before nine o'clock in the morning, and Tempest had met Ivy at the Locked Room Library in San Francisco, where Ivy was working part-time as a library assistant. The private library specializing in classic mystery fiction was located on the first floor of a converted Victorian house and open to the public six days a week. The library wouldn't be opening for another hour, but Ivy was opening that day and couldn't be late, so they'd agreed to meet there.

Ivy unlocked the door of the train-car replica that served as the small library's meeting room, which could be reserved by book clubs as a meeting space during open hours.

It wasn't a true replica, but curved, black-paneled walls built to resemble a steam train, with large wheels and gears on the exterior. Everyone could tell it was a train, and mystery fans would also be reminded of the steam train from *Murder on the Orient Express*.

To work as a meeting room, the interior recreated a lounge car, with a narrow meeting table with plenty of seats for people to gather, and a bar at the far end.

"You look like death," Ivy said, then winced. "Bad choice of words. But you do look like you didn't sleep at all last night."

"It was impossible to sleep." Tempest slid into the closest seat. Normally this was a comforting room—it was the heart of a library, how could it not be a joy?—but now its close walls felt confining. She stole a glance at the curved ceiling, wondering yet again how something could have been hidden inside Secret Staircase Construction's renovations for Lavinia. "I was hanging out in a room with an invisible dead body last night—"

"Who mysteriously materialized from more than fifty miles away within minutes. I read about it after I got your text."

"What you didn't read," said Tempest, "is that my grandfather is the prime suspect."

Ivy's eyes grew wide. "That can't be right."

"The whole situation is like something out of these old books you consume like breathing air." Tempest stood from the cramped seat and looked out the train-car windows at the library filled with mysteries. "That's why I'm here, even though I know how busy you are. I'm hoping you'll have some insights."

Ivy joined her at the window. "I appreciate that you reached out, but you don't need to pretend I'm any more than a sounding board."

"You're more than—"

"Tempest. You're the one who figured out what happened to Cassidy. You're the one who understands misdirection from your years of honing stage magic. I'm happy to help, but you don't need the false flattery. As a magician, you've already spent your life creating the misdirection imagined by my favorite Golden Age of detective fiction author."

Tempest smiled. "John Dickson Carr." She and Ivy had become close friends as small children when they realized they were more obsessed with the mysteries in Scooby-Doo episodes than their peers. From there they moved on to reading the adventures of classic kid sleuths like Encyclopedia Brown, Nancy Drew, Trixie Belden, and The Three Investigators, then on to Sherlock, Dupin, Poirot, Marple, Queen, Merlini, and John Dickson Carr's most popular sleuth, Dr. Fell, who gave a famous locked-room lecture in *The Three Coffins,* in which the portly sleuth described all the possible ways an impossible crime could have been committed. At sixteen, Ivy had continued on their childhood path, disappearing into the world of books, while Tempest threw herself into magic.

"You can do this," Ivy added.

Tempest filled Ivy in on the restraining order that gave Ash a motive and how he was currently being held by the police.

"Is your grandmother cutting her trip short to get home to him?"

Tempest shook her head. "A storm in the Scottish Hebrides is raging, so we weren't able to reach her. We've been trying, but wireless towers are down from the storm."

"You know so many people there. Could you send someone from the mainland? I'm sure Nicodemus would—"

"Nicky would if he could perform real magic." Tempest had known Nicodemus the Necromancer since she was a kid. The Scottish stage magician had been the one to spot the talent of her mom and aunt when they debuted their Selkie Sisters magic act as teenagers at the Edinburgh Fringe Festival.

"Is his health that bad these days?"

"His arthritis makes it tough to perform some of the sleights he used to, but it doesn't prevent him from traveling. But Grannie Mor and her friends are on one of the many islands that's only accessible by boat. There's no bridge."

"You mean," said Ivy, "there's no way to tell Morag that her husband is the prime suspect in a murder?"

"Grandpa Ash isn't guilty, so I'm sure they'll figure that out. Only . . ."

"Only the whole thing seems impossible."

"Meaning they'll go for motive plus the fact that he's the one who had blood on him."

Ivy stared at her. "He *what?*"

"He thought Corbin might still be alive, so of course he was going to try to help him."

Ivy groaned. "He accidentally drew attention away from the real culprit." She gasped. "Wait, did anyone *ask* Ash to examine the body?"

"You're thinking the person who asked Ash to examine him is the guilty party?" Tempest shook her head. "Except nobody did. He jumped into action all by himself."

"You don't think—"

"Of course not," Tempest snapped.

Ivy held up her hands. "I don't think so, either. But from everything I've heard about Corbin from Lavinia . . ." Ivy's hands flew to her mouth. "Lavinia?"

"I hate to think so, and I can't see how she or anyone else at that table managed it. That's what I wanted to talk through with you this morning. It seems like *nobody* could have done it—yet at the same time, one of the people at the séance had to have done it. Lavinia, her mom Kumiko, your book club members Ellery and Sylvie, Victor, and my grandfather. It wasn't me. It's not Sanjay or Ash—"

"How do you know it's not Sanjay or Ash?"

"You're kidding."

"I know *everyone* there. I hate to think it's any of them."

"And I hate the helpless feeling of sitting around while my grandfather is being held by the police—how long can they do that anyway? Twenty-four hours? Forty-eight?"

"I've read too many classic British mysteries to have the faintest idea how the U.S. police and court systems work. For all I know, we have barristers." Ivy paused and waited for a reaction from Tempest. When she got none, she went on, "That was a joke, by the way. Only the last bit. I know we don't have barristers here. Um, I think. We need more inspiration. Hang on."

Ivy moved away from the train-car windows facing the library to the windows facing the wall. There wasn't much to look at—until Ivy activated the moving faux background that made it look like the train was chugging through the countryside.

Tempest watched as a field of vineyards sped past, accompanied by the chugging sound of a steam train. As the background images sped up, so did the sound of the train.

"If they're focusing on my grandfather, they're not looking as hard for whoever really did kill the Raven. And there's no way the police will be able to wrap their heads around the four impossibilities."

Ivy perked up. "*Four* impossibilities? Not just that he was seen fifty-something miles away right before he landed on my book club's meeting-room table?"

Tempest didn't have room to twirl around in the cramped train-car meeting room, so she instead took three deep breaths and took herself back to the previous night. "It's all so messed up."

"I should have been there with you at the séance. I'm sorry—"

"You had to study. I know that. You need to finish your degree so you can apply to graduate programs."

Ivy bit a pink, chipped fingernail. "But I didn't end up studying. I've been so burnt out from everything lately that I binge-listened to a true-crime podcast my sister recommended. I didn't even crack a book."

"It's okay. There's nothing you could have done. Sanjay was running the fake séance. Lavinia sat between the two of us."

"Meaning you two would know if there was any jiggery-pokery, like using a dummy's hand instead of her own."

Tempest couldn't help smiling at Ivy's use of one of the expressions her favorite fictional hero, Dr. Fell, used. "True. Unless she used her feet."

Ivy gasped. "You don't think—"

"Like you said, we can't rule anyone out."

"Victor is the only one who had no connection at all to Corbin."

"I'm not so sure about that," Tempest said slowly, thinking back on Lavinia's expression when she looked at Victor. "I think he and Lavinia might be seeing each other. I can't be sure, but why else would he be invited? And the way she looked at him suggested something was going on."

"So we can't rule anyone out based on not knowing Corbin."

"We did a full tour of Lavinia's Lair right before the séance, and Corbin's body wasn't hidden anywhere. A caterer, with two other witnesses, was stationed right outside the main door—which is the only way in or out—the whole time. There's no other way out, except for smashing the windows—which have mallets next to them as a safety feature in case of a fire, but nobody got in or out that way. It was impossible for anyone to get into or out of the room we were in."

"I know. I helped build it, so I know there aren't any secret passageways."

"Yet shortly after the séance began and Sanjay summoned Corbin Colt's spirit, Corbin landed on the séance table, dead, with a knife sticking out of his chest, but none of us had broken the circle. Not only that, but the knife turned out to be fake, like a stage prop."

"And all of this happened a few minutes after he appeared on a livestreamed video from fifty-five miles away." Ivy drummed her fingers on the table. "That's the biggest impossibility."

"It's obvious that a fake knife didn't kill him, so something else did. That part of the situation was only briefly 'impossible' in the truest sense of the word. But it's still baffling, because *why do it?* He was staged like that for some reason."

"To draw your attention away from something else!"

"If that was the reason, it was incredibly effective." Tempest thought back to the séance, when she thought the knife handle was attached to a real knife. "Misdirection. Staged misdirection."

"Which points to you, Sanjay, and your grandfather—but you three are the ones I know aren't guilty."

"I thought you said—"

"I don't *really* think one of you three is guilty. I'm merely pointing out that you're all viable suspects to the police. Even if Corbin could really turn himself into a raven—which I'm not saying is the case," Ivy added hastily, "someone still stabbed him to death. Oh! His new girlfriend. That *Happy Hour with Hazel* woman."

"She wasn't there at the séance. She has the best of all alibis: she both wasn't there *and* was seen on a live-broadcast show. She *could have* faked the interaction and instead recorded it earlier. Except that we know it wasn't recorded ahead of time."

Ivy raised an eyebrow. "How do you know?"

"Because people were asking questions. Which she responded to. Live."

"Tricky, yet doable." Ivy drummed her fingers together. "It's one of the key methods of making a crime appear impossible. A time shift is a classic device."

"But *why* would she do it? She wasn't at the séance, so what did it get her? It's also complicated and so many things could go wrong. That's one thing I never understood about so many of those puzzle-plot classic mysteries. I love their clever plots, but there needs to be an answer to *why* someone would go to such effort."

"To kill Corbin."

"How would making it seem impossible help her do it?"

"Because," Ivy said, "it gives her a fake alibi."

"She doesn't need one. She truly wasn't inside Lavinia's Lair with us."

Ivy raised an eyebrow. "Are you sure?"

"Very. Even if I'm wrong—which I'm not—I can't imagine how she'd fake that live interaction without one of her fans catching on. So yes, she's suspicious, but I don't know how or why she's involved yet."

"There's way too much we don't know. Not like when we had all the pieces of the puzzle last summer, but just couldn't see it." Ivy hesitated. "I'm sure the police are investigating all this, so you'll learn more soon. I appreciate this as a cerebral challenge, but you don't really need to—"

"Hang on." Tempest grabbed her buzzing phone from her pocket. The goofily smiling face of her dad lit up the screen, but when she picked up, his voice was the opposite of light-hearted.

Tempest gripped the edge of the train-car's meeting table as she listened to his unbelievable words. She tried to calm herself by focusing on the faux scenery speeding by, but the vineyard background had given way to a tumultuous mountain pass.

"What's going on?" Ivy whispered as Tempest hung up.

"I no longer have a choice." Tempest's voice shook as she spoke. "This isn't just an intellectual puzzle. I have to get involved. My grandfather has been arrested for the murder of Corbin Colt."

# Chapter 13

shok Raj was released on bail late that afternoon. Sooner than Tempest had expected, and she was grateful for small mercies. Her dad's information that Ash had been arrested was correct, but a judge had let him go on an exorbitantly high bail, financed by Fiddler's Folly as collateral—plus an ankle monitor. Her grandfather also had to relinquish his passport.

"It's a trick," Tempest said, pacing back and forth across the tree house deck. "As soon as we figure out how the trick was done, you'll be cleared."

"Tempest," her grandfather began.

"Ellery and Sylvie never let go of your hands, right? That proves you didn't do it."

"*None* of the participants let go of each other's hands. The detectives confirmed it with everyone."

"Which is why it's a trick."

"And why Detective Rinehart and the district attorney believe I'm the only one who could have done it. I got his blood on my hands when I attended to him, which they believe I did to cover up for the fact that I'd touched him when I killed him. His body was warm. He hadn't been dead long at all. One of us in that room killed him."

"But they don't even have a murder weapon. The knife was fake—"

"They found a blade inside him," Ash said softly. "The murder weapon was never missing like they thought at first. It was there the whole time. And I have a motive."

Tempest felt herself in danger of squeezing her fingernails so tightly into her palm she'd draw blood. Her tension eased infinitesimally when she opened the kitchen's junk drawer and saw what she'd hoped to find. She picked up the pack of Bicycle playing cards.

"That's why they might *suspect* you." Tempest began shuffling the deck of cards. "But *arrest* you? Lavinia has an even bigger motive—and it's her house. You would still be in jail if you didn't know Judge Washburn."

"But I *do* know her, so I'm home." Ash chuckled and adjusted his Panama hat. "She has such a charming son. I don't know why his primary care doctor hadn't been able to properly diagnose his illness, thinking it was allergies. It was as clear as day on the Ohlone Greenway."

Tempest remembered the story. Ash had been riding his bike from Hidden Creek to Berkeley to bring Darius and the rest of the crew a hot lunch packed in tiffins, and stopped to help a woman whose son was having trouble catching his breath. "Thank you," the judge had said. "He just has bad allergies." Ashok had not been convinced, and asked her to have his doctor check for Lyme disease. He wrote down his suspicion and his contact information. The judge called Ash a few days later to tell him he was right and to thank him.

Tempest would have felt marginally better if Judge Washburn had been the trial judge assigned to the case. But the ethical judge would probably have recused herself if that had been the case. She was only the judge drawn for the preliminary hearing to determine what would happen to Ash as he awaited trial.

That story wasn't unique. Grandpa Ash had saved so many lives. Including hers. That's what he did. When Tempest was an angry sixteen-year-old, raging at the world for its wicked capriciousness after Aunt Elspeth's death from what they thought was a tragic accident, Ash was grieving but still managed to be her rock. She couldn't imagine having survived that dark time without him.

"Don't look so forlorn." He kissed her forehead. "All will be resolved."

"How can you say that?"

"My biggest complaint," he said, ignoring her question, "is that they didn't make the coverage of this beeping monstrosity extend beyond half of the yard!" He lifted the leg of his trousers and wriggled his ankle. "It doesn't even reach your house. I can't come over to cook for you."

"When do you ever come over to cook for us in Papa's kitchen?"

"That's not the point." Ash frowned and stepped back into his own kitchen. "I can't go to the market, either. And your grandmother isn't here to go for me."

"I can go. Not a problem. Make me a list."

Ash sighed. "I never taught you how to properly pick out fruit. You were a teenager by the time you lived with us in our Edinburgh flat. You had no interest in cooking with me."

Tempest grimaced. "I'm lucky you never gave up on me despite how dreadful I was in every possible way."

He pressed his nose to hers. "I would never give up on you, Tempest."

"Let's see if you still say that after I bring back a bag of mushy potatoes and unripe mangoes." Tempest could shuffle a deck of cards with one hand, like she was currently doing, but she couldn't cook an edible baked potato.

"Local California mangoes aren't in season. No mangoes on my list." He scribbled a few items on a piece of gridded scratch paper and handed it to her.

"You'll be okay while I'm gone?" she asked.

"I'll make some phone calls. I made sure my phone is set so any calls from Morag will come through even if I'm on the phone."

Cell phones had become popular in Europe before the U.S., so Grandpa Ash had been an early adopter. Since Tempest had deleted all her social media accounts after the sabotage that had wrecked her career and after learning that most of her old "friends" had abandoned her during the scandal, she rarely used her cell phone these days. Her eighty-year-old grandfather was probably far ahead of her with the latest apps.

"Give her my love when you two are able to talk."

"Tempest." Ash tried to catch her eye. "You're only going to the market, right?"

"I have a couple of my own errands to run—"

"Tempest. No investigating."

"Did I say I was investigating?"

"You think I don't know that look in your eye? I doubt Lavinia is a danger to anyone else, but I don't want you to provoke her."

The cards slipped from Tempest's fingers. "You think Lavinia is the killer?"

Ash sighed. "I suspect so. I also suspect she'll come forward if I'm not cleared. She's a good person. Corbin was not. His body was still warm, you know. I can't say as precisely as the medical examiner, but he hadn't been dead long. Which makes sense. Lavinia had a good reason to kill him with all of us there at the party."

"Why?"

"So *nobody* could be charged. But then I bungled her plan when I examined the body."

Tempest was processing this theory when a knock sounded from the front door below.

"Time for you to go!" Ash said. "I need proper snacks for my guests. You understand everything on the list?"

"Your guests?"

"I can't go to the world, so I'm bringing the world to me."

On her way out the door, Tempest passed Ash's guest, a man she'd met before, who she was fairly certain was one of her grandmother's musician friends. She said a brief hello before leaving them to chat and heading to her jeep.

Which had a flat tire. She glanced around uneasily. She didn't sense the presence of anyone lurking about.

The car was parked in the driveway. On closer inspection, nothing nefarious had been done to it. She found the culprit: a long nail sticking out of the tire. As careful as they were about cleaning up the Secret Staircase Construction workshop, sometimes errant screws and nails lost their way.

She groaned when she realized she'd already used her spare tire. She hadn't replaced it.

"Can I help?"

She glanced over her shoulder and saw Gideon Torres walking her way from the workshop. She didn't need help changing a tire. She was better at it than most guys she knew. "You don't happen to have a spare tire, do you?"

"Not one that'll fit your jeep. But I'm done helping your dad get the workshop set up, so I can take you somewhere if you need a lift."

The sound of laughter floated down from the tree house.

"Is your grandfather having a party?"

"He said if he can't go to the world, he's bringing the world to him."

"He's holding court?"

That got a smile from Tempest. He was right. That's exactly what her grandfather was doing.

"Your dad filled me in about his arrest," Gideon continued. "I'm really sorry."

No false platitudes from Gideon. His words were genuine. He was perhaps the most genuine person Tempest knew. When Gideon Torres spoke to you, he gave you his undivided attention. Tempest doubted he fully understood the very concept of multitasking. It was both charming and frustrating. He didn't even own a cell phone. He claimed he didn't need one, without considering that other people in his life needed him to have one to reach him.

They'd gone on a grand total of one proper date, after the murder business had been cleared up. It had been a good one, but they'd both been so busy with multiple jobs and travels that it had proven impossible to find time for a follow-up—especially when one of them didn't have a cell phone and often lost track of time when carving a piece of stone. And now months had gone by. She was grateful that, surprisingly, there was no weirdness working together. Though he was a year younger than her, he had always struck her as being mature for his years.

"I hope my grandfather invites over that private investigator he knows," said Tempest as another roar of laughter sounded from the tree house deck.

"You think he needs one?"

"Maybe. In that huge Rolodex of contacts of his, he's got just about every occupation one could imagine."

"You could look at the Rolodex to find the PI."

"He's got it under lock and key. He knows I'll try to clear him if I have the chance. He doesn't want me investigating."

"But you're not listening to him."

"Of course not." Tempest studied Gideon's face. "You in to help?"

# Chapter 14

I don't get it," Gideon said as they got into his baby-blue Renault. "Ash's got his contacts locked up where his magician granddaughter can't get to them, but surely he knows you'll see the people coming and going from his house."

"By then he can have warned them not to indulge me."

"Hmm . . ."

"You're not starting the car." Tempest shifted impatiently in the seat.

"Because there's someone else walking up the driveway toward the tree house."

"We already established that he was holding court."

Gideon shook his head. He wasn't looking at Tempest. His gaze was directed toward the tree house. They couldn't see the structure itself from the car, yet his focus was still intense. That was his way, she'd learned. Total focus. He wasn't of this century.

"Someone," he said, "is already leaving. These aren't casual visits. Ashok is up to something."

"The woman going up to the house looks familiar." Tempest was sure she remembered the long blond hair that stretched to the woman's waist and the distinctive gait of her footsteps. "I know her. But not in this context."

"You mean she's not a friend of the family."

"No." Tempest thought for a moment before she came upon the memory. "She's a circus performer. I've seen her sideshow act in San Francisco."

"Why would your grandfather invite a circus performer over?"

"It's not for entertainment. . . . I'm going to talk to the musician who's leaving. You can see what's going on with the circus performer. They're probably sitting on the deck, so stay back, but see if it looks like anything odd is happening."

"Odd?"

"You know. Strange. Sinister. Startling."

"'S' words. Got it."

Tempest gave Gideon a raised-eyebrow scowl, then jogged after the man she'd recognized as being one of Grannie Mor's musician friends. She was pretty sure he played the acoustic guitar and that his wife was an artist.

"I didn't get to say a proper hello," Tempest said when she caught up with him walking toward the bus stop. "How are you?"

"Lovely of you to ask," he said in a boisterous voice. "Of course I'm wishing I could reach Sarah."

"What?"

"Oh? I assumed that's why you were asking. My wife is on the artist's retreat with Morag—the now-infamous *unreachable* retreat. Ash and I were putting our heads together to come up with how to reach them. Until the ferries are back in service, even if we could reach them, they can't get back to us."

Tempest wished him well after chatting for another minute, then jogged up the hillside slope in search of Gideon. The musician—whose name she still didn't remember—had been a dead end.

She found Gideon half-hidden behind an oak tree.

"They're speaking quietly," she whispered. "This is too far to hear them." From this vantage point, they could see a good portion of Ash and his latest visitor.

"As close as we can get without being observed. Did you see that?" Gideon pointed.

"He gave her a box of sweets to take with her."

"There was a wad of cash poking out of that box of orange sweets."

Tempest would have seen it if he'd used sleight of hand to do it. But the fact that he'd simply handed her a gift of food was so normal for Ash to do that Tempest hadn't given it another thought.

"She's not even five feet tall," Tempest murmured. "She can slip through the smallest of openings and contort herself to fit inside impossibly tiny spaces."

"Your grandfather is from a family of traveling magicians, right? You think he's nostalgic and wants her to perform while he's stuck at home?"

"No." Tempest watched. "She's going to steal something for him."

"Wait, *what?*"

"Go back to the car."

"What are you going to do?"

"Just go back to your car. I'll meet you there in a minute."

She followed the circus performer and caught up to her as the woman was unlocking the passenger-side door of ancient Volkswagen Rabbit parked on the street outside Fiddler's Folly.

"Fleur, right?" Tempest smiled and extended her hand. "I

saw your sideshow performance in San Francisco a couple of years ago. Your fire-eating is top notch. I'm Tempest."

Fleur left the box of treats on the seat and turned to face Tempest with a warm smile. It seemed genuine, but her forehead was creased with worry. "That's lovely of you to remember."

"I didn't know my grandfather had seen your show as well."

"I know him from busking. Most people don't put anything in the tip jar, even when they take a photo of me. Your grandfather didn't take a photo, but dropped a fifty-dollar bill into the jar."

Tempest's heart sank. Gideon was right. He was probably only extending his generosity further. It was hard to make a living as a performer.

Fleur paused to smile at the memory before continuing, "Usually the only people who give large tips make a big show of waving a twenty-dollar bill around, so whoever they're with will see how generous they are. But Ashok was alone. He folded the bill to make it look like a five, but I know the difference. Just as well as I know the type of person who does that. He wanted me to find it later and not know who put it there, just to be happy that I'd made someone smile that day."

"That definitely sounds like my grandfather. I'm surprised he didn't slip a home-cooked meal into your tip jar. He probably would have if it wouldn't have leaked all over the money."

"He was on his bike on his way to deliver some meals that smelled phenomenal, so he didn't stay long. But he visited again on his ride home. He'd saved me two cookies." She frowned. "I'm really sorry he was arrested."

"I'm glad you came to visit him. I didn't think his arrest

had been reported by the media yet." Tempest bit her lip, hoping she wasn't overacting. "I'm so scared to read what they're saying about him online that I haven't even looked." She broke off and stifled a fake sob.

"Don't worry," Fleur assured her. "I didn't come because I saw him in the news. Your grandfather called me."

"He did?"

Fleur frowned. She realized she'd said too much. Tempest tried not to smile. "I didn't realize you two were close enough that he'd call you."

"We weren't. I mean, we're not." Fleur stumbled over the words. "He must've wanted to talk to a fellow performer."

Tempest gave Fleur her best Cheshire-cat smile. "I know about the money. The money he gave you *today*. It was a lot more than fifty dollars."

Fleur returned her smug smile with a stage smile that didn't reach her eyes. "He's such a *generous* man."

"I'd hate for him to do something that would negatively impact his trial. He doesn't know the American legal system like he does the Indian and Scottish systems." That wasn't strictly true. Morag was a huge fan of American police-procedural TV shows and he'd learned more than he cared to know about law enforcement in California when his daughter had vanished.

"I knew from your stage show, *The Tempest and the Sea,* that you had a wild imagination. It's good to see your troubles last year haven't dampened that imagination."

"Whatever he's asking you to do," Tempest said, "just make sure it's not something that's going to blow up in his face. I'm not nearly as forgiving as my grandfather."

# Chapter 15

**Y**ou struck out, huh?"

Tempest slammed the car door and sunk down in the seat, disconcerted by Fleur's parting words. "Follow that car."

Gideon laughed.

Tempest raised an eyebrow.

He stopped laughing. "You're serious?"

"We might as well try."

They lost Fleur less than five minutes later, as soon as she got on the freeway at a spot that split in two directions. Fleur crossed two lanes quickly to take the highway they weren't expecting and Gideon wisely chose not to cause a traffic accident. Tailing someone in a distinctive baby-blue 1960s Renault shipped over from France wasn't the best way to be inconspicuous.

Once they gave up, Gideon drove them to Hidden Creek's town center, which consisted of a small main road that retained a historical Main Street feeling. It was packed with small shops and cafés, like Lavinia's Veggie Magic, with a tree-filled hillside behind one side and a more modern plaza on the other. The more modern plaza included a multilevel parking garage and a midsize supermarket where Tempest thought she'd be able to get the items on the list for her grandfather. Twice a week, the plaza also held a farmer's market. This afternoon, they found a corner of the outdoor parking area filled with food-truck pop-ups.

Hidden Creek couldn't quite decide if it was a small town or a metropolis. Though near bigger cities, it hadn't been able to grow as much because of the constraints of the steep hillside and the underground creek that prevented buildings from being packed into every spot. The parking garage was relatively new and was a nice way to encourage people from nearby towns to visit both the cute main street and the amenities in the bigger plaza, but the town quickly abandoned charging for parking after experiencing the unintended consequence of people coming to town but circling nearby residential streets in search of free parking.

"Tacos?" Gideon asked as he maneuvered into a parking spot. "Rewind. I'm sure you can't think about eating at a time like—"

"No. It's a good idea. I'm starving." She hadn't realized how hungry she was until she saw the food trucks. She hadn't eaten all day. "If my grandfather has taught me nothing else, it's that it's important to take time to eat." She could have added *with people we care about* if she'd finished her grandfather's thought out loud, but she didn't want to weird things up between her and Gideon.

They split up as they each picked a different truck to order from. Tempest felt her tension ease slightly as she stepped into the line behind four others.

Tempest loved pop-ups. Not only food trucks, but temporary shops and experiences of all kinds that popped up in unused storefronts or outdoor spaces. She knew it was partly that she was a product of her generation, but she also loved them because so many of them strove to create the same effect as magic: presenting a surprise to the participant that brought them a sense of wonder. They were fleeting. Special. And they could be absolutely wondrous if you did them right.

She was thinking of implementing that pop-up theme to the farewell stage show she was planning. Since it was a one-off performance, she wanted it to feel special on multiple levels. She hadn't yet told her manager, Winston Kapoor, the full extent of what she was planning. Winnie would never approve.

Tempest had struggled for months to come up with a story that made a worthy follow-up to her first big headlining show, *The Tempest and the Sea.* Story came first. Always. Magic wasn't really about tricks. Not if you wanted an illusion to be memorable. It's easy to fool people. It's hard to make them gasp with wonder and get so swept up in a story they feel like a kid again.

After her name had been cleared of the charge of orchestrating a dangerous stunt that went horribly wrong and endangered lives, Tempest agreed to perform one final live televised show. That way she could go out with a bang, both bringing closure to her fans and setting herself up with a nice payment to get her started on building her own house in Hidden Creek, and to help her dad's business get back on its feet.

The problem? Her show didn't yet have an ending to its story.

Her farewell performance had to be a personal show. She'd followed in the footsteps of her mom and aunt, who'd been famed illusionists when they performed as the Selkie Sisters in Edinburgh thirty years ago—before they both died by magic. Emma and Elspeth Raj, with their otherworldly presence, spinning stories of their supposed origins as the daughters of a mythical selkie from Scottish lore and an Indian sailor, caught between the words of land and sea. Their grand illusions drew upon classic magic and used simple-yet-captivating devices like a magic lantern that cast mysterious shadows and wires hidden by mirrors and careful lighting.

After Aunt Elspeth and her mom were gone, Tempest created her own version of their story of the sea. A way for her to bring them both back to her, and give both herself and her audience a satisfying happy ending that didn't exist in real life.

For her farewell show, she knew she'd begin with their story. But this time, the ending would be far different. This time, the ending would be—

"Miss?" the man at the window asked, startling her from her thoughts. "What would you like to order?"

She'd been so caught up in the memories she hadn't realized she'd moved to the front of the line. She shook herself and ordered fluffy bao buns stuffed high with grilled chanterelle mushrooms in barbecue sauce. The food truck was called "Toadstool and Steam" and featured a steampunk-style illustration of a giant mushroom with a toad wearing a monocle and eating a bao bun.

Okay, so maybe it was sometimes the name and logo of a truck that were the most unique things about it. But the food was still damn good.

She made a note on her phone to look up where she could find the latest venture of her chef friend Juan, who'd taken over the Tandoori Palace restaurant when its previous owner retired and renamed it Odisha to Oaxaca, with a cool logo designed by his girlfriend. He'd reimagined it as a fusion restaurant with Indian dishes he'd perfected as head chef at the Tandoori Palace, mixed with his grandmother's Mexican influence. It was going so well that she'd heard he'd opened a couple of pop-up food trucks, but she didn't know when and where she could find them.

The winter air was crisp, so she and Gideon took his crispy tacos and her stuffed bao buns back to the car. There they'd also have more privacy than the crowded bar-height communal table a dozen others were gathered around.

"I love that food culture here is finally catching up to France and the Philippines," Gideon said after savoring a bite of his taco.

Tempest raised an eyebrow. "I know you get so caught up in your stone-carving you forget to sleep, but have you been living under one of those rocks? California has always had amazing tacos."

"But so many more people actually *appreciate it* now."

She couldn't answer, since she was fully appreciating her own meal and didn't want to rush to swallow the soft and savory bite.

Gideon finished his first taco and set the remaining one on the dashboard. He looked out the window for a few moments before turning to Tempest. "I'm sorry I wasn't there that night."

"You're not the gruesome type."

He shook his head. "But I'm the observant type. I wish I could have been there, since I might have seen something that would help exonerate Ash."

She smiled. "It wouldn't have mattered. Your superpower of being the observant one because you don't have a phone to scroll on was irrelevant that night. Sanjay took everyone's cell phones before the séance. None of us were obsessively scrolling on our screens. We were all paying attention. But that didn't matter. It was completely dark."

"Wait. Then how did you see him with the knife in his chest and know to turn on the lights?"

Tempest froze. "The light. . . . It flickered on for a few seconds."

"Weren't you all seated around the table holding each other's hands?"

He was right. How had the lights flickered on? She closed her eyes and thought back on what she'd seen. She knew her memories would be muddled and unreliable at this point because of the trauma, but was there anything clear still there?

Her eyes popped open. "The light didn't come from overhead. It was the fake fire."

"The projection of the cozy fireplace?"

"It was menacing the way it silently cast light and shadows. Like when you held a flashlight beneath your chin to tell a ghost story."

"Tempest. That projection is activated by a remote control. If you're sure nobody let go of anyone's hand . . ."

Tempest slipped her foot out of her sneaker without using her hands and wriggled her toes at him. It was difficult in the small space of his European car, but she'd done far more dramatic contortions in much tighter spots.

"You're saying someone used their feet?" Gideon attempted to look skeptical, but he wasn't very good at it. He had too generous a personality for skepticism.

"They could have. It's easy."

"Maybe for magicians like you or your grandfath—" He broke off when he realized what he was saying.

He wasn't wrong. That remote wasn't simply a button you could smash on and off with the ball of your foot. Someone clever had activated the soft, flickering light at that moment. Someone who'd just killed Corbin and now wanted everyone to see that they were seated at the table holding hands. The more Tempest pieced together, the more it looked like everything had been staged in such a precise manner for a reason.

"What about Sanjay?" Gideon added hastily. "How well do you really know—"

"It wasn't Sanjay."

"But you know it wasn't you or your grandfather. Someone put a lot of work into setting up a murder that looks a lot like a trick. It was Sanjay's séance."

"It wasn't him. Truly. But thank you. You've helped me clarify my thoughts. This wasn't just a murder. Someone was trying to cast suspicion in a particular direction." Tempest balled up the empty wrapper of her bao bun in the palm of her left hand and squeezed.

"I know you're frustrated—"

"You're not as observant as you think you are if that's what you think is happening." She blew on her hand, then uncurled her fingers one by one, revealing an empty hand.

"Someone wanted Corbin Colt's murder to look like the work of a magician," Gideon whispered.

"A magician who's also a doctor and would surely examine the body. Someone is trying to frame my grandfather."

# Chapter 16

We're not going inside," Gideon said the next morning as he and Tempest rang the doorbell at Lavinia's house.

They were bringing a basket of Ash's cardamom cookies along with a savory lentil stew and freshly made chapatis. Tempest shivered as they waited on the porch, both from the cool breeze and from her fear that someone was framing her grandfather.

She'd called Detective Rinehart and told him what she'd remembered about the lights that had flickered on during the séance, suggesting he check out the remote control. From his non-reaction, she couldn't tell if he already had that piece of information or whether he wasn't showing his hand. It was doubtful it would tell them anything regardless, since anyone in that room could have innocently handled the remote. Tempest missed Detective Blackburn more than she thought possible. Blackburn had been the one who worked the case of Tempest's missing mom. *The vanishing*, he'd called it. He hadn't told her everything, but he at least reacted like a human and told her what he could.

Even when others gave up quickly and said Emma Raj had

a mental break and was either dead or had run off, Blackburn kept working all the angles. He'd shut down the Whispering Creek Theater for such a long time that the chief of
police had to step in to release the crime scene. He hadn't
known Emma's disappearance was related to proving her
sister was murdered. Tempest hadn't known it at the time,
either. Blackburn hadn't been perfect, but he cared. What
would they have been able to find out if they'd known what
was really going on?

"You okay?" Gideon asked.

No, not really. Her grandfather was probably going to
prison. Her mom was probably dead. Her own life was only
slightly more put together than a hot mess.

"Just chilly," she said instead. It was true as well. Just not
the whole story.

"I'm surprised Ash wanted to give a sympathy basket to
Lavinia," Gideon said softly, "since she's one of the prime
suspects."

Tempest avoided his gaze.

Gideon groaned. "Ash didn't put this basket together, did
he? This was *your* idea to question the suspects. This is a
terrible—"

"I'm not stupid enough to go alone. I have you." She gave
him the most charming smile she could muster and rang
the doorbell again.

Lavinia Kingsley's home was far up the Hidden Creek
hillside from Tempest's family's house, with a view of the
San Francisco Bay, the Bay Bridge, and the Golden Gate
Bridge—as long as it wasn't foggy. Today, it was foggy. And
cold enough for Tempest to see her own breath.

Hidden Creek's hillside was filled with idiosyncrasies,
courtesy of an earthquake early in the previous century,
which had sent much of a natural creek underground. It

could be a jarring experience, if you weren't used to it, to be out to dinner at a restaurant or on a morning stroll and hear the lapping water of the creek when there was no running water visible, regardless of where you looked. The creek showed itself here and there, nestled into the hills near especially lush vegetation.

It was Kumiko who answered the door.

"Some food from my grandfather." Tempest held up the basket. "I'm sure you've heard about his arrest, but he didn't—"

"Of course he didn't harm Corbin," Kumiko snapped. "We all know that. He had the audacity to try to help that undeserving man. Ashok's heart is too big." She looked curiously at the basket. "What did he send?"

"Various breads, a stew, and cardamom cookies."

"Ash sent me his cardamom cookies?" Her face lit up. She opened the box of cookies on top, took one out, and took a bite, clearly not worried about poison like she had been when she thought her son-in-law had broken into her daughter's home. "He remembered I love them."

"For both you and Lavinia."

Kumiko's face fell. "She's still sleeping. Or trying to. It's been a terrible ordeal."

"We don't want to disturb her," Gideon said. "We're just dropping off food and extending our condolences. C'mon, Tempest."

They walked back toward Gideon's car. Kumiko closed the door behind them.

"Don't even think about it," Gideon said as they approached the car.

"What?"

"You're looking at the basement door."

"It's called 'Lavinia's Lair.' Not a basement." Tempest failed at pulling her eyes away from the crime-scene tape.

"It's also an active crime scene."

"I haven't done anything." She still wasn't looking at Gideon.

"Now you're gravitating toward that basement door."

"Am I?" She took a couple more steps toward the door. Bright yellow tape crisscrossed the frame, blocking the entrance. They'd know if she went inside. The door was probably locked anyway. "And it's a lair, remember?"

"Let me take you to get a new tire. Then I need to get to work."

Tempest sighed and spun on the heel of her ruby-red sneaker to face Gideon, who was leaning against the rounded hood of the car with his arms crossed. "Kumiko doesn't think my grandfather killed Corbin."

"She could have been acting polite. She could also still be watching us." He nodded toward the main house.

"Kumiko *isn't* polite," Tempest answered once they were safely inside the car. "And she took a bite of that cookie. She knew it was safe."

"You think *she* killed her son-in-law?" The idea flustered him enough he dropped the keys at his feet.

Was that a flutter of curtains coming from the house? "Or she knows who did."

# Chapter 17

G ideon dropped Tempest and her new tire back at Fiddler's Folly. Tempest knew he had work to do, so she assured him she could change a tire herself. It was true.

After doing so, she checked in on her grandfather, who
was happily chatting with an elderly man and a thin and
energetic greyhound who resembled its owner. The trio were
breakfasting at the outdoor dining table.

With her grandfather hardly noticing she'd departed,
Tempest slipped into her jeep and headed to the outskirts of
town. She had a meeting with the property manager of the
Whispering Creek Theater. She'd considered canceling, but
she could at least get the key today.

*Facing her fears.* That's why Tempest had signed a lease to
rent the empty theater. The plan was to practice the show
she was producing later that year. She'd gone back and forth
to Vegas a few times in the last couple of months, letting
her young friend Justin watch Abra while she was gone, but
after she'd sorted out logistics, now came the important part:
What *story* was she going to tell during her farewell show?

She knew, of course. Part of her had always known. *If* she
could pull it off.

This was the theater where her mom had vanished. Tempest wanted, more than anything, to find out what had really happened to her mom and aunt, to tell their stories. Justice. Closure. She wasn't sure what it was. She only knew she needed to bring things full circle here. As soon as her grandfather was cleared, she'd figure it out.

The theater's parking lot was empty except for a lone car. An electric SUV with shiny silver paint. Tall weeds grew through crevices in the asphalt in most of the lot, but the SUV's owner had selected a far-away spot in a pristine area the weeds hadn't yet conquered. Stepping out of her jeep, Tempest stepped around a bunch of flowers she only knew as "sourflowers," those bright yellow flowering weeds from her childhood.

A couple of playhouses had continued to use the theater in the year after Emma Raj vanished, but after a few strange incidents, rumors spread that the theater was haunted. Not serious rumors, but theater types were superstitious already (she knew never to say the name of "The Scottish Play"). Most likely the bigger motivating factor was that nearby theaters had better management and amenities. Performances migrated elsewhere, and for the last two years, Whispering Creek Theater had sat empty.

The property manager stood in front of the vaulted wooden door that led into the run-down theater, a distasteful look directed at a spiderweb. In a motion disguised nearly as skillfully as something Sanjay or Tempest could have done, she wiped the web aside with a tissue and was smiling brightly as soon as Tempest reached her four seconds later, leaving no evidence a spider had even looked at the theater's door.

"I don't mind a few spiders," said Tempest.

The woman's smile faltered. "I wasn't made aware of the current condition. . . ."

"It's fine." Tempest swept her eyes over the abandoned building, a combination of excitement and trepidation building every moment. She didn't miss many things about Las Vegas, but she missed the gasps from the audience. Their spontaneous smiles. The sense of wonder replenishing their childhood dreams.

"I can give you the number of a good cleaning team, if you'd like."

"It's really fine. I don't mind."

The confused property manager handed Tempest the keys and, after a few pleasantries that must have been mandated in a customer-service training manual, retreated from the abandoned theater to her pristine vehicle. Tires screeched as she pulled out of the empty lot.

The heavy wooden door squealed so loudly as Tempest pulled it open that it nearly disguised a different sound. Another car pulled the parking lot.

A woman with hair as pitch-black as Tempest's, though rail straight instead of wavy, sat behind the wheel. After turning off the engine, nothing happened for seven seconds. Indecision? Lavinia Kingsley stepped out, her face splotchy and subdued. Dressed in a black dress that reached her ankles, she looked the part of a grieving widow.

"My mom said you stopped by." Lavinia's dress billowed as the wind picked up. "I thought you might be here."

*Alone.*

Even if Lavinia had good reason to kill Corbin and wasn't a deranged serial killer, Tempest still didn't like the idea of being alone with her in the deserted parking lot under the barren hillside above that was too steep and rocky for homes. They had only a few birds for company. Oh, and one squirrel. Though the squirrel was running in the opposite direction. Its floppy tail disappeared around the trunk of a tree.

"I wanted to thank you for bringing over the food from your grandfather," Lavinia said. "Those cookies are Ma's favorite. More than anything at Veggie Magic." She hesitated. "I'm sorry for what happened to him."

"He didn't—"

"I know he didn't hurt Corbin. Even with what he . . ." She hesitated again. "You know about what happened between them?"

"The restraining order."

"I didn't want Corbin to do it. He could be so vindictive. Darius and Ashok knew I tried to stop him. I couldn't stop him, but I made sure Ash got a free meal whenever he came to Veggie Magic." She shook her head. "Your grandfather wouldn't even let me do that for him. He always left so big a tip that it covered everything."

"That sounds like him."

"I know he'd never kill anyone. We all know that."

"Except for that new detective and the DA."

"I told them to look into Corbin's fans. That's all that makes sense. People are passionate about books. His books evoked strong feelings in his readers. They're the kind of people who would create a bizarre death for him. That has to be it." Lavinia squeezed her keys as the words poured out of her.

"You told the detective?"

"I even gave the police some of the strangest letters." She paused. "Corbin wasn't always like this, you know. When I first met him, he was a completely different man. He loved writing and everything related to it. By the time my café was a success, I was living a full life, with hobbies I truly enjoyed like my book club. But Corbin? His career had gone the opposite direction. He started refusing to come to Veggie Magic because it was so successful—he said it was because it was crowded and noisy. We never managed to have children, and we were each so busy pursuing our separate lives that I shouldn't have been surprised by his affairs. I was angry, yes. I wanted him out of my life. But I didn't really want to kill him. I was just angry when I spoke to you. I didn't—"

"Is that why you followed me here?"

"You say it like—" She broke off and swore. Then laughed. Not a timid or fake laugh, but a throaty, unstoppable howl. "Email and text messages are the worst. I thought I was helping put you at ease by coming. So you could look me in the eye and know I didn't kill him."

Lavinia didn't step closer to Tempest, but she did as she said and looked Tempest in the eye. In front of a theater where hundreds of people once told lies for a living, the apparent sincerity was less convincing.

"You don't have to worry," Tempest said. "The police aren't focused on you."

"I don't want you to think I'm the one who did it, either." A look of disgust came over Lavinia's face, but it wasn't directed at Tempest. She unclasped her hand, revealing indentations in her palm where she'd been gripping her keys. It was more than a depression in the skin. Something sticky. Had Lavinia drawn blood? She wiped her palm on the skirt of her dress and turned back.

Tempest could have taken the opportunity to let Lavinia leave, now that she'd said her piece, and get to work at the theater. But Lavinia had been ready to share her thoughts. That's why Tempest had made up a story to go to Lavinia's house that morning in the first place. Lavinia might have facts that could get Grandpa Ash cleared.

"You really think it was one of his fans?" Tempest called after her.

Lavinia paused at the door of the car. "Who else would do such a thing?"

"None of them were in the Oxford Comma with us."

"You think his death is an impossible crime like in one of the books we read in the Detection Keys book club?"

"It is."

Lavinia turned her face to the sky. The cool wind blew her hair around her face. "I know you're right. I wish you weren't."

"How long have you known the women in the book club?"

Lavinia tucked her hair behind her ear and gave Tempest a frosty stare. "Long enough that I'd hate to think one of them is responsible. But after Corbin's betrayal . . . I know better than to trust someone simply because I've known them a long time. But the women of the Detection Keys . . . we understand each other."

"You named the club after the famous British club of mystery writers."

That got the hint of a smile from Lavinia. "You're right. The name pays homage to the U.K.'s Detection Club, the group of writers who founded the social club during the Golden Age of detective fiction. We're not writers, but we love their books. Each of us has a name that begins with one of the letters in the word 'KEYS.' It was Ellery who thought of that, since she loves puzzles. I'm Lavinia Kazumi Kingsley, so I'm the 'K.' Ellery and Sylvie are obvious."

"And Ivy is your 'Y': Youngblood."

"It all came together at Veggie Magic. Sylvie and Ellery were two customers who loved to linger after their meal to talk about mystery books. They always tipped generously, so we didn't mind that they stayed so long. One day I heard Sylvie and Ellery bemoaning their book club, in which the women only wanted to read the hot new books recommended by celebrities and often spent more time picking out the wine for the meeting than actually reading the books. I'd also seen Ivy reading classic mysteries by herself at the café. I proposed the four of us get together for a trial book club meeting over coffee before Veggie Magic opened for the day. Sylvie was skeptical about inviting Ivy, since Ivy is so much younger than the rest of us. She suspected that Ivy thought of classic mysteries as a fad, like high-waisted jeans and fanny packs."

"I bet Ivy knew more than any of you."

"She did. It was clear straight away that even though she was young, she was a perfect fit."

"Plus she made the 'KEYS' possible."

Lavinia turned her face back to the sky. "I never should have let your grandfather insert himself." The warmth that had been palpable in Lavinia's voice when she spoke about the Detection Keys was gone. Now her voice was cold. Ominous, even. It was like she was a completely different person. "I knew something was going to happen that night." Lavinia snapped her gaze back to Tempest. "I knew. Ever since Corbin wrecked my typewriter—"

"It wasn't him."

"What?" Anger flashed in her eyes.

"He was in New York meeting with publishing people at the time. He only got back the day before the séance."

"No. That's impossible. It had to be him. Maybe he asked one of his twisted fans to do it for him. Whatever it was, he was behind it. He was like that character, the Raven, from his first novel."

Tempest felt her skin prickle. Did Lavinia believe he could turn himself into a raven? "You don't really think—"

Lavinia laughed. This time it was a haunting, shrill laugh,

like a banshee from the pages of folklore come to life. Tempest had never heard such a sound from Lavinia before. Was it grief, or something more?

"I don't think he flew from Forestville to Hidden Creek," Lavinia said, "if that's what you mean. But his attempt to turn around his literary decline transformed him into a man so different from the one I married nearly thirty years ago. His quest consumed him. He's the Raven, all right."

# Chapter 18

Tempest left the theater an hour later, satisfied that it had potential to work as a performance space. No creaks sounded on the stage even when she landed hard after a running flip and a backbend kickover. Part of her wished she could exorcise the memories that filled her with trepidation. But they also gave her strength.

When she stepped out of the theater back into the parking lot, the sun was high in the sky and momentarily blinded her. She wasn't entirely certain she saw it—but she heard it. Another car was peeling out of the parking lot at high speed. Maybe it was just her imagination. The theater wasn't on a dead-end road. It was simply on a road not frequently used that led to the steepest part of the hillside with barely any development. Still, she hurried into her car and locked the doors.

When she reached Fiddler's Folly a few minutes later, a small woman with long blond hair divided into two braids was leaning against one of the ancient oak trees on the street in front of the house, looking like a pixie who'd stepped out of the knot of the tree. The circus performer, Fleur.

Tempest parked on the side of the street instead of continuing up the driveway.

"I didn't have your number." Fleur stepped away from the tree and shook loose a piece of bark from her hair, giving her an even more elfin presence. "I have no idea what your schedule is, so I almost gave up."

"You decided to tell me what he asked you to do?"

Fleur twisted one of the braids in her hand, then watched it unravel as she let go. "I can't do what he asked. I need to tell you, in case you can help instead."

Tempest waited, not wanting to push. Two birds flapped their wings overhead and took flight from the tree above.

"If Ash killed that man," Fleur continued after a full eight seconds, "I have no doubt he deserved it."

"He didn't—"

"If you want to help him, I'll tell you what he wanted me to do."

Tempest wanted to convince her there was no way her grandfather was a killer. But any argument she made would have been counterproductive. "Please," she said instead. "Tell me what he wanted you to do."

Fleur twisted her hair around her finger once more. "He hired me to retrieve a book."

"A book?"

*"And Then There Were None."*

"An Agatha Christie novel? Why did he want an old mystery novel?"

"I don't know. Not exactly. He made me promise that no matter what happened, I wouldn't look inside the book he asked me to find for him."

Tempest shivered. What did her grandfather not want Fleur to see? This was getting more and more strange. She needed to bring the conversation back to the one thing she knew—or at least strongly suspected. "He asked you to get it because you can contort your body and get through small spaces?"

She gave a single nod. "I asked if it was a rare first edition or something. He assured me the item was nothing of value. *Except to him.*"

"Where were you supposed to get the book from?"

"A private house."

"Breaking and entering?"

Fleur shook her head firmly. "No. He specifically asked me to look for open windows. People never think to close windows that they don't expect a human body to be able to fit through." She grabbed hold of her heel and extended her leg until it was over her head. "No breaking in. Just entering through unconventional means."

"You'd do that for him? How much did he pay you?"

Fleur dropped out of her contortionist pose. "Not as much as he offered to give me. But hell yes. He's a good man. I know he didn't kill that man. I wish I could have helped, but I need to give the money back."

"Because you couldn't follow through."

"I don't do security systems. Especially high-end security like that house."

"Where exactly are we talking about?"

"The house owned by the woman known on the internet for her *Happy Hour with Hazel* show."

Tempest stared at her. "That's Corbin Colt's new girlfriend." The woman involved with one of the impossibilities surrounding Corbin's baffling death.

"I know. Ash didn't lie to me. He told me exactly what I'd be getting into."

Tempest swore. Why did her grandfather need an old book

of Corbin's? "You said he asked you not to look inside. And that you didn't 'exactly' know what was in the book. What did you *think* he meant?"

"He said the book was important for this case against him."

Tempest's mind bounced from possibility to possibility. How could a book exonerate Grandpa Ash? "He didn't say how it would help his case?"

"I got the feeling something was written inside the book. That's why he'd say he didn't want me to open it, right?"

"He's been talking to the police with his attorney. He should have—"

"I told him exactly that. If this book would prove his innocence, he should tell the police and they could seize the book as evidence." Fleur twisted a curl of hair around her fingers so tightly her fingertips turned white. "Ash said *they wouldn't understand* what's inside. He made me promise not to go to them. Or to look. He stressed that at least three times."

This couldn't be good.

"I agreed," Fleur continued, "but I had no intention of keeping the second part of my promise. I understand not trusting the police, but if I was going to take so big a risk, I was going to see what was inside. That would be my reward. Helping your grandfather—and *knowing*."

Tempest looked at this unexpected woman. "You don't care about the money."

"Of course not." Fleur spoke the words as if they were distasteful. "If I did, I could have chosen a much easier profession. I also don't care if your grandfather is guilty. Ashok is a good man. If he killed that writer, I have no doubt that man deserved it."

"He didn't. Whatever is written inside that book is important to proving his innocence, like he told you."

"But I won't ever know. Hazel's house has a full-on security setup. If you ask me, she thinks she's a bigger deal than she is, thinking she needs so much security to keep away fans."

Tempest thought back on what she and Ivy had discussed about Hazel interacting with her fans. *Could it* have been a trick? Was her video filmed ahead of time?

"You okay, Tempest?" Fleur asked.

"I just wish I knew what was going on."

"I wish I could help. Take care, Tempest." Fleur turned, but instead of walking down the street to her car, she began walking toward the house.

"Don't return the money," Tempest said.

Fleur turned back.

"He'd want you to have it," Tempest added. "I know he would."

Fleur nodded slowly. "Maybe. But of more import to you, if I go talk to him, he'll know he needs to figure out another plan. It looks like he's not the only stubborn one in the family. Just remember, whoever retrieves that book for your grandfather, they'll have to contend with top-notch security. Ash is treating this like a game. It's not."

Whatever was going on, it was certainly a game to someone. How had Hazel worked the trick with her livestream? Was Corbin's new girlfriend involved in Corbin's death? Tempest couldn't ignore Hazel's part in someone's game any longer.

# Chapter 19

L et me get this straight," said Sanjay. "You're attempting to get past the state-of-the-art security system of an internet celebrity to steal a book belonging to a dead man that your grandfather desperately wants but won't tell the police about."

"Pretty much." Tempest was stretched out on the bean bag in her bedroom, on the phone with Sanjay as she looked up at the pinprick stars on the ceiling above that formed a skeleton-key constellation.

"You can't do it alone. At least wait until I'm done with these shows and am back in town."

"That'll be days from now. Time I don't have if I'm right that someone is framing Ash."

Sanjay swore in Punjabi.

"Thanks for being a sounding board." Tempest closed her eyes and imagined he was there with her for one last moment. "I know you need to get back to your rehearsal."

"They can wait."

"Break a leg." Tempest clicked off, then slipped down her secret staircase and across the grounds to the tree house.

Her grandfather had invited his attorney, Vanessa, over

for lunch, along with her wife, Dahlia, and their daughter Natalie. The idea was to have a practical meeting between Ash and his attorney, since he couldn't leave Fiddler's Folly, but sociable Ash couldn't resist inviting the whole family. There would be no talk of legal matters during lunch, but Vanessa had driven separately from the rest of her family so she could stay for a private meeting with her client afterward.

"Ms. Raj!" six-year-old Natalie squealed from the open front door of the tree house. "Mamma V said I could ask you if you could get Abracadabra from his castle for me to play with."

"I'll get him in a minute," Tempest said with a smile. Abra's grand bunny hutch was indeed built with turrets to look like a fairy-tale castle. Not that Abra appreciated the castle motif, but he enjoyed the space, since he couldn't roam free twenty-four hours a day. "Let me say hello to your parents first, and then I'll go get him."

The adults were gathered in the kitchen as Ash stirred the fragrant contents of a cast-iron skillet with a wooden spoon and Darius fixed a carafe of iced tea. Dahlia wrapped her arms around Tempest as soon as she spotted her behind her daughter. Tempest hugged her back.

"Let me know if there's anything else I can do." Dahlia gave her one last squeeze before letting go.

Dahlia was Ivy's older sister, which is how they'd met Vanessa, though they'd never had need of her legal services until now. Dahlia shared the same naturally red hair as Ivy, and you could guess that they were sisters, but you'd never mistake one for the another. Contrasting Ivy's petite frame and penchant for pink, Dahlia wore vibrant colors that showed off her numerous curves, sported thick-rimmed cat-eye glasses in bright yellow, and spoke with a loud and confident voice that matched.

Tempest grinned back at her. "You've already helped us get the best lawyer."

Vanessa gave Tempest a much briefer hug, but a smile just as warm. "Good to see you, Tempest."

Dahlia hooked her arm around Tempest's elbow. "Nat wants to play with Tempest's bear-size bunny. We'll be back with him in a minute. Between the two of us, we should be able to carry him. Right, Tempest?"

Natalie giggled and waved goodbye.

"I can carry my bunny by myself, you know." Tempest closed the door behind them.

Dahlia held a finger to her lips. "After you. I can't tell which direction we're supposed to walk."

From this vantage point, in the thickest section of trees on the property, it was possible to imagine the tree house was the only dwelling for miles. If no traffic was passing on the residential street below, and if the wind blew in the right direction, the sound of the hidden creek that gave the town its name filled the air, sounding almost like a raging river after heavy rainfall. Tempest led the way to the Secret Fort with Abra's hutch.

"She'll come looking for us if we're not back in ten minutes," Dahlia said once they'd cleared the tree house. "That doesn't give me long to convince you to stop."

"Stop what?"

"Vanessa is an amazing attorney and your grandfather is innocent. She'll get him acquitted if it goes to trial. You don't need to investigate."

"Says the woman who writes about true crime."

Dahlia's glasses slipped down her nose as she stepped over

a gnarled tree root. "Historical cold cases are totally different. Nobody is alive to come after me if I poke my nose in the wrong place."

"Who says I'm investigating?" Tempest knew Ivy wouldn't have ratted her out.

"Wow." Dahlia stopped in front of the partially constructed stone tower. "That's the most spectacular bunny house I've ever seen."

"Come on in." Tempest stepped through the doorway that lacked a door, into the stone structure without a roof. Abra's castle-style hutch took up only a small corner of the tower, but the sprawling hutch gave Abracadabra a lot of room to explore. The gargantuan gray lop-eared rabbit came to the main door of the hutch to greet his visitors.

Dahlia knelt in front of the hutch. "I should have brought him some food so he'll like me."

"He's eaten enough as it is." Tempest scooped Abra into her arms. With so many people fussing over him, he'd gained several pounds since she'd moved home. "He likes being scratched between his ears."

"Don't distract me with a cute pet."

"You were desperate to help me investigate last time—"

"Which was a terrible, terrible idea. Can I hold him? Hey there, little guy. Oh my God, he's heavy! I stopped picking up Nat before she got this big. No, I've got him. Forget about what my past self told you. I'm an older, wiser woman than I was last year. I have gray hair now. Look." She tilted her head toward Tempest, revealing not even a hint of gray. "Gray. Hair."

"There's no gray."

"Really?" She swore. "I thought I spotted a couple the other day. Van says I need to act older for some of my sources to take me more seriously. Good thing my next interview is with a guy my age. But still, gray hair or not, I'm older and wiser than I was when I tried get involved."

"It was only a few months ago."

"Different calendar year." Dahlia straightened and adjusted Abra in her arms. "One of my New Year's resolutions is to stop giving friends bad advice."

"That's a strangely specific resolution."

"You haven't been home long enough to know you should never listen to my advice. I convinced one of my girlfriends to dye her hair white. It looks really stylish on a lot of people. On her? Not so much. People kept thinking she was her daughter's grandmother."

"Ouch."

"I told another friend she should do the wasabi challenge at a restaurant, to eat a whole rice ball filled with wasabi, to make the restaurant's wall of fame."

"No." Tempest's throat and stomach ached psychosomatically when she thought about eating such a large amount of spicy Japanese horseradish.

Dahlia bit her lip. "I'm afraid so. She's still not speaking to me."

"But you're telling me not to investigate on my own. By your logic, that means I should."

"But my gut is telling me you should investigate. What I'm saying out loud is the opposite of my real advice."

"That makes no sense."

"I think I'm going to fall over."

Tempest took Abra back from Dahlia. "Did Vanessa ask you to talk with me?"

"God, no. Vanessa is the most professional of professional professionals. Did I mention she's a professional? I know absolutely nothing about the case. It's not like on TV how everyone tells everyone else their legally protected business.

How is every single TV lawyer not disbarred? My sister didn't give you up, either. I've known you since I was a kid."

"I've been gone a long time. A lot has happened."

"Life happens to all of us. Just because I haven't known you in years, doesn't mean I don't know you." Dahlia ran her fingertips over one of the rough stones of the unfinished tower. "Whatever you do, please be safe."

"I will."

Abra squirmed in Tempest's arms as they made their way back to the tree house, as if he could sense the fact that she was lying.

"Sometimes I hate how smart you are," Tempest whispered to the bunny.

Natalie played with Abra on the deck, which was effectively an extension of the kitchen. Ash had grown up with a traditional South Indian kitchen, with no real distinction between the outdoor and indoor spaces of the kitchen, and he'd created the same feeling here. The sliding door to the deck was almost always open, even when the weather was bad. Between the awning and the protection of the sprawling oak tree, there was plenty of protection from the rain.

"When do we make the pizza?" Natalie asked.

Ash chuckled. "Do you want to help?"

She scrambled up from her spot sitting cross-legged with Abra on her lap and joined them inside.

"I'm making the jackfruit topping for the pizza," Ash said, "but I need someone who can roll out the turmeric pizza dough."

He scooped a ball of orange-tinted dough that had been rising on the counter, set Natalie up at the breakfast-nook table, and showed her how to roll out the dough into two

pizzas after she washed her hands. They topped the two pizzas with a tomato-jackfruit sauce and mozzarella.

"It's like magic," Natalie said as she watched the crust rise
and the toppings bubble through the oven's glass door as the
pizzas baked. "I want to be a baker."

"Not a writer like Mommy D?" Vanessa asked.

"Both." Natalie grinned.

They ate the pizzas at the deck's dining table, talking
about food, movies, and a new clothing shop that had
opened downtown that carried amazing shoes, according
to Dahlia—basically anything except for the case. Natalie
was riveted by the conversation about how large a jackfruit
grows once Ash explained that they often weighed more
than fifteen pounds—heavier than Abra.

"Can we plant a jackfruit tree next to my lemon tree?"
Natalie asked after she'd had a second slice of pizza.

"I don't think they grow in this climate, Nat," Vanessa
said.

"It's true," Ash confirmed. "But I have a secret." He disappeared into the kitchen and returned a few seconds later
holding an empty can with a label showing green jackfruit.
"Shh. Don't tell my secret."

"Want to see Abra's house before you leave?" Tempest
asked Natalie.

"His castle!" she squealed. "Come on, Abra. I'll take you
home." He came when she called him and hopped down the
stairs at her side.

On the way to the Secret Fort, a whirring noise came from
the Secret Staircase workshop, the last of four structures
on the property. Her dad and grandfather were still at the
tree house with Natalie's parents, but someone was making
noise inside the workshop.

"Why are you stopping?" Natalie asked. "Are you tired from carrying Abra?"

"That's either your aunt Ivy or my friend Gideon, who I want to talk to. Let's take a detour."

Hoping it might be Gideon, who was hard to track down due to his lack of cell phone, Tempest moved Abra into the crook of her left arm and slid open the barn doors with her free hand.

It wasn't Gideon.

This was a much larger person. One hiding behind a mask.

# Chapter 20

Tempest didn't step into the workshop. She would never be one of those characters in Ivy's books that her former-maybe-once-again BFF deemed Too Stupid To Live.

The masked man held a whirring circular saw in his large, calloused hand. He switched off the saw as soon as he saw his visitors. He raised the face shield covering his face. Victor's bearded face came into view.

Tempest let out a breath she didn't realize she'd been holding. The mask wasn't a disguise. It was to keep out dust and debris from the wood he was sawing through. It was foolish of her to have been so on edge when she first saw him.

Or was it?

Victor grinned at her. "Hi, Tempest. And who's this?"

Tempest trusted Victor to help her build her own house and to have her dad's back on a building site. But she'd been wrong about people before. Victor had only been working with Secret Staircase Construction for the past three months. What did she really know about him? He was one of the people at the séance, and he wasn't supposed to be working on any building project she knew of. That's what had put her on high alert even when she saw who it was.

Tempest kept hold of Abra as she crouched down at Natalie's side. "I'll show you Abra's house a little later. This workshop is dangerous, with lots of power tools like that one. I'll meet you back at the tree house with everyone else in a minute. You can follow the path back up the hill?"

Natalie nodded. She waved goodbye and ran off.

Victor pulled the face shield all the way off his head and stretched his neck. "You don't trust me." He didn't look hurt. More amused than anything.

"Is there a reason I shouldn't?" Abra attempted to kick free of her arms, sensing her continued discomfort.

"There's a reason you *should*. I'm here because I want to help clear your grandfather."

Tempest eyed the wooden panels on the tabletop where he'd been working. "You have a theory about how the killer maneuvered Corbin Colt's body into place."

He grinned. "I was working on ideas on paper at my place. But I had to test my theory. That's what I'm doing here."

"Is that a jungle gym?" Tempest stepped around the table to a set of bright blue bars like you'd find on a playground. There were often strange new things that appeared in the barn-like workshop, but she hadn't seen a jungle gym in there before.

"Borrowed from my sister's backyard. Actually, 'borrowed' is the wrong word. Her kids are in college now, so she'd rather have the space for a garden."

"You're going to outfit the jungle-gym bars with the contraption you built."

"Bingo." He rubbed his hands together with excitement. "I started off with really complex ideas, but quickly realized it had to be as simple as possible to work in practice."

Tempest could imagine him as a kid dreaming up Rube Goldberg machines to perform simple tasks with overly complex, but fun, engineering.

"I thought of it," he continued, "as soon as the shock of seeing him . . ." Victor trailed off and his eager smile fell away. "I've never seen a dead body before. Not outside of a funeral, I mean. That was . . . *terrible* isn't even a bad enough word to describe it."

"Horrifying," Tempest whispered. "Absolutely horrifying." Abra nuzzled her hand, sensing her sadness just as he'd sensed her fear moments before.

"That has to be why I didn't think of it right away, when I could have checked—"

"I did. I checked. Sanjay did, too."

"Did you—"

"We didn't see anything."

"It would have been disguised. The mechanism and its harness could have been painted to look like the ceiling."

Tempest shook her head. "Sanjay attached things to the ceiling when he set up for the séance, and the police arrived before anyone could take anything away."

"A smart criminal could hide it so they wouldn't find it in their first pass," he suggested, but his voice was no longer confident. He must have known he was grasping at straws at this point. "Those walls of the little pub in Lavinia's Lair don't reach the ceiling. Something could have been rigged to move a body into the room."

"Something we're just not seeing?" Something hidden in plain sight . . . What were they missing?

"Don't be so skeptical." Victor tugged nervously at his beard. "I have to be right."

"Why?"

"Because if I'm wrong," Victor said, "it would mean that

someone at the séance is truly responsible for his death. But if I'm right, it could have been anyone."

"I want to believe that, too, but you're forgetting one important thing. Even if your contraption works and the killer used something similar; even if the police didn't find it in time and the killer had time to sneak in and remove it; even if all those things are true, there's the time of death. Corbin was killed *once we were all in that room together*. So even if we find a cleverly concealed hiding spot where he was tied up or unconscious, it doesn't answer the question of how someone slipped away." Or how he traveled fifty-five miles within minutes. Or why they staged him like they did.

Victor gripped the edge of his wooden contraption in frustration. "Maybe there's a way to add an automated knife-thrower. . . ." He caught her eye. "I guess none of this is too realistic since there was no evidence of tampering with our design when the room was searched."

"It was a good idea, though."

He kicked the table, sending three large screws to the concrete floor below. "A good idea doesn't clear your grandfather or—" He broke off abruptly.

"Or *what?*" Tempest struggled to keep hold of Abra, who didn't like kicking.

"I don't like accepting what that means."

"I know." Tempest held Abra close. "That there's no getting around the truth that someone in that room killed Corbin Colt."

# Chapter 21

After the unexpected diversion, Tempest made good on her promise to show Natalie Abra's house in the Secret Fort before going back to the main house to move forward with her plan to clear her grandfather. Sanjay was the rational choice for someone to help her with her wild idea, but he was performing out of town.

Ivy was still at work and Gideon wasn't answering his landline, but she knew he often let it go through to his answering machine—a real live answering machine!—if he was working on a sculpture. Tempest sent Ivy a text and left Gideon a message. Ivy texted her back to say she was in, but after half an hour there was still no word from Gideon.

She drove to Gideon's house in Oakland and let herself in through the side gate. His studio door was open and she spotted him in front of a slab of limestone with a tool in each hand. She'd been right. He was chiseling on a stone creature. She froze when she saw what it was.

A raven.

No, that was just her imagination. It was a bird with large eyes and a long beak. But not necessarily a raven. And its body wasn't just a bird. The bird head blended into the body of an amphibious creature.

"Raven-lizard?" she asked.

He pulled an air filtration mask from his face. "Crow and salamander. A commission requested the combo. I'd never done one like it. It's a challenge."

Though he'd never carved this exact creature before, it still radiated the magical feeling that came through with every stone he touched. The expressions on the faces of his stone carvings made them seem like living, breathing creatures. It didn't take a big stretch of the imagination to think of them climbing off their perches, stretching their necks, and walking or flying off into the wider world beyond Gideon's backyard.

"I left you a message on your answering machine earlier."

"The beak was tricky, so I've been here the whole time with Cas."

"Cas?"

"Crow-and-salamander." He wiped stone dust off his hands and led her to an answering machine as big as a shoebox. It looked like one she'd seen at the indoor section of a salvage yard she'd visited while looking for knickknacks for a house whose owners wanted multiple sliding bookcases—yet the owners weren't readers. They wanted a certain vintage aesthetic.

He pushed a black plastic button as big as his thumb and played back the message before deleting it. "I'm in."

"I didn't even tell you the details of my plan in the message."

He shrugged. "I figure that's because it's bad enough you didn't want any evidence left behind."

"Then why did you say you were in?"

"Because it's bad enough that you need help. What do you need me to do?"

Gideon and Ivy were both in. A former stage magician, a librarian-in-training, and a stone carver planning a heist. What could possibly go wrong?

☠☠☠

"Maybe we're after a cipher," Ivy said an hour later. She'd arrived at Gideon's house after getting off work at the Locked Room Library, and Tempest had handed her the notes she'd compiled already. They were now sprawled in front of his stone fireplace shaped like the open mouth of a dragon, with both paper notebooks and electronic devices spread across the floor. "Corbin could have used that particular edition of *And Then There Were None* as the key to a coded message your grandfather needs to decipher."

"Why would he do that?" Gideon asked.

Tempest shook her head. "I've been thinking about something that makes more sense. Agatha Christie loved to populate her novels with characters who all had something to hide. *And Then There Were None* especially. If my grandfather thinks Corbin wrote something important inside this book that could clear him—"

"The characters," Ivy squealed.

"I have no idea what you two are talking about." Gideon looked from Ivy to Tempest.

"Parallels." Tempest stood and made sure there was room for her to spin. She pushed off into a pirouette. Then another. It all made sense. She came to a halt in front of the haunting fireplace. "Corbin Colt's debut was so successful because of the creepy, well-written story, but people also noticed the subtle social commentary and real-world parallels. He loved doing that. It makes sense he'd scribble notes into the books of other authors."

"You mean assigning the roles of real-life people to characters in that book?" Gideon asked.

"People," said Tempest, "with something to hide."

"Who were at the séance," Ivy murmured.

"His killer," Tempest said, "could be named inside the book."

Nobody spoke for eleven seconds.

"I don't know." Gideon ran his fingers along the stone hearth he'd carved. "It's a big leap."

Tempest shrugged. "I know. I'm probably wrong. We have no idea what's written inside that book. Which is why we need to get it." She pointed back at the pile of papers and devices they'd been using to plan the break-in.

"Right," Ivy said. "Back to work. It's scary how much information about Hazel and her house is available online. I didn't know Hazel wasn't her real name."

"She calls herself that because of her green-flecked hazel eyes," Gideon said.

"No, really?" Ivy deadpanned. "The photos of her and her mom show they've got the same eyes."

"The ones taken on an unnamed Caribbean island?" Tempest asked. "I think that's her aunt, from the captions. She can't decide how much she wants to share online versus how much to keep private. She was born on an undisclosed Caribbean island, where her family is from, then raised since elementary school somewhere in the U.S."

Real estate photos of her house were publicly available from previous online listings, and Hazel shared enough snippets of her life online to get a good idea of what her living situation was. She'd lived alone before Corbin moved in. No pets or kids underfoot. Like Fleur had said, it was a house with an extensive security system. At least that's what two signs stuck in her yard warned would-be burglars. Hazel wasn't stupid. She was a minor internet celebrity living alone. Of course she'd have security.

"I brought these." Ivy tossed a pile of Donald Westlake novels onto the coffee table. "Heist capers."

"Don't those heists always end badly?" Tempest asked.

"Hmm." Ivy scooped the books back into her bag. "Maybe another time."

"We're doomed," Gideon said half an hour later. "We can't defeat a security system. We don't even know if those little signs are really the company she uses."

If they'd been a real crew of thieves, they could have disarmed an alarm. But that wasn't in the cards.

"We also have to remember she could be involved in Corbin's death," Tempest added, "since she's mixed up in the trick that had thousands of her fans seeing Corbin in two far-apart places within minutes. Dozens of fans would have had to fake their 'live' interaction with her and lied about it, which seems really risky. We don't know what she's capable of. We need to figure out how to defeat her security system *and* be careful around her."

Gideon groaned.

"Gideon is right," Ivy said. "It looks pretty hopeless."

"Not if we stop trying to plan a heist," Tempest said.

Ivy scowled at her. "You're giving up?"

"No. I'm saying we use the skills at our disposal. We don't plan a heist. We plan *a trick*."

# Chapter 22

Their best option was to steal the book while Hazel was home, with her never realizing anything was wrong. Tempest proposed the magic-trick-style plan that could allow them to pull it off.

Ivy would play the role of a woman Corbin had dated, to distract Hazel while Tempest searched the house. Ivy would have to read Hazel's reaction to decide whether to spring the revelation that Corbin was dating other people at the same time or commiserate as an ex-girlfriend about the loss of a man they had both once loved.

Gideon had worked as a stonemason on government jobs where things like retaining walls were needed, and he had a vest and a hard hat he could use to look like an official city construction worker doing work outside her house. The hillside near Hazel's house could reasonably be in need of shoring up. A surveyor in an orange vest and a hard hat that shielded his face from view wouldn't be memorable as an individual.

"You'll both make enough noise to cover my actions inside the house," said Tempest, "and you'll also serve as a force."

"A force?" asked Gideon.

"It's a concept in magic where you basically force an audience member to do what you want them to do, even when they think they're doing it of their own free will."

"Like picking a specific card," he said.

"Exactly. You'll be making noise on the side of the house where we think the main room and Corbin's study are located, forcing Hazel to see Ivy in the kitchen rather than the living room."

"I still can't get over how terrifying it is," Ivy cut in, "that we can get so much information about Hazel and her house online. It's not even like we hacked anything."

Tempest nodded. "I'm guessing she has cameras in addition to an alarm, which is why it's so important that she never know something is wrong to pull up any video feeds."

"And why we'll be in disguise if she does."

Tempest's makeup-artist contacts were in Vegas, which would do them no good here. But with Ivy's distinctive auburn hair, they realized all they had to do was buy a brown wig. That was enough to have her not be recognizable as herself.

"The timing is important, too," said Tempest. "Within a half-an-hour window in the mid-morning, Hazel usually posts a photo online of a beautifully staged coffee, tea, or smoothie."

"I saw that," Ivy said. "She doesn't do a video then, but it's the first happy hour of the day, according to Hazel."

"According to the online version of herself," Tempest added. "So there's a good chance she'll be at home during that time, and also that she'll have fresh drinks in the kitchen."

Tempest next taught Ivy how to wipe her fingerprints off a glass, which they decided would be a good idea before Ivy departed. They expected Hazel would offer Ivy something to drink, but they didn't know what, or what she'd serve it in, so they practiced with a mug, a tumbler, and a wine glass similar to the one Hazel photographed berry smoothies in.

"If we were in a movie," Ivy commented, "I'd simply have false fingertips with different fingerprints."

"If it were a movie," said Tempest, "we would know someone who could turn off that alarm system."

Ivy grinned. "And if it was a comedy, we'd place an advertisement and find a hapless unemployed burglar to help us. Oh! And they'd end up getting trapped in the house inside Hazel's impenetrable safe room, which they'd disappear from, and then we'd have to puzzle out how they—"

"Okaaaay," said Tempest. "It's clearly time for a break."

"I think," Gideon said, "that this is one of those situations where one laughs so they don't cry. You want some leftover lumpia from my mom that's in the fridge?"

"Obviously," said Ivy.

After their snack break of mouthwatering vegetarian lumpia that Gideon's chef mom had made with homemade pastry wrapping and jackfruit interior, they went over the plan again.

"One last thing," said Tempest. "None of our cars are inconspicuous." Tempest's red jeep, which was recognizable to a fault; Gideon's baby-blue Renault, a car more commonly seen in France; and Ivy's pink moped, which wouldn't hold the three of them even if it would make the fifty-five-mile trip.

"We could borrow a car," Ivy suggested.

Gideon groaned. "Is that a euphemism for stealing one? What have I gotten myself into?"

Tempest smiled. "You mean your sister's generic station wagon?"

"Yup. Nobody ever pays any attention to that thing."

Ivy left on her moped to ask her sister about borrowing her car the next day.

"Hang on," Gideon said as Tempest walked to her jeep. "I want to show you something first that I think you'll appreciate."

Gideon led her back to his studio. He whisked a white sheet off a sculpture, and Tempest immediately knew this was the one he'd stayed up all night working on.

"Marble?" Tempest ran her fingers over the smooth stone of the three-foot bas-relief carving—a slab of stone with an angel emerging from it.

Gideon nodded. "It's a new stone for me. I've only done small experiments. . . ."

"She's beautiful." The angel's face was fully formed and free of the stone slab. Her wings were set into the stone, and there was a sense of movement as if Gideon had captured the moment in time before she stepped forward out of stone.

"She's not quite done yet." He tossed the sheet back over the marble. "That's not what I really wanted to show you. Come on out back."

It was nearly pitch-black now. With the flip of a switch, pinpricks of fairy lights illuminated the yard. Larger bulbs hung over a patio table. Landscaping lights were placed strategically on the ground, highlighting the best features of the carved animals and casting shadows onto the wood fence. In one corner of the fence, a gargoyle's shadow danced with the shadow of a griffin.

"It's spellbinding," Tempest said as soon as she could speak.

"Good. I'm thinking of doing the lighting like this at the gallery art show I've got planned."

"You're selling these?"

"Of course."

Tempest felt a stab of sadness at the thought of never seeing these magical stone creatures again. "How can you bear to part with them?"

Gideon stepped inside for a moment and returned holding a black-and-silver camera that looked like something from the 1940s. Maybe even earlier.

"I've already documented them." He held up the hefty camera. "And I've got my memories from carving them. I've seen them come to life. That's the best part. Here. Let me take your photo with them."

"Where do you want me?"

"You're perfect." He held her gaze before looking down into the viewfinder on top of the camera. His words referred to her placement in the photograph, but his eyes told her the words meant something completely different to him.

In another time and place, without everything else going on in her life, she could have easily returned the feeling. Even now, she felt the strong pull of Gideon's presence. She didn't know what she'd do if he didn't hurry up and take the picture.

She let out a breath as the box gave a *click*. "I'm guessing I don't get to see a copy."

"Not until I develop the film." He wound the camera before looking up. "I like it that way. It's a mystery for now. It's much more satisfying to wait and see what things look like in the future. Don't you think?"

If he was waiting for her to figure out her life, he'd have a long wait.

# Chapter 23

Pebbles struck her bedroom window as Tempest was getting ready for bed later that night.

She crossed the room and drew back the curtains. Looking out the window, she spotted Sanjay walking away, toward the Secret Fort. Typical. He assumed she'd heard him, since he had good aim, and that she'd follow. She grumbled that he was, of course, correct. She put her shoes back on and slipped out of the house.

Typical Sanjay. He must have come back early, since the last time they'd talked she'd been clear she was going to move forward with the heist the following day without him. What *wasn't* typical was for him to be passive-aggressive about it.

A battery-operated camping lantern illuminated the unfinished stone tower that Tempest would be converting into her own small home. For now the space only contained Abra's spacious bunny hutch along with a wooden table they'd moved into the tower to look at drafting plans on site.

A bowler hat rested on the table next to the lantern—but the man next to it wasn't Sanjay.

The man who stood before her, holding Abra in his arms, looked nothing like he had before, yet she knew it was him.

He'd done that on purpose, when she thought she knew him. She remembered his words so clearly, when he showed her he wasn't who she thought he was: *An easy idea to remember but a difficult man to recognize. What color are his eyes? How tall is he under his slouch?* He'd been right. She didn't know anything about him.

Except for what he was.

"Moriarty," Tempest whispered. She hadn't been prepared to find the man who'd evaded capture back in Hidden Creek and standing on her family's land.

His lips ticked up into an amused smile. "Moriarty? Really?"

Tempest recovered her composure and shrugged. "The name I knew you by was fake. Ivy and I thought 'Moriarty' was appropriate."

"You wound me, Tempest. I have no desire to harm you. You should know that. Although I do appreciate the vote of confidence in my intellect. But really, you should call me Gabriel, since I'm your guardian angel."

Tempest snorted. "I don't think so. Put Abra back in his cage."

"He likes me." Moriarty scratched behind Abra's floppy ears. The rabbit cuddled back.

"Judas," Tempest mumbled to the bunny before meeting Moriarty's amused gaze. "What are you doing here?"

The smile fell from his lips. "I understand why you didn't tell me your suspicions before we knew each other. But now that I know . . . I'm truly sorry, Tempest." He had what looked like genuine sadness in his eyes.

"Stop talking in riddles. If you were as smart as you think

you are, you would have noticed I'm busy with a family cri-
sis."

"That's why I'm here."

Tempest's stage instincts kept her from expressing the
constriction she felt in her throat. She made sure her voice
would be steady when she spoke. "The police are very interested in your whereabouts."

"I see you making a move for your phone. I wouldn't do
that if I were you."

She paused, but only for a moment. "You're my self-
declared guardian angel. You're not going to hurt me. You
have nothing to threaten me with."

"I'm not threatening you. I'm telling you I'm here to help.
Your grandmother isn't up to what she says she is."

Tempest felt the skin on her arms rise into goosebumps. "I
don't know what you hope to accomplish by bringing up my
grandmother and lying—"

"I'm sorry I didn't know what was really going on with
your family curse. I should have suspected." Again, there
was sadness in his eyes.

He was manipulating her. He had to be. "Why are you
really here?"

"If you hadn't noticed, dearest Tempest—"

"Do not," she growled, "call me that."

"In time. . . . If you hadn't noticed, I'm much more observant than the average person. That's why I also know how
special you are."

"Pointing out your superiority isn't the smartest way to
win someone over."

He smiled. "I've always thought of you as my equal. It's
quite rare. That threw me off balance. That's why I didn't
approach you directly when I first saw you. I've never been

in such a position before, but you're a remarkable woman, Tempest. *Shhh.* Now you know my secret."

"Your secret that you're a stalker?"

"Sticks and stones . . . but must you be so cruel?" He said the words with a smile on his face. "I know how independent you are, so I won't take it personally. That's why I'll still give you this information I found about your gran. She didn't go to Scotland to go on an art retreat with her girlfriends."

"Of course she went to Scotland—"

"Your attention to detail is failing you now. I didn't say she's not in Scotland. I said she didn't go there *for* an art retreat. She's looking into what really happened to her eldest daughter. She wants to lay the Raj family curse to rest."

Tempest used to hate the clichéd expression that time slowed down. But there are some moments when it turns out to be absolutely true. There was no way Moriarty was telling her the truth, and yet . . . what if he was?

"How do you—"

"I fear you wouldn't like the answer." He picked up the bowler hat that didn't look anything like Sanjay's up close.

Tempest glared at him. She couldn't let herself get distracted by the past until her grandfather was cleared. But after that? If Moriarty could help her find the truth . . . was it worth it to make a deal with the Devil?

# Chapter 24

You look more like a mime than a burglar," said Gideon.

It was the next morning. Tempest was dressed all in black, with her long dark hair pulled under a winter cap. She couldn't find her black gloves, so her hands were covered in white.

"I was going to say 'goth model,'" Ivy chimed in, "but 'mime' works, too."

The three of them were sitting in Dahlia's old station wagon in the parking lot of a campground near the river that ran through Forestville. It wasn't the season for camping or swimming, so theirs was the only car in the lot, as they'd hoped. This was the location they'd scoped out ahead of time that was walking distance from Hazel's house for Gideon and Tempest, and that Ivy could drive to without Hazel seeing where she went when she drove away.

Tempest hadn't been talkative on the drive. She was still distracted and distressed because of the visit from Moriarty. She couldn't believe she was actually entertaining the thought, but . . . what if he was right? She couldn't let that distract her now. She told herself that's why she didn't mention Moriarty's appearance to either Ivy or Gideon. But was it the truth?

Gideon donned his hard hat and opened the back of the car to get the bag of tools and orange cones.

Tempest reached his side as he closed the back. "I wish we'd gotten you a cell phone. We could have bought a burner phone."

"Like I said before, it wouldn't matter. I'm the distraction. Not a lookout." His eyes were barely visible under the hard hat, which was the idea, but she could still feel him looking intently at her. He squeezed both her hands. His fingers lingered longer than they should have. "See you back here in about an hour."

Tempest slid back into the car.

"I know you're keeping something from me," Ivy said as she adjusted her wig in the rearview mirror.

"I've told you everything I'm going to do. We went over every contingency we could think of—"

"That's not what I mean."

"Now isn't the time for hinting. I have to start walking over to Hazel's house in a few minutes."

"Fifteen," Ivy snapped. "We agreed we should give Gideon time to establish himself before you get in place and I knock. What happened to that precision you're famous for?"

"The timer is already going on my phone. I'll know when I need to leave. You're jumpy because you're nervous. I won't be upset if you want to back out—"

"No! God, Tempest. I'm not abandoning you. We're doing this. I just wish you'd tell me what's really going on."

"I've told you—"

"No. You haven't. You've told me only what you want to. You don't really let me in. You don't let anyone in. You're following the same pattern of keeping things to yourself."

"I'm trying to clear my grandfather. I can't lose him, Ivy. That's the most important thing."

Ivy's expression softened. She nodded. "We'll talk later. For now, I know what we need to do."

☠☠☠

Hazel opened the door for Ivy. As they'd expected, Hazel held a beautiful mug in her manicured hand.

Tempest was far enough away that she couldn't hear their quiet conversation, but she could see them. Once Hazel ushered her inside, Ivy used the sleight of hand Tempest had shown her to make sure the door didn't lock shut behind her. If that hadn't worked, or if Hazel led Ivy to a living room directly next to the front door, their back-up plan was for Ivy to ask to use the bathroom and then leave a window open for Tempest. It appeared this back-up plan wasn't needed. At least not yet.

In his construction gear, Gideon was running a loud power tool next to the retaining wall close to Hazel's property. The wall faced the living room. This was their "force" to get Hazel to lead Ivy to her kitchen rather than to the living room next to the front door. He'd refused to touch the wall itself—a stonemason's code of honor?—so he instead drilled a shallow hole a few feet from the wall.

Tempest made sure her hair was fully tucked under her cap and walked casually up to the door. Her plan had been to listen for the sound of Ivy fake-crying, but Gideon's jackhammer drowned out the sound of everything coming from inside the house.

Another sound rumbled. A car. No, not just a car, but a delivery truck. One that slowed as it rounded the curve in the road. How did a delivery truck even fit on such a narrow winding road? The truck came to a stop. The driver killed the engine.

Tempest darted around the right side of the house. She didn't dare stay where the delivery driver could see her, which meant she couldn't see them, either. At least the incessant sound of Gideon's jackhammer drowned out the sound of her feet skidding across the dirt.

*A former stage magician, a librarian-in-training, and a stone carver. What could possibly go wrong?*

As it turned out, quite a lot.

"Delivery," a voice called as its owner rang the doorbell. A few moments later, the truck's engine started up again.

If Hazel came to the door, she'd immediately see that Ivy had left it unlocked with a piece of plastic. Tempest pressed herself up against the wall of the house, staying clear of a nearby window. Could she make it back to the front door in time to remove it before Hazel got there?

"I hope you understand it's my nature as a city girl." Ivy's raised voice came through the door. "So many packages are stolen from porches, I'd feel so much better if we bring yours inside. No, don't worry. I'm already up. I'll get it. You've already been so hospitable fixing me tea in the kitchen."

*Thank you, Ivy.* She'd told Tempest everything she needed to know.

The original plan was for Ivy to dab her eyes with an irritant to get her fake tears flowing as she talked to Hazel about her memories of Corbin. When Tempest heard Ivy's crying escalate in volume, Tempest would sneak in through the unlocked front door. Ivy must have realized how hard it would be for Tempest to hear them from the kitchen.

A large black bird flapped its wings from a branch of the enormous Douglas fir tree only a few yards away. It was high on the large tree, so she couldn't get a close look at it, but she also couldn't look away from the agitated bird. It couldn't be a raven, could it? She was letting her imagination run away with her.

After waiting thirty seconds, Tempest let herself into the front door and found herself in a sunken living room. She knew she needed to stay focused and move quickly, but what she saw in the living room made her unable to move on. Above the fireplace, a five-foot-high painting of a black raven looked out over the room. The raven's blue-black wings were outstretched as if in flight. The wings shimmered. She thought, at first, that they were real feathers. And there was something else. Two words, written in calligraphy with a silvery paint. *Nam Fitheach.*

Was that Gaelic? There was no way she was taking time to look it up on her phone.

She really needed to leave this room. The raven's obsidian eyes bore into her, as if it could see her soul. The storm clouds behind the bird appeared to be moving ever so slightly. Or perhaps it was the wings of the raven. It had to be a trick of the light. Or something to do with the intensity with which she was staring at the raven's inquisitive eyes.

Tempest pulled her eyes away from the unsettling image. What she saw next didn't make her feel any better. A silver amulet with a deep-blue stone eye at its center rested on the mantle, underneath the painting. A talisman to ward off evil?

She forced herself to turn away from the display and look for where she needed to go. The hallway. Yes. The hallway was what would lead her to the bedrooms and home offices. She couldn't see any of the doors off the hallway from the living room, so she tentatively poked her head into the hall.

The first piece of luck since arriving was that Hazel hadn't knocked down any walls of the old house to give it an open floor plan. Tempest could move through the rooms without too much fear of being seen.

The first room she came upon was filled with camera and audio equipment, but no books or notebooks. Not Corbin's office. This must be where Hazel filmed her show. Across from it was a bedroom and bathroom. At the end of the hallway was another small office, this one lined with books. A whole bookcase was filled with occult titles, with sections divided by bookends in the shape of ravens. Another contained hardback thrillers. The third and final bookcase was stacked with multiple copies of each of Corbin Colt's books, with one shelf devoted to the two literary awards he'd received for his debut novel, *The Raven.*

Tempest hurried to the shelf of thrillers as murmurers of voices came from the kitchen.

There were no Agatha Christie novels on this shelf. Nor on any of the others.

"You need to leave."

Tempest knocked her shoulder against the bookcase as she whirled around. One of the stone raven bookends teetered precariously.

But the voice hadn't come from the doorway of Corbin's office. It was farther away than that. Hazel was asking Ivy to leave.

"I'm sorry to have distressed you!" Ivy cried. "I loved him, too."

Tempest caught the bookend before it could fall. Her eyes darted around the room as she rubbed her shoulder. There were no closets in this room. An old black trunk was pressed up against a wall, underneath a desk with a large monitor.

She yanked on the trunk. It scraped the hardwood floor as she tugged. The sound was mostly masked by Gideon's distant jackhammering.

Inside were dozens of notebooks. And one book.

The book in the trunk wasn't *And Then There Were None*. Not exactly. The large hardback was a collection of three Agatha Christie novels, including that one. But this had to be the book they were looking for.

Voices grew louder. Hazel was showing Ivy out. *It was too late for Tempest to leave through the front door.*

Tempest tucked the book under her arm and went to the room's single window. Thankfully it didn't have a screen she'd have to break. She unlatched the window and tugged upward.

The window didn't budge.

She set the book down and yanked upward with both hands.

Nothing.

If she was about to be caught, she needed to know what was inside the book before it was taken away from her. She opened the front cover, revealing a book plate with Corbin's name. Instead of a usual title page, a thicker page began the book. A thick sheet that hid the real purpose of the book.

This wasn't a real book. It had been hollowed out in the center.

A handwritten manuscript lay inside.

Fifty or so pages of handwritten pages rested inside the false book. Tempest didn't have time to read it right then and there, but she froze when she saw the title scrawled on the first page: *The Vanishing of Ella Patel.*

Her mom's disappearance had been called "the vanishing of Emma Raj." "Ella" was so close a name to "Emma," and "Patel" was a short Indian surname like "Raj." He wasn't even trying to disguise his intentions.

Tempest had to know what was in those pages. Using all her strength, she shoved the window frame. It nudged open two inches. She shoved again. That did it. The window slid open wide enough for her to slip through the opening.

She dropped the book outside the window onto the ground, then followed it out the window herself. She tugged the window frame to close it behind her, picked up the book—then ran.

Corbin Colt had stolen her family's story. He had been writing a book about her mom's disappearance.

That's what her grandfather was after. The story the Raven had stolen from her family.

# Chapter 25

Tempest only stopped running once she'd reached the campground parking lot a mile away.

She shouldn't have been breathing as hard as she was. She hoped it was merely proof that burgling wasn't for her, not that she'd already gotten so badly out of shape now that she was no longer practicing a taxing physical routine and performing on stage most nights.

Dahlia's station wagon was idling in the parking lot. No other cars were around.

Tempest peeled off her cap and gloves and slipped into the passenger seat. "We good?"

"She hates me," Ivy said. "Or rather, she hates fake-brunette me who was another of Corbin's mistresses. But I don't think she suspected anyone else was in the house."

Tempest didn't feel too guilty about their ploy. After all, Hazel herself had been having an affair with Corbin while he was married to Lavinia.

"She wanted me to leave because I'd upset her," Ivy continued. "I'm sorry I overdid it and couldn't buy you more—" she broke off as Tempest held up the fat book.

"I got it." Tempest opened the book, revealing its hidden

contents. "A handwritten draft of an unpublished manu-script."

"No way," Ivy whispered. "I thought his books were duds lately. Why would an unpublished manuscript of his be worth something to Ash? Did Ash lie about it not being something valuable?"

Tempest removed the papers, noticing that she'd ripped a couple of them in her haste earlier. "Look at the title." She could barely look herself.

"*The Vanishing of Ella Patel,*" Ivy read. "Ella Patel . . . It sounds kinda like your mom's name, Emma Raj, doesn't it?"

Tempest swallowed hard. "It's too close to be anything else. Lots of people called my mom's disappearance *the vanishing of Emma Raj.* This has to be Corbin Colt's barely disguised fictionalization of my mom's disappearance."

Patel was a Gujarati name, never mind that her family was Tamil. Indian surnames were tricky anyway. Her grandfather was Dravidian Tamilian, and Tamils rarely used surnames at all until recently. Instead, they used the first initial of their father's name, along with their own first name. But that was hardly the thing Tempest should have cared about at that moment.

"*This,*" said Tempest, "is why Ash threatened Corbin Colt. It's even worse than I thought. It's not just that Corbin had written an essay about my mom that was in poor taste. *He wanted to write a novel about her.*"

"That's even more of a motive. That's why he wanted it back?"

The car sputtered. Tempest had forgotten the engine was still running. "I don't think Dahlia's car likes sitting still."

"It took me a minute to get it started earlier. I can't risk turning it off again. I'd better—" Ivy gasped. She grabbed the rearview mirror and stared at whatever horror it showed her.

Tempest whirled around in the bucket seat. "Gideon." She croaked out a laugh. "It's only Gideon."

"I can't see his face," Ivy whispered.

"That was the whole point of him wearing that hard hat."

Ivy grasped Tempest's arm. "Does he always saunter like that?"

Tempest stared at the man walking toward them with a slightly lopsided gait. *Did he?*

"It's fine, Ivy. He's walking like that because he's carrying a heavy bag. It's Gideon." She was 90 percent certain. Maybe 80 percent.

Ivy let out a sigh of relief as Gideon reached the car and took off the hard hat.

"You got it?" Gideon asked after he dropped the bag into the back and slid into the back seat.

Tempest held up the open book with the false interior.

"*The Vanishing of Ella Patel,*" Ivy said. "A fictionalization of Tempest's mom's disappearance."

"That's awful," Gideon said. "Can we talk while driving? This place gives me the creeps. I could have sworn there was a raven following me back here."

Ivy pulled out of the lot. "Why would you say that? Don't say that."

"As soon as we're out of this eerie small town, I'll be fine."

"Seat belts," Ivy said as the tires screeched on a tight turn she was driving far too quickly for.

Tempest barely noticed the seat belt pulling tight and cutting into her stomach as she flipped through the handwritten pages. Corbin Colt's penmanship was neat but simultaneously difficult to decipher. He wrote in cursive, which she'd learned at school, but his handwriting was scrunched together, often overlapping and slanted, reminding her of letters written in Victorian times when the authors tried to conserve paper by writing not only with small, precise lettering, but also at different angles.

As a canopy of pine trees whipped by beside the car. As the small road transitioned to a highway, she squinted at the tangle of looped letters and attempted to read on.

The manuscript notes began with a book club closely resembled his wife's book club, including a member named Alice who discovered her love of books after being named after *Alice's Adventures in Wonderland*. And here it was. On the next page a new character moved into the neighborhood who closely resembled Tempest's own mother. There was no mistaking it. Even more similar than the name "Ella Patel" was the character herself—a woman originally from Scotland who was a magician who made the Statue of Liberty disappear, like David Copperfield had done. Then, Ella herself disappeared. *Vanished*. The book club took it upon themselves to investigate.

"You okay?" Gideon asked. "Tempest?"

"There's no question. This is about my mom." She stared at Ivy. "Your book club never investigated my mom's disappearance, did they?"

Ivy took her eyes off the road for a fraction of a second to flash a befuddled look at Tempest. "Why would we do that?"

"Did anyone have an affair with another member's significant other?"

Ivy reddened. "Just because I found Corbin attractive, that doesn't mean I'd—"

"I didn't mean you." Why was Ivy so flustered? "I was thinking of Ellery. There's someone in Corbin's manuscript named after—"

"It's a piece of fiction, Tempest." Ivy's voice was clipped. Was she protesting *too* much?

"I don't get it," Gideon said. "This piece of fiction was

hidden inside a book. Was Ash worried the police would find it? Why would they care?"

"I don't know. . . ." Tempest flipped through the folded pages. "This will take me a little while to read. His handwriting isn't meant for a moving car."

"Wouldn't there be other copies?" Ivy asked.

Tempest shook her head. "From the look of this, this is just his handwritten draft. I read an old article about him where he bragged about how he followed the writer's path of the literary greats before him and only turned to a computer as a distasteful necessity."

"If he didn't publish anything from those pages. . . ." Ivy let her voice trail off.

"We're looking at the only copy in existence of Corbin Colt's fictionalized version of my mom's disappearance."

# Chapter 26

vy and Gideon dropped Tempest at home, where Tempest wanted to be alone while she made sense of Corbin Colt's handwritten manuscript pages.

Tempest had already fixed her flat tire, so she could have gone anywhere, but she knew where she wanted to go. The secret garden in her own backyard.

The garden was tucked away behind the kitchen at the back of the main house and hidden behind a high wooden fence covered in ivy. There was no gate in the fence. Nor was there a door from the house to step into the garden. Not a visible one, at least.

Next to the kitchen sink and its picture window with a view of the magical garden sat a grandfather clock. The clock itself told time perfectly, yet it was only an illusion that it needed a pendulum. A separate clock face had been placed atop a cabinet of secrets that had been built to look like a clock. Past the ornamental copper pendulum was a door to the secret garden. The five-foot-tall door of the cabinet remained locked until you gave a boost to the carved griffin climbing the side of the clock.

Tempest helped the griffin climb an inch higher, activating

the glass door showing the pendulum. Pushing the pendulum aside, she crawled through the grandfather clock and emerged in the secret garden.

The garden was one of her mom's projects. Grannie Mor had kept it thriving in recent years and left one of her easels there to paint inside the private garden. Snapdragons and English primroses filled the cozy space with vibrant pops of color. Tempest's favorite was the red hummingbird sage, which did indeed entice hummingbirds to visit the garden.

She went back to the beginning of the manuscript. After the title page with the looped cursive title, *The Vanishing of Ella Patel*, the first page began with the book club. And with a bang. Alice ducks as a glass vase hurtles toward her head. The glass vessel shatters into hundreds of miniature shards that gleam like diamonds in the light beaming into the room through a stained-glass window. Several of the diamond-like fragments of glass land in Alice's brightly dyed hair. Melodramatic dialogue follows, with an accusation that Alice is having an affair with another member's husband.

The next page jumped from the unnamed small town to New York City, where Scottish immigrant and stage illusionist Ella Patel meets the sinister Angel Diablo. Angel fools her with his superficial charm and secretly steals her money. The two are soon married by a minister, but the minister is actually the Devil in disguise. When the fictionalized version of Emma Raj vanishes, the book club puts their differences aside to investigate.

Even removing the bit about the Devil, the story in the manuscript was nothing like Tempest's parents' true relationship. In real life, Darius and Emma joked that their partnership could be summed up with two sentences that said it all: *What happens when a carpenter and a stage magician fall in love? They form a business that builds a touch of magic into people's homes.* Tempest's parents created Secret Staircase Construction after falling in love. They were inseparable from the day they met, shortly after Emma arrived in California from Edinburgh, and had more than twenty happy years together before Tempest's mom vanished.

The sunlight shifted through the trees overhead. Tempest's charm bracelet caught the light. She paused reading to run her fingers across the smooth charms that always calmed her mind and reminded her of so many good memories of her mom. The top hat, Janus-faced jester, handcuffs, lightning bolt, selkie, book with the title *The Tempest*, fiddle, and smallest of them all: a key. With Ivy's help, she'd figured out the secret of the charm bracelet last summer. Though it no longer held a mystery, it was the last gift her mom had given her and it brought together so many elements of their shared love of magic.

Tempest shoved the handwritten pages back into the book. The words made her memories of her mom feel tainted.

She wanted to scream, but that would only worry her grandfather, who would no doubt hear her from the tree house. Instead, she twirled three pirouettes, coming to a stop in front of the purple snapdragons. There wasn't enough room to do anything in the garden besides spin, but she didn't care. She arched her back and flipped into a backbend kickover.

She landed with her feet stomping a patch of nasturtiums. The destruction didn't help her feel better. She was avoiding the manuscript. She flipped open the cover of the book so violently the spine cracked and several sheets of paper fell to the ground. She snatched the pages from the earth, grabbing a clump of dirt in the process. Which was appropriate considering the words her eyes fell upon. *Grave robbing.*

Tempest's breath caught. The manuscript described not a

fictional plot device, but a real-life event. One that had be-
fallen Tempest's family. One that wasn't public knowledge.

*Corbin Colt knew about the body snatching.*

In a final indignity to Tempest's beloved aunt, her body
was one of several moved during a string of grave desecra-
tions that took place ten years ago, shortly after Elspeth Raj
was killed. A macabre prank that went way too far. One that
paralleled a grisly crime from over two hundred years ago.

Edinburgh's most famous body snatchers, Burke and Hare,
were neither Scottish nor body snatchers. They were Irish-
men and murderers. That small issue of truth didn't stop
a mythology from developing around them, which continued to the present day, with everything from pubs to escape
games named after the infamous pair.

The University of Edinburgh was a hub of education during
the Enlightenment. Breakthrough medical advances were
on the horizon, except there was a problem. There weren't
enough bodies for students to learn on. When two skilled
laborers who'd traveled to Edinburgh in the 1760s for the
backbreaking work of building North Bridge realized how
much money body snatchers made by selling fresh corpses
to medical schools that needed cadavers, they saw an opportunity. Burke and Hare didn't wait around at cemeteries
for new bodies. They formed a plan to get lonely men drunk
enough to smother them without much difficulty. They
killed sixteen people before they were caught.

Tempest admitted the chilling story held a certain gory ap-
peal for people who enjoyed horror films and ghoulish ghost
stories. She would have been one of them herself, if not for
how the story had touched her own family two hundred and
fifty years later.

Shortly after Aunt Elspeth was killed on an Edinburgh
stage on that fateful day ten years ago, a group of drunken

university students thought it would be fun to dare each other to dig up graves, like body snatchers had done. It might have been an initiation into some college club. They didn't actually do anything with the bodies, but desecrated half a dozen graves and animals got to the bodies that had been removed, carrying off the extremities of several bodies, including one of Aunt Elspeth's hands.

Elspeth's right hand was never recovered.

As if Tempest's grandparents hadn't been through enough, they had to suffer this indignity for their beloved daughter. The press and public expressed outrage and summarized the macabre history that had led to such a horrific desecration. The authorities succeeded in keeping names out of the paper, so it was never publicly reported that Elspeth Raj's grave was one of the ones disturbed.

But now, here in Corbin Colt's manuscript of *The Vanishing of Ella Patel,* Ella's sister had died in an accident, and her grave desecrated *in the exact same way* it had been in real life, with her right hand taken.

In the manuscript, the hand was taken by a person collecting body parts for a supernatural entity who derives power from taking the body part that helped that person be special—the eye of a painter, the ear of a composer, *the hand of a magician.* That wasn't what had happened in real life, but still, the parallels couldn't be a coincidence.

*How did Corbin know?*

What else did he know about her mother's vanishing?

She kept reading, but her phone startled her and she dropped the pages once more. The wind was picking up and they scattered across the secret garden. She glanced at the screen as she chased pages. She didn't recognize the number, so she silenced it and scooped up the pages, no longer in any sort of order. A short time later—or it could have been longer, since she'd lost all sense of time—a loud knocking sounded at the front door of the house. She ignored it and kept turning pages.

The plot was even worse than she thought possible. Her hands were trembling as she turned over a sheet of paper with the words "the final chapter" printed in block letters at the top of the page. She knew she'd missed several pages of plot after scooping up the scattered pages, but she couldn't look away from the ending. Angel Diablo was the murderer who orchestrated the grave robbing of his sister-in-law, killed his wife Ella Patel, and hid her body where nobody would ever find it.

*Corbin Colt was implicating Tempest's father, Darius, as his wife Emma Raj's killer.*

# Chapter 27

Darius wasn't answering his phone. He didn't immediately return Tempest's text, either. She looked at their shared work calendar and saw where he'd be today. He was only a few miles away. She could easily go to him. She hurried through the grandfather clock with the book and grabbed her car keys.

"I'll take the book," a voice said as she reached the driveway. Detective Rinehart. He was waiting near her jeep, next to Gideon. *Why was Gideon there with the police?* He stood with his hands in his pockets, looking helpless.

"Book?" Tempest's heart thudded in her ears.

"The police in Forestville received a call reporting a theft," Rinehart said. His dark eyes bore into her. Judging her. *He knew.* "A window the homeowner was sure she'd locked was open, and a trunk with her recently deceased boyfriend's important keepsakes had been moved. A boyfriend who happens to be Corbin Colt. And a homeowner who happens to be someone we've already interviewed extensively regarding his mysterious death."

Tempest didn't speak. She could barely breathe. They'd been so careful, all for two tiny details to have tipped off the audience. On stage, she'd never have been so sloppy. But she'd never have performed with only one day's practice compared to a hundred.

"Miss Bello was already suspicious because she couldn't find any information online searching the name of a supposed girlfriend of Corbin's who'd visited her home," Rinehart continued. "She looked to see if anything was missing from the trunk, and it was."

"A trunk?" Tempest spun around and dropped the book from her hand into her bag. She wasn't defeated yet.

"Don't walk away from me," Rinehart said.

"I'm not walking away." She turned back around. "You said there was a missing trunk. We've got a lot of steamer trunks in our house. I was leading you inside to look at them."

"A book. I'm looking for a book. It was stolen out of a trunk. I want the book."

"I don't know what—"

"Don't make it worse for yourself. You were holding a book a second ago. You've got the Agatha Christie book in that bulky bag of yours. I expect Torres here knows what's going on. When I got here, he was banging on your front door."

*Gideon had been trying to warn her.* She'd been so obsessed with reading Corbin Colt's character assassination that she'd done this to herself.

She hesitated before reaching into her bag. Rinehart had said *the Agatha Christie book.* Not *the manuscript.* Was it possible he didn't know the hardback book was a secret hiding spot?

"I can come back with a warrant if I need to," he added, though the words weren't harsh. They were almost regretful. Detective Rinehart was keeping up appearances, dressed in a serious and well-pressed suit similar to the one he'd been wearing that fateful night of Corbin Colt's murder, but the self-assuredness she'd seen in his raven-like eyes the other night was gone. The case was getting to him.

"That won't be necessary. I've got it somewhere in here." Tempest fumbled in her bag for several seconds. "Sorry . . . I've got so much in here. . . ." She popped a piece of gum in her mouth—one of the many things in her bag—then handed Rinehart the book with the manuscript inside.

He slipped it into a plastic evidence bag. "Why go to all the effort for an old book?"

*Anything but the truth about what it says about Papa.* "It's worth a lot of money now that he's dead. There's a bookplate with his signature inside the cover."

Rinehart shook his head. "From what I've heard about you, I didn't take you for a person who'd steal something valuable to make a quick buck."

"It was my idea," Gideon cut in. "All of it. It's tough to make it as a stone-carving artist. I didn't think anyone would miss it, but it would really help me."

It was a good lie. Gideon was skin and bones these days. Obsession and lack of sleep got him there, not lack of funds for food, but he looked the part of a starving artist.

Rinehart shifted his gaze from Tempest to Gideon. "I could arrest you for that admission."

Tempest opened her mouth, but Gideon was quicker. "Maybe that'll drum up interest for my creative work. All publicity is good publicity." He held out his wrists.

The detective sighed, but didn't make a move. "Miss Bello doesn't wish to press charges. She only wants to retrieve a book she knows Corbin Colt cared about, since he'd mentioned it to her."

"Why'd you put the book in an evidence bag?" Tempest asked. "Aren't you just going to return it to Hazel?"

"Until the murder is solved, it's evidence."

"You've already arrested my grandfather," Tempest snapped.

Rinehart's frustrated expression shifted. Sadness? Regret? "My hands were tied. The district attorney felt there was enough evidence. . . ."

"Does that mean you're still looking at other suspects?"

"As far as I'm concerned, we don't yet know what really happened. There are too many things that don't add up."

"So you're—"

"You did the right thing handing over the book. Don't make this worse. I'll be in touch."

☠☠☠

Once the detective had gone, Tempest studied Gideon's face. "Why'd you say it was your idea?"

He shrugged. "You're the one whose life it would ruin. You've already been dragged through the press and social media. You have your farewell show coming up before you get to start your life here for real. I don't even own a cell phone. Is someone not going to buy one of my sculptures because I have a criminal record?" He shrugged. "It doesn't matter much to my life. But it matters to yours."

"He could have arrested you."

"Don't get me wrong—I'm glad he didn't. I don't think my heart has ever beat quite that quickly. But you're the one who'd be ruined if you were arrested." Gideon was watching her closely. "Hang on . . . You were chewing gum a minute ago. . . ."

"Is that a crime?"

"That's why you were looking so flustered when you went through your bag. You *weren't* flustered. You were creating misdirection."

"Plan B." She squeezed her eyes shut. "I never should have put the manuscript pages back inside the book, but I wasn't expecting to be found out. I tried to dump the pages out into my bag before handing over the book, but they were wedged too tightly inside. I couldn't get them out using sleight of hand. My only hope was if the detective didn't realize there was something hidden *inside* the book. It sounded like he doesn't know that. Yet."

"You used gum to keep the book shut."

"I don't know if it'll work, but I had to try."

"Why? They already know your grandfather had a reason to be angry at Corbin. How can the manuscript make it even worse?"

"Because Corbin Colt spells out exactly how he believes my father killed my mother."

"So if they open that book and read that manuscript—"

"Even if they free my grandfather, based on what's in that manuscript they'll turn their attention to my dad. I need to figure out the truth about who killed Corbin Colt before the police figure out exactly what they have."

# Chapter 28

Tempest called her dad once more. He still didn't answer. She grabbed her keys.

Ten minutes later she screeched to a halt in front of the house where her dad's calendar said he'd be that afternoon.

"Can I help?" asked a woman kneeling in a bed of white and yellow flowers in the front yard.

"I'm Darius's daughter. Is he—"

"Are you Tempest?" She pulled off dirt-covered gloves and stood up. "It's lovely to meet you. Did your charming father leave something at the house?"

"He's not here?"

"Afraid not. He left an hour ago."

"Sorry to bother you. We must've gotten our signals crossed." Tempest stumbled back to her car. *Where was her dad?*

She arrived back at Fiddler's Folly eight minutes later. Her dad's truck wasn't in the driveway, so she hurried to the tree house to speak with her grandfather.

"Have you eaten?" Ashok was stirring a pot of something that smelled delicious, wearing a smile on his lips and a plaid newsboy cap on his head.

"I promise I'll eat something shortly. But we might not have much time." She'd wasted too much of it already. "Why did you ask Fleur to steal a book from Corbin's new girl-friend's house?"

The smile vanished from his lips and the wooden spoon slipped from his fingers and clattered to the kitchen floor.

"You shouldn't have interfered."

"You shouldn't have asked someone to steal—"

"The man is dead, Tempest. His notes are irrelevant."

"Except that they're clearly not. Otherwise, you would have accepted the small risk that his draft would have been discovered where it was hidden."

With a shaking hand, Ash turned off the stovetop burner, then collapsed into a seat in the breakfast nook. Tempest rushed to his side, but he held up his hand and shook his head. "I'm all right. And you're wrong. It wasn't a small risk. Rinehart would have found it when he dug into Corbin's past for motives."

"Why would he keep digging?"

"I don't think he truly believes I'm guilty. It was the pros-ecutor who insisted on my arrest. A high-profile case where I had motive and physical evidence against me. I was trying to beat Rinehart to finding Corbin's notes. Because—" he stopped himself.

"Because you knew that the manuscript would implicate Papa."

Ash nodded sadly. "You got it from Fleur? How did you know she—"

"She wasn't able to get it," Tempest explained. "Hazel's house has a good security system."

"Then how?"

"It doesn't matter. But I found it."

"And read it?"

"Most of it. I didn't think to take photos of it before Rine-hart showed up."

"He has it now? *Ada-kadavulae*. You let him—"

"I didn't *let him* do anything. He's a law enforcement offi-cer and I had stolen property." She softened her tone as she added hastily, "He didn't arrest me, or anyone, even though Gideon tried to take the blame and say I had nothing to do with it."

Ash grunted. "Gideon is a good lad. But you two shouldn't have put yourself in the position for the detective to seize the manuscript."

Tempest raised an eyebrow. "If you'd told me what you were doing and why it was important, we wouldn't have needed to."

"I was protecting you."

"And look where that got us."

Ash clicked his tongue. "How bad does the manuscript make your father look?"

"Bad." Tempest looked at her phone again. No missed mes-sages from her papa. "I know his story isn't true, but it gives him a motive—if he knew what Corbin Colt wanted to do."

"He knew," Ash said. "Your father and I both knew."

"That's why you really threatened him when he got a re-straining order against you. It wasn't just that essay he wrote on the first anniversary of her disappearance."

Ash nodded. "That's what we thought at first. But when I ran into him in town and expressed my dismay at exploiting our family's tragedy, he laughed and said I needed to get used to it. He couldn't resist gloating about the novel he was writ-ing, so he told me some of the ideas he was playing with—but then said he'd said too much."

"I can't believe Lavinia was okay with him writing about our family." Tempest said.

"Lavinia didn't know anything. At least not that she admitted. I believed her. They hadn't been close in quite some time, and she never read his work. I looked up more about him online to learn more about his weaknesses. He knew a lot about the occult, for his thrillers. In some of his interviews he said things that made me suspect he believed, or at least was frightened by people he interviewed for book research. With the history of our family curse, I thought I could use superstition against him. That's when I went to his house to talk with him. I was hoping to reason with him, but if that didn't work, I thought I could frighten him by saying if he published such a novel that the Raj family curse would come for him."

"Did my dad know what you were up to?"

"He wanted to come, but I know his temper. I'm better at controlling mine. I went alone. I thought I could be more . . . convincing. I couldn't stop Darius from emailing Corbin, though. Corbin wanted to get a restraining order against your father as well, for the email, but it wasn't a threat of physical harm, only a message expressing anger. I was the only one who'd 'physically assaulted' him. By glaring at him so menacingly that he fell and hurt his ankle. Supposedly. He wouldn't let me look at his ankle, but I suspect he was faking the injury."

"That's why he tried to have you arrested for assault."

Ash clicked his tongue. "That nonsense was thrown out. But something I said got through to him."

"Because he never published it."

"The pages he waved in my face were enough for me to know how far he'd gotten," Ash said. "I saw where he put them. It was a big Agatha Christie volume, including that book of hers where everyone is hiding something—which I'm sure Corbin found amusing. He didn't know I had seen where he put it, thinking himself clever to wait until I left to get his wife after he'd fallen. I lingered in the doorway longer than he thought, because I hoped to see him walking normally on his 'injured' ankle. I didn't catch him in a lie, but I saw his hiding spot. I didn't know if it would still be there for certain, but I expected an author would never throw away his own work."

"You could have easily stolen it before now. When it was at his house he shared with Lavinia. Why didn't you?"

"Don't you see? It was never *the pages themselves* that were a threat. It was the man himself. What he could do with the *idea* for his book. It wasn't a polished manuscript. It was a draft of a story filled with thinly veiled lies about our family. If that was the only place the story was left, I had to get it."

Tempest groaned. "That's why you wrangled an invitation to the séance!"

"Darius said Lavinia was having a bonfire with the book notes he left behind, to banish his presence. I wondered if it might be there. If it was, then we could be done with it for good. That's why I wanted a tour of the space as well, but I saw that it wasn't in the box."

"That's why you were so nosy."

"I didn't know she was going to kill him."

Tempest studied the lines on her grandfather's face. Lines from a long and interesting life, filled with both love and tragedy. He looked as if he truly believed what he was saying, yet he wasn't judging Lavinia for killing Corbin or blaming her for his own current predicament.

"You still think she did it?"

Ash let out a long breath before speaking. "I wouldn't blame her. If she's guilty, I don't believe she'll let me take the blame, if this goes to trial. But no, I'm not absolutely certain."

"Oh! I just thought of one thing we can be certain of that's good news for once. Even though I made things worse by finding that manuscript that implicates Papa, he can't be implicated. He wasn't there at the séance."

Ash lifted his hat and ran a handkerchief across the beads of sweat on his head. "Technically, that's true. . . ."

"Technically?" Tempest repeated.

"Your father wasn't in the room with us, but he was there. Right outside. I was going to search the papers Lavinia was going to burn and toss any pages related to our family out the window for Darius to pick up—"

"Because she's said she'd read from the pages first," Tempest whispered.

"But they weren't there. I texted Darius right before the séance began that the plan was off."

Tempest groaned. That was bad. "Does the detective have your cell phone records?"

He tugged at the tip of his newsboy cap, straightening the hat before yanking it off with frustration. "I believe that's part of the evidence against me."

Only then did Tempest notice the kitchen counters were filled with food. Cardamom scones, at least three varieties of cookies, multiple mason jars filled with blackberry preserves, two jars filled with a bright yellow spread of some kind, and various breads. This wasn't his usual balanced assortment of food.

He was stress-breaking.

Following her gaze, Ash's eyes lit up for the first time since the start of their conversation. "You can taste-test for me." He scooted out of the breakfast nook and opened the two glass jars with the mystery yellow substance. "Try these two versions of lemon curd on a scone and see which you prefer."

"We were talking about—"

"Humor an old man."

Tempest scowled at him, but she accepted a plate. Sinking her teeth into the first taste test, Lemon Curd Number One on a bite of cardamom scone, she closed her eyes and let the sweet and tart flavors blissfully intermingle and make her forget her troubles.

"*Chuvaru irunthalthan chithrangalum padamum poda mudium.*"

Tempest opened her eyes and smiled. Though her knowledge of Tamil was virtually nonexistent for the purposes of proper conversation, she remembered many of the sayings her grandfather had taught her. These words were familiar. "'Only when you have a wall can you paint or hang pictures.'"

Ash smiled. "Very good. Which means we must keep up our health and energy, because unless we have strong walls, whatever we hang on them will collapse."

She took another bite. "This is amazing. Your scones are even fluffier than I remember. Is this topping so sweet because it's from the bag of lemons Natalie brought you from her beloved lemon tree?"

"Don't be silly, Tempest. It's the sugar."

Tempest started laughing so hard she couldn't stop. She threw her arms around her grandfather.

"Good. Now finish the scone and I'll make us dinner."

"Anybody home?" a voice called from the foot of the stairs. Her papa was back.

Tempest flew down the stairs and met him halfway. "You weren't answering your phone, and you weren't where your calendar said you'd be. Is everything okay?"

Darius kept walking and ran a hand across his face. "I was in a meeting."

"Can't new jobs wait—?"

"Vanessa found us a good private investigator, not the guy Dad has in his Rolodex. She's looking into Corbin's fans."

Ash clicked his tongue and frowned at his son-in-law. "Shouldn't I have been consulted?"

"I okayed it." Darius poured himself a glass of water and drank it over the sink before turning back to them. "I knew you wouldn't do what's necessary—"

"Stop it!" Tempest screamed. "Both of you. You're each trying to protect each other, and me, but by keeping things from each other, we're all making things worse—myself included. We need to start telling each other everything. That's the only way to clear both of you."

"Have you eaten?" Ash asked his son-in-law. "Tempest has a lot to report. It's going to be a long night."

# Chapter 29

Tempest repeated to her dad what she'd told her grandfather about Corbin's manuscript, in more detail this time.

"I would have killed him myself if I'd known just how damning his manuscript was," Darius said.

Ash clicked his tongue. "Don't say that."

"It's just an expression." His eyes said otherwise.

"It was awful." Tempest couldn't help shivering as she remembered those words scrawled in the hand of a dead man. "How did he know about the grave robbers?" she whispered.

"It can't have been a coincidence." Darius paced across the kitchen floor. "He knew Emma's sister's grave was one of the ones desecrated."

"It wasn't a difficult secret to figure out," Ash said as he stirred a pot on the stove. "The press simply didn't ask the right questions to discover the full list of names of the graves disturbed. The story the media told was of university students running wild and student clubs with initiations that went too far."

"Corbin made up the part about her grave being specifically targeted," Tempest said. "Right?"

"Of course," her grandfather said quickly. "Sensationalist fiction. Along with his nonsense about it being a supernatural entity collecting body parts." He visibly shivered.

"It's kind of good how bad it is," Darius said.

Ash grunted.

"I'm serious, Dad. Angel Diablo? It's like a cartoon-character supervillain name. Nobody who reads that will take it seriously. The cops can't possibly think I did the things that character did." Darius's voice didn't sound as confident as his words.

"I wish I'd had a chance to read everything," Tempest said. "The pages got mixed up so I saw the end before I'd read them all."

"The damage is done," said Ash. "How much worse could it get?"

☠☠☠

Tempest brought Abra in from his hutch to keep them company as the continued their tense discussion, because it's a scientifically proven fact that it's impossible to be entirely devoid of hope with a curmudgeonly lop-eared rabbit hopping around at your feet.

In the cozy kitchen, they ate a dinner of spicy chana dal and cucumber and red-onion raita, using the already-baked sourdough as dipping bread. The tart sourdough flavor worked surprisingly well to complement the spicy lentils.

They hadn't reached Morag yet, which added additional stress to an already anxious meal, which they ate with their cell phones face-up on the table—something both Ash and Darius usually frowned on. Tempest declined a call from her business manager, Winston Kapoor, who wanted on update on how show planning was going. She'd ignored his texts and emails, so he was resorting to actual phone calls now. She knew she'd have to get back to him at some point.

After scooping second helpings onto plates to make sure his family was well fed, Ash got down to business. "Darius, why don't you give us a report from that private investigator of yours. Since you hired them without my knowledge, at least you can tell me what you've learned."

"None of Corbin's fans have serious criminal records. Not that she's found so far. At least none of the ones who've said things about him online."

"Lavinia said she gave his paper fan mail to the police," Tempest cut in.

Darius nodded. "I'm told they're looking into it, but our own investigation can't hurt. Vanessa thinks focusing on the fans is the way to go."

"It wasn't a fan," Tempest snapped. Then it dawned on her. "Reasonable doubt for the jury? But we're nowhere close to a trial. We need to stop things from getting that far. Is the PI looking into the people at the séance?"

He shook his head. "Like I said, she's focusing on other angles. You have any specific questions?"

"A couple hundred. But for the PI, two. First, was Ellery having an affair with Corbin?"

"The purple-haired woman?" Ash asked.

"In Corbin's manuscript," Tempest explained, "there's a character named Alice with dyed hair who's named after Lewis Carol's *Alice's Adventures in Wonderland*. In real life, Ellery is named after literary character Ellery Queen and obviously her purple hair isn't natural. Alice is having an affair with the husband of one of the other book club members. Since there are so many parallels to our family, I bet there are other parallels as well."

"That manuscript is filled with lies." Darius flexed his jaw and arm muscles as he spoke. Tempest doubted he was aware of the action, and she hoped if he ever had to testify in court, he'd get a good coach first. He looked as if he was ready to bring Corbin Colt back from the dead to murder him once more. A jury could easily believe such a muscular man was more than capable of tossing a dead body onto an encircled table without making a noise or breaking a sweat. Especially with the anger that contorted his face when he spoke of Corbin Colt.

"You'll still ask her to look into Ellery," Tempest asked, "to see if there's any evidence she was having an affair with Corbin?"

Her dad gave her a single curt nod.

Probably best to change the subject away from the manuscript. "One more thing I'm curious about. It would be good to know if Lavinia and Victor—?"

"That question I can answer already," her dad said. "They're dating. But their relationship started after Lavinia filed for divorce. They met when we began working on the plans for her renovation."

"I wondered why he was at the séance," Ash said. "He could have helped Lavinia commit the murder."

Darius swore. "A conspiracy?"

"Two people is a partnership, not a conspiracy," Tempest pointed out as her thoughts began to spin. Would any of the impossibilities be answered if it was two people working together? "If their secret—"

"It's not a secret. Lots of people know. My guess is they're being kinda private about it since they don't know where it's going."

"We've had too many separate conversations," Ash said

as he brought mugs of coffee and a platter of cookies to the table. "Let's go over what we know once more."

"Starting with you." Tempest pointed a shortbread cookie at him. "You've had at least a dozen people visiting you during your tree house confinement."

Ash chuckled. "All but one really were social visits. I truly believe Lavinia will confess."

"If it's her." The cookie in her fingers snapped in two. "Even if two people were working together, I don't know what that tells us. It still looks impossible. I've tried to figure it out with Sanjay and Ivy, but I'm still missing something."

Tempest abandoned the cookie and explained in more detail what she and her friends had thought through about the four impossibilities so far. The Raven's impossibly quick flight from Forestville to Hidden Creek being a trick she hadn't yet figured out, the fake knife placed into a real stab wound as misdirection with a purpose they didn't yet know, no hiding spot big enough for Corbin to have been tied up in Lavinia's Lair, and no mechanisms to have moved Corbin's body onto the table while the séance circle remained an unbroken chain of hands.

Ash clicked his tongue. "You should have included me in your misdirection conversations with Ivy and Sanjay."

"You were indisposed at the time." Tempest was glad her grandfather hadn't noticed how little she'd eaten. She'd employed dinner-plate misdirection, moving her food enough to disguise that much of it was still on the plate.

"Those cookies are cold. Let me make something fresh for dessert—"

"It's fine, Dad." Darius put a hand on his father-in-law's shoulder.

Ash frowned, but a moment later he gave them a sly grin

and showed them his open palm. A fraction of a second later, a quarter appeared between his thumb and forefinger. "Why is this coin in my hand?"

"Because you're doing a coin trick," Tempest answered.

"False." He tossed the coin into the air. He didn't even make a move to catch it in his hand.

Tempest followed the arc of where the coin would have landed. An oversize paper version of a coin appeared on Abra's fluffy gray back. The bunny shook himself and the paper fluttered to the kitchen floor.

"Where did you come from?" Tempest asked the bunny as she scooped him up. "I thought you were napping under the table."

"You didn't notice Abracadabra wake up because you weren't looking in the right place. You know better than that. You should focus on what you know. Not following leads you should not have followed." Ash cupped her cheeks in his hands and leaned over Abra to kiss her forehead. "You have a brilliant mind, but it doesn't always take you where it should. You understand misdirection from stage magic, and your oldest friend is an expert on impossible crime novels. *This* is what you should be doing."

"Armchair detecting?" She couldn't resist a smile.

"Exactly." Ash grinned. *"Armchair* being the key word."

"I thought you didn't want me helping at all."

"You're my granddaughter. You're going to help whether I like it or not, so at least I can keep an eye on you."

Ash's phone rang, startling all three of them. It was after ten o'clock already. Who could be—

"Morag!" he cried.

Tempest and her dad cleaned up the dishes in the kitchen, giving them time to catch up privately.

Ash came inside as they were finishing up and reported

that Morag was well and that ferries were starting up. She'd be on the first one and Nicodemus would meet her and get her onto a flight home.

Was it true that Grannie Mor had been looking into her daughter Elspeth's death in Edinburgh, which was tied to Emma's disappearance in California five years later, rather than going on an artist's retreat?

Now that Tempest had read Corbin Colt's manuscript, she didn't believe for a moment that her dad had desecrated her aunt's grave and killed her mom as Corbin's story had posited—but Corbin had known more than a casual observer should have. How did he know so much about the body snatching? *Could Corbin Colt could have been involved with her mom vanishing?*

# Chapter 30

Sunlight streamed into Tempest's bedroom. She'd fallen asleep while digging into research on Corbin Colt on her phone and forgotten to close the curtains. Her phone lay under her arm, which now bore a rectangular impression.

She rubbed her arm and tapped her phone. Nothing. It had only had 5 percent battery life the last time she'd noticed before falling asleep. There was an endless amount of content on Corbin Colt she could have read, so she'd told herself she would only research until the phone battery died. She'd nearly made it.

Not that she had much to show for it. There was plenty of information about Corbin online—some fact and some fiction—but nothing that connected him to the Raj family aside from living in Hidden Creek and the single essay published on the one-year anniversary of Emma Raj's disappearance. In the essay Corbin explicitly said they had been quite close (a lie) and obliquely hinted that he had ideas about what had really happened to her when she vanished. Yet after that essay appeared, nothing. Was that because of her grandfather threatening him? Whatever was going on, his manuscript proved that Corbin Colt had known a lot more about Tempest's family than she'd ever realized.

Tempest plugged in her phone and headed to the bathroom to smooth out the rat's nest of hair she always woke up with when she didn't tie up her thick black hair before going to bed. When she stepped back across the floorboards of different lengths and colors pieced together to form the image of a skeleton key, her phone was blinking from where it rested on top of her old steamer trunk she used as a dresser. She'd missed a call during the night and a voicemail was waiting for her.

"Sorry to ring you so late," her grandmother's voice said in the recording, "but we *didnae* have a chance to speak earlier and I thought you might still be awake. I'm at the airport awaiting my flight. I wanted to hear your voice, and to thank you for sending the professor to get me. Such a charming young man. Why haven't you told me about him before? Ta. See you soon."

*The professor?*

*No. No, no, no.* It had to be Moriarty. Sherlock Holmes's nemesis James Moriarty was a professor.

Nicodemus was supposed to be picking her up. *What had Moriarty done to him?*

Tempest phoned her grandmother back. The call went immediately to voicemail. It wasn't her grandmother's voice on the outgoing message. It was Moriarty's.

The message was short: "Call me," followed by a phone number beginning with her own area code.

The somber tone conveyed a serious urgency that frightened her nearly as much as the fact that his voice was on her grandmother's phone. She hadn't gotten a handle on her guardian-angel adversary. She called the number.

"This isn't funny," she said before he could speak. "The members of my family aren't pawns you can use—"

"Don't worry," Moriarty said. "She's fine. I would never hurt anyone you care about. I wasn't using her. I—"

"Why are you even in Scotland?"

"I'm a man of the world, Tempest. I enjoy travel. And helping those I care about."

"You didn't fly to Scotland to take my gran to the airport." She wasn't even going to ask how he knew. She didn't want to know the answer.

"I needed to talk with her to help you both. I'm the only person who knows she's looking into your mom's and aunt's murders. I know you want to figure out what happened to them. I really am here to help."

"How exactly do you think you can help?"

"I'm good at asking important questions."

"Did you upset her?"

"It's insulting to her that you think of her as a frail old woman."

Tempest bristled. "She's nothing of the sort. I'm more concerned that when she finds out you who you really are, she'll hurt you. Badly. Then she'll be arrested for your assault."

Moriarty chuckled. It wasn't a lighthearted sound. It was cold. Clinical. Like if you'd explained to a robot what a chuckle was. Or a sociopath.

Tempest swallowed hard. "How did you dispose of Nicodemus? If you hurt him—"

"I don't know what I have to do to convince you I'd never hurt anyone you care about. I know you think of Nicodemus the Necromancer as something of a mentor. His act is a bit over the top, you know. All of those devils whispering in his ear? I know it's in the tradition of classic stage magic, but I quite prefer your style of honoring the classics by making them your own. Then again, I prefer your magic to anyone else's."

The phone went silent. Not just the absence of speaking, but a faint hum she hadn't been aware of until it was gone also vanished. Her screen assured her the call hadn't dropped, and two seconds later Moriarty spoke again.

"I need to sign off in a minute. Before I go, I should tell you—"

"Wait. Is my grandmother on that flight she was supposed to be on?"

"She's somewhere over the Atlantic as we speak. She even received an upgrade to first class. And she's none the wiser that I subtly asked her for information pertaining to your family curse and her daughters' murders." As he spoke the last few words, his tone shifted. "I'm truly sorry, Tempest. But you must believe me. Your grandmother is the least of your worries. I didn't think I needed to be concerned about your grandfather's predicament, but I was mistaken."

"He'll be much better as soon as my grandmother gets home to him."

"I'm not so sure about that."

"You can make the most innocuous things sound sinister."

"The world is a sinister place, Tempest. As you know all too well. Which is why I'm glad you called me back. I'm glad I could assure you your grandmother and mentor are safe, and I always enjoy hearing your voice, but that's not why I wanted to talk with you. I need to tell you something."

"Then go ahead and tell me," Tempest growled.

"I wouldn't trust that detective who's been assigned to the case."

"Of course you don't trust detectives."

"This has nothing to do with me. Detective Rinehart isn't what he seems."

"If you're trying to tell me something, go ahead and tell me."

"Patience isn't one of your virtues. No matter. You have so much else going for you I'll forgive that."

Of all the impossibilities she was trying to solve, this impossible conversation had now topped the list.

"Until ten years ago," Moriarty said, "Detective Austin Rinehart didn't exist."

"He's only been a detective for ten years? Not the most experience possible, but still a lot—"

"Precision with language. I appreciate that. Allow me to clarify. Austin Rinehart, who is currently a detective in Hidden Creek, California, only came into existence in the world ten years ago. Before that, the man didn't exist."

"What does that even mean, *he didn't exist*—"

"I really do need to sign off now. Be careful, Tempest."

Her phone beeped. Moriarty had hung up on her.

Tempest tried calling him again, but it went directly to voicemail. She squeezed the phone.

She was going to kill him. He'd ingratiated himself to her grandmother and left her with a bombshell that the detective who'd put her grandfather in jail was a fraud.

He had to be lying. Or mistaken. Or it was a sick joke.

No. None of those alternatives made sense. She believed him when he said he didn't want to hurt her. Not that she trusted him, but she believed that in his own twisted mind *he* believed his own words.

She looked up the detective online. The Hidden Creek PD didn't include a staff list on their website, but she found Detective Rinehart several other places online in his official capacity. He was truly a detective with HCPD.

But . . . that's not what Moriarty had taken issue with. He said Rinehart *didn't exist* until ten years ago.

Tempest switched from her phone's browser to her phone contacts.

"Tempest?" Ivy's voice on the other end of the line was groggy. "Oh, God. What's wrong?"

"Sorry. I forgot how early it was."

"What's wrong?"

"I shouldn't have called."

"It's early even for early birds." Ivy yawned. "I'm awake. Whatever you called about, tell me."

"Can you use your librarian-in-training superpowers to look something up for me?"

"Like, right now?"

"If it's true, it's a problem I should know about sooner rather than later."

The sound of a book, or something like it, falling to the floor came through the phone, along with a grumble from Ivy.

"I've got a pen and paper," Ivy said a moment later. "What do you need?"

"Detective Rinehart, the guy investigating Corbin Colt's death. Someone suggested that he didn't exist until ten years ago."

"What, like one of Corbin's fans saying the detective investigating their hero's death is a supernatural entity, and he's ten years old in raven years or something?"

"Something like that. . . . Can you help me look him up to reassure me he's just a regular guy who became a detective? A general search didn't get me anywhere."

"*The Raven* is getting to you."

"Everything is getting to me."

"I'll put my information-science skills to work. Call you back when I have something."

☠☠☠

Tempest called Nicodemus while she waited for Ivy. She used a video call, since they always liked to see each other from across the world.

"Tempest!" He was in good spirits, so that was something. And he was in his house, with his magic memorabilia behind him. Magic apparatuses as well, so he was in the workshop beneath his living quarters. She caught a glimpse of several automata behind him. The fortune-teller in a glass booth who told your fortune by dealing Tarot cards, a handwriting automaton who could write several short messages, and her favorite miniature automaton, a woman made of wire who sat at a toy piano and played a melodious tune when wound. A framed poster of the Indian Rope Trick peeked out from behind the automata.

"Why didn't you take my grandmother to the airport, Nicky?"

"It's nice to hear your voice, too, my dear. Didn't she tell you her flight was delayed?" He swore. "Don't tell me they changed her flight again. Airlines these days, I tell you—"

"They did. She got another ride to the airport. Don't worry." No need for both of them to be worried.

"I'm sorry I missed her. But I don't see a missed call. . . ."

"Don't worry about it. She's fine. She—"

A banging knock on her door at the bottom of her secret staircase nearly made her drop the phone.

"Tempest?" her dad called from behind her door. "We need to see you."

*We?*

"My dad's calling for me," she said to Nicodemus. "We'll catch up later."

"Everything all right?"

"I have no idea."

She ran down the stairs in her pajamas and bare feet. The members of the Secret Staircase Construction crew had seen her with grimy arms, sawdust in her hair, and covered in sweat. They could deal with plaid pajamas and bare feet.

But when Tempest opened her bedroom door, it wasn't a member of the crew with her dad. It was a uniformed police officer with a solemn expression.

"It's Sylvie." Her dad ran a hand across his face. "One of the members of Lavinia's book club who was there at the séance that night."

"I remember her. What's happened?"

"She's dead."

# Chapter 31

Tempest pulled up in front of Lavinia's house.

A bloody handprint had been discovered on a window-pane inside Lavinia's Lair—next to two feathers of a raven. The fingerprints in the blood matched Sylvie's.

Tempest drove over as soon as she was done giving her statement to the officer who'd arrived at Fiddler's Folly and found Darius in the workshop. Since Tempest and Ash had both been at the séance, and the crimes might have been connected, the officer wanted to speak with both of them. Separately.

The officer asked more questions than he answered, but Tempest learned this much: in addition to the blood, there was "other evidence" leading them to be concerned that Sylvie had been killed. But Darius's initial information when he banged on Tempest's door wasn't the full story. *There was no body.* The police were treating it as a missing persons case, not a murder. Not yet. This was a possible kidnapping, but a suspected second murder.

For a brief moment, Tempest thought there was a silver lining. Her grandfather was confined to the tree house by his ankle monitor. There was no way he could have harmed

Sylvie. But that wasn't strictly true. Ash had been in contact with numerous people. He could have hired someone. It wasn't true, but the police would be sure to look into it.

Tempest walked along the outskirts of the crime scene tape surrounding Lavinia's Lair. She caught a glimpse of the bloody handprint on the window. A streak of red stained the glass as if a hand had desperately tried the break the glass but been dragged away.

A sound from above drew her gaze from the bloodied windowpane. A flock of black birds circled overhead. Tempest considered what to do next. Whatever it was, it would definitely *not* include a movie night to watch *The Birds* with Ivy.

A figure came into view. In her wheelchair, Lavinia's mother, Kumiko, was wrapped in a soft black shawl that Tempest couldn't help but think looked like it had been made out of the feathers of a large black bird. This was a woman who everyone underestimated. Tempest wouldn't make that mistake.

"Things look bad for my daughter," Kumiko said.

"I know," Tempest murmured demurely. No. Who was she kidding? She wasn't capable of acting demure.

Kumiko gripped the handles of her chair with frustration. "Lavinia isn't guilty. I want you to find her—and clear her."

"Find her? Isn't she talking to the police like the rest of us did?"

Kumiko looked up at the birds that were still circling. "My daughter wasn't at home when the newspaper delivery man saw the bloody handprint and called the police."

"She was already at Veggie Magic?"

Kumiko shook her head. "I thought you were intelligent. If I knew where she was, I wouldn't have asked for your help. I'm not as mobile as I used to be. I need you to *find her*. Therefore, she is missing. I'm worried she might have been harmed herself, but the police don't seem to find that theory compelling."

"You tried calling her?"

Kumiko threw her hands into the air. "I have done everything I can think to do. My daughter knows that someone around that table killed Corbin. We all know it wasn't a fan. It was someone at that séance table. *Someone in that room with us.* Unless you believe in Corbin's fantastical supernatural plots. Which I don't. I know it could have been your grandfather."

"You don't really think—"

Kumiko cut her off with a wave of her hand. "I don't *think* so. I don't know for certain, either." She paused. When she spoke again, her voice was softer. It held a vulnerability Tempest hadn't heard before. "Lavinia is my only child. My husband is gone. Now that someone has kidnapped that vile woman, they're trying to make it look like Lavinia did it."

"Because Sylvie was attacked here."

Kumiko made a noise between a grunt and a sigh. "Do keep up. I believed you were the smart one. They're not treating my daughter's disappearance as a kidnapping, because there's no physical evidence. They're considering the possibility that she *fled*."

"The person who harmed Sylvie could be keeping Lavinia hostage to make her look guilty."

"I don't know what's happening. What I do know is that we both want to help prove the innocence of our loved ones, and that you solved a murder last year. We can help each other."

"You know something that could help me clear my grandfather?"

"I have the key to the basement. Lavinia's Lair. After the police have gone, I can let you inside so you can look for whatever clues you need."

Tempest considered the proposition. She knew Kumiko didn't trust her, and Tempest didn't trust Kumiko. Not only because of her interest in her grandfather, but because she'd been there the night of the séance. Tempest knew not to underestimate a woman just because she was physically frail and in a wheelchair recovering from a bad fall. But she also understood Kumiko wanting to help her daughter, just as Tempest wanted to help her grandfather.

"If we work together," Tempest began, "we have to explore all options. Wherever they lead."

"You can believe in my and my daughter's guilt all you want," said Kumiko. "We're both innocent. I'm not afraid of the truth."

"Tell me what you know."

Kumiko had learned that Sylvie's neighbor was the first to report her missing, even before a newspaper delivery person had seen the bloody handprint and called the police. Before the blood was found, the police hadn't taken any action. An adult can forget to turn off their alarm clock, and though it is irresponsible to leave a barking dog inside, it was hardly enough for her to be officially "missing."

But after a frantic newspaper delivery man described the blood on the window, the police woke up Kumiko to let them into the basement and then sent officers to question everyone involved in the first murder.

"Sylvie's neighbor heard Sylvie's door slam at around five o'clock," Kumiko said. "They share a wall, so it's not unusual for her to hear things. She went back to sleep until Sylvie's alarm clock went off at five thirty and continued blaring through the wall, along with a barking dog. The neighbor complained about the loud alarm to the building manager. At six, she complained once more. The manager finally agreed to open the apartment door. They found the apartment empty except for an agitated dog, who bolted out to the bushes. Her neighbor called the police, but they explained there was nothing they could do. At six thirty, the newspaper delivery person saw the handprint reflected in the window with the light of his head lamp."

There were definitely advantages to being underestimated. Tempest hadn't gotten nearly that much information from the officer who'd questioned her. Both Sylvie and Lavinia were missing—or worse. But even with that much information, there was far more they didn't know.

"Only Sylvie's blood was found inside Lavinia's Lair?" Tempest asked.

"What was *missing* might be even more important." Kumiko paused to scowl at the birds circling overhead. "The rug in the entryway has been removed. So was one of the mallets next to the windows. The ones your father's crew insisted on placing in case of an emergency so there would be a second exit. One of them is gone."

Tempest winced. The metal mallets were strong enough to break glass. She didn't want to think about what they would do to a skull. "The amount of blood suggests she's dead?"

"It's not the amount of blood." Kumiko pointed to a spot of ground beyond the crime-scene tape. "There are drag marks leading to the driveway."

Tempest winced. This was bad. So bad. "As if a rolled-up rug, holding something long and heavy, had been dragged away." Could someone be alive under those circumstances?

Tempest's phone rang. Both of them jumped.

"Ivy, sorry I missed your earlier calls. A lot has happ—"

"Tempest. I don't know what's going on. But whatever internet weirdo told you about Detective Rinehart had it right. I can't find anything about him before ten years and three months ago. It's like he didn't exist."

# Chapter 32

One of the reasons stage magic can look truly impossible, like something supernatural is responsible, is because the magician has practiced for hundreds of hours and has taken every detail into consideration. The use of misdirection is central to any illusion, be it a magic trick like the ones Tempest performed—or a murder made to look impossible. But misdirection only works when it's set up perfectly. One mistake and the house of cards tumbles down. Tempest needed to find just one loose card. That would be enough to send the house tumbling down to reveal what was behind the trick.

The problem was that unlike Tempest's exhaustive knowledge of her own illusions, where she knew every last detail down to the centimeter and second, she was missing too many pieces of the crimes going on around her to see the trick. Too many gaps in her knowledge.

She looked to the silver charm bracelet she'd worn every day for the last five years. The top hat, Janus-faced jester, lightning bolt, fiddle, selkie, book, handcuffs, and key. Each was a symbol related to her and her mom's shared love of magic.

The top-hat charm was a reminder that the history and

foundations of magic were important to learn before rushing forward. If you sped too quickly to get to the spectacular ending, you'd skip the necessary steps to get the end result you wanted. In a magic performance, that would mean revealing what was up your sleeve. In this real-life trick she needed to unravel, that would mean too much guesswork derailing her from finding the true solution.

Before jumping to conclusions about Detective Rinehart and before looking through Lavinia's Lair for clues about Sylvie's disappearance, Tempest knew she needed to learn more about what exactly had happened that morning.

☠☠☠

Sylvie's apartment building was a run-down '60s-style building dominated by slabs of drab concrete and looked rather like a motel you'd find on a lonely stretch of highway. The front doors of all the units in the U-shaped two-story building were accessible from the outside. The second-floor walkway was covered by a flat roof that extended to shield each doorway from rain. It hadn't been an especially rainy winter, yet the rain gutter was dirty and bent.

Sylvie's apartment was on the far end of the second floor, directly above the building's laundry room, so there was only one option for a next-door neighbor who would have heard her alarm clock and called the building manager. Tempest knocked on the door of Sylvie's neighbor and introduced herself as a concerned member of Sylvie's book club who wanted to help.

"What was your name, hon?" the sprightly woman asked from the doorway. She held a tumbler of iced tea and an unlit cigarette in one hand and rested the other against the door frame. Her gray hair was tied in a bright pink scarf and she wore a matching pink sweatshirt over silver leggings.

"Tempest."

"Tempest what?"

"What?"

"Your surname, hon."

"Raj. I'm Tempest Raj."

The woman pursed her lips as she stretched her skinny neck to look up at Tempest. "Middle initial?"

*Middle initial?* Was this a scam to steal her identity? "Um . . ."

The woman laughed, then knelt and scratched the head of a corgi that had snuck up between her legs. "I'm not trying to steal your Social Security number or anything. But I suspect you're lying about the book club. Sylvie told me how it was perfect that each of the members had a name that made up the word 'KEYS.' A silly membership criteria, if you ask me! But there it is. You're not one of them." She rumpled the corgi's ears as a larger dog approached them. Compared to the playful corgi, the collie stood rigidly, looking down his nose at the smaller dog.

"No," Tempest admitted. "I'm not a member."

"Why do you care about figuring out what happened to Sylvie?"

"I love my grandfather dearly. He's one of the most generous and loving men you'll ever meet."

"That's nice, hon. But what does that have to do with—"

"He was at an event with Sylvie where a man was murdered last week, and now he's a suspect." She didn't think it would help to add that he'd been arrested.

"Terrible all 'round." The woman shook her head. "Sylvie was so shaken when she got back."

"The police are focusing on my grandfather, even though I know he's innocent. He didn't hurt Sylvie, either."

Sylvie's neighbor gave her corgi one more playful pat before standing. "Let's chat in the courtyard. These two are getting along fine. Be back soon, fellas." She left her iced tea, but tucked the unlit cigarette behind her ear, picked up her phone, and spun a gargantuan set of keys around her diminutive index finger before shutting the apartment door behind them.

"The collie is Sylvie's dog?"

"Lord Peter misses her already. He's quite devoted. I'm Laura, by the way. This way." She led them to a wooden bench in the central courtyard, next to a stone fountain devoid of water.

Tempest let her host pick if she wanted the sunny or shady side of the bench. Laura chose the sunny side. She played with the cigarette but didn't light it. On closer inspection, the cigarette was rumpled, as if it had been handled hundreds of times, and had a large crease in one spot where it might have rested between two restless fingers. If Tempest had thought a Sherlockian deduction would have put Laura at ease, she would have made an offhand remark about how it was commendable that she'd quit smoking. But sharing observations about personal habits that people hadn't freely shared rarely ended well.

"You think you can figure out what happened to Sylvie better than the police?"

"I have to try."

"Sylvie loves that dog. That's how I knew something was wrong. Maybe she'd leave early and forget to turn off an alarm clock. But leave Peter? Never. Not even if there'd been an emergency. No, I knew something was wrong."

"You two have known each other a long time?"

"We're friendly, but not friends, you know? More like dog-mom friends. I know she loves vinyl records because she gets LPs mailed to her, she's a big reader—though she gets books at the library—and she adores her dog. Her dog is even named after a character in some book. When I first met her, I thought the 'Lord' bit of Lord Peter's name was because Peter's such a regal dog. Turns out it's the name of a fancy British fella in one of Sylvie's favorite books. She's lived here with Peter since I moved in nearly a decade ago."

"She's been here that long?"

"I know she doesn't look like someone who'd live here. She used to be well-off, as I understand it. An advertising exec. Her job moved to New York. She didn't. I pressed her on that once. Since she seems so New York, you know? I always imagined her looking in her element stepping out of a taxi in New York or London—not that I've ever been to London. But from the movies."

"What did she say?"

"She stayed for a man." Laura tucked the rumpled cigarette behind her ear and shook her head. "Nothing good ever comes from giving up your dreams for a man. I have personal experience on that one. Sylvie's man wasn't quite Lord Peter something-or-other, she said, but as close to him as you can get in the real world."

"What happened?"

"He died. He was ill for a long time, I take it. It was hard on her. She never put her career first. Before you know it, you're past middle age and invisible. It happens before you realize it. Don't let life pass you by, Tempest."

Tempest felt herself smiling. Her life was a mess, but she was certainly living it fully. And protecting her family as best she could.

"I'm working on it," she said, "Starting with helping make sure my grandfather isn't held responsible for a crime he didn't commit. You didn't hear anything else odd this morning, did you? I know about the door slamming, the alarm going off, and Peter barking."

"What do you do for a living, Tempest?"

Tempest couldn't tell if Sylvie's neighbor was being friendly or evasive. "I'm working for my dad's home-renovation company."

"You look like a nice young woman. I know you're worried about your grandfather, but honey, the police are better equipped to find out what she was up to."

*What she was up to?* "Why did you say it like that?"

"Like what?" she blinked at Tempest.

"Sylvie was up to something?"

"Of course, hon. She's in that silly book club where they only read mystery novels. I'm more of a romance reader myself."

"What does the book club have to do with anything?"

"Sylvie was lonely. She lived through her books. Especially ones about a gentleman who sticks his nose into other people's problems to solve mysteries."

"You think Sylvie was doing the same thing?"

"Oh, I know she was. She saw something that night of the murder. I don't know what it was. We aren't that close, you know. But the last time we ran into each other and walked to the dog park together, I got the feeling she was close to putting the pieces together. Along with someone else in that book club of hers."

"You told this to the police this morning?"

"Of course, hon. But I didn't know anything specific, so I don't know how seriously they took what I told them. Like I said, when you get to be my age, you're pretty much invisible."

Had Sylvie gotten too close to the killer's identity? What had she discovered?

# Chapter 33

Sanjay answered his door with wild hair sticking out at all angles and bare feet peeking out from beneath pajama pants. Tempest found herself slightly disappointed he'd taken time to pull on a T-shirt.

"Oh, goodie. You're welcoming me home with death donuts." Sanjay smoothed down his hair as he led her inside his loft apartment. It didn't work and it sprang free as soon as he let go.

"These are store-bought." Tempest placed the paper bag of donuts on his kitchen island. "One hundred percent free from chili pepper."

He grinned as he peeked inside the bag. "You remembered my favorite was jelly-filled donuts."

Tempest didn't have the heart to tell him everyone's favorite donuts were the jelly-filled kind. They hadn't eaten enough donuts together for her to know his favorite.

"You were still asleep?"

He nodded. "Some of us still have nocturnal careers."

"Then you haven't heard the news."

Sanjay paused with a donut inches from his mouth. "I don't like the sound of that."

"Sylvie was attacked."

"Is she okay? God, you weren't with her—"

"I wasn't. I found out when a police officer showed up at my house. They don't know if she's okay. She's missing."

"But you said she was attacked."

"They know that because there was blood."

Sanjay eyed the donut oozing with crimson-colored raspberry filling. With a shudder, he abandoned the donut.

"When you're not on stage," he said, "you really have the worst timing. Since you've spoiled my jelly donut, go ahead and tell me what's going on."

While she told him what had happened at Lavinia's Lair and what she'd learned about Sylvie investigating Corbin's death, he got his espresso maker started.

"Lavinia is the one who attacked Sylvie?" His eyes bulged.

"Don't interrupt. I've nearly got you caught up." She concluded by telling him what she'd learned right *after* meeting with Sylvie's neighbor, which was the reason she'd driven across the bridge in hopes of finding Sanjay at home. "After I left Sylvie's apartment building, I got a call from Kumiko that the police had found Lavinia. She spent the night at Victor's house. Which, if the timing holds up, gives her an alibi for the attack on Sylvie that took place at her house. The two of them are giving statements to the police now."

"The attack took place *inside* Lavinia's Lair?"

Tempest nodded.

"Was the door forced?"

"I don't think so. You're thinking someone had the key." Tempest grimaced. "Which Lavinia just changed. Leaving Kumiko as the most viable suspect in the attack on Sylvie."

Sanjay froze with his hand raised to take a bite of a donut with bright yellow lemon-curd filling. "I was right all along?"

"The more I think about it, the more it seems like you were

right. Lavinia appears to have an alibi for Sylvie's kidnapping or murder, so we overlooked the person who didn't need an alibi. An elderly woman in a wheelchair."

"You poked a hole in my theory earlier, saying her scuffed shoes were her pre-accident shoes. Did you learn they were new after all?"

"Who says someone needs to be able to walk to kill people? Have you noticed Kumiko's arms?"

"Um, I'll have to go with no."

"They're amazing. She used to be a rower when she taught at Oxford."

Sanjay frowned at her as he thrust a tiny espresso cup into her hands. "You could have told me that fact before."

"I didn't realize it was relevant. It's less relevant for Corbin's murder than the attack on Sylvie. None of us at the séance have an alibi for his death, but if Kumiko is the only one without an alibi when Sylvie was attacked, that's a different question."

"Even if you're right that Kumiko could have attacked Sylvie and dragged her body away with her badass rower's arms, *why*? Why would she do it?"

"Maybe because she doesn't want my grandfather to go to prison. She's fond of him. If my grandfather hadn't gotten himself a last-minute invitation so he could look for that damn manuscript—"

"Then a doctor wouldn't have been there to insist on examining Corbin and getting blood on himself. It makes sense. . . . I just don't know." Sanjay ran a finger around the edge of his espresso cup.

"You're the one who thought she was guilty in the first place."

"I wasn't *exactly* joking."

Tempest glared at Sanjay, who was still looking delightfully rumpled with his unkempt hair. "Put on your shoes." She tossed back the espresso shot.

"Why?"

"Because otherwise," said Tempest with a wicked curl of her lip, "I'll do something terribly inadvisable without you."

☠☠☠

"I can't believe I'm letting you talk me into this." Sanjay pulled his bowler hat more tightly around his head.

"You were mad I didn't wait for you to break into Hazel's house."

"That was different."

"How? How was that different?"

"*Shh.* Keep your voice down. I'm trying to concentrate."

"If you want to be more conspicuous," said Tempest, "you're doing a great job. If anyone is watching, that security-blanket hat of yours is as distinctive a calling card as possible."

Sanjay reddened. "Exaggeration does not become you. Do you want my help breaking into Victor's house or not?"

She'd meant to practice lock picking, not for this explicit purpose but to keep her skills sharp and to never stop learning ways to improve her craft as an illusionist. But it hadn't happened yet. Her understanding of pins, keyways, and tension wrenches was still mostly theoretical.

This was her reason for surprising Sanjay with donuts. From Kumiko, she'd learned that Lavinia was on her way to Hidden Creek with Victor. Kumiko didn't know what Tempest planned to do with this information.

"You're sure he doesn't have an alarm?" Sanjay asked. For the fourth time.

"Ninety-five percent sure."

"Ninety-five? What kind of answer is that?"

"A truthful one. I've been here before. I didn't see an alarm."

The lock clicked open. They held their breaths. No alarm. At least not one that made noise.

She'd previously gone to Victor's house to see some of the models he'd built in his home office. They were going over ideas for the small house she wanted to build on the Fiddler's Folly property using the Secret Fort built by her mom as the main structure.

"What are we looking for?" Sanjay asked as he peeked out from behind a closed curtain.

"Anything suspicious."

"No way." Sanjay gripped the curtain.

"Is someone coming?"

Sanjay turned slowly around. "No. I meant *no way*. I can't believe there's nothing in particular you're looking for. Nothing! Why did we even break in?"

"I told you—"

"Right. To look for 'something suspicious.' Like a handwritten confession he wrote on the walls of his workshop."

"Let's go." Tempest led the way to Victor's home office on the second floor.

"I was joking!" Sanjay called after her.

"I know," she called back from the top of the stairs. "But his home office is the best place to start."

On a large drafting table, they found dozens of sheets of graph paper with ideas for a mechanism that could hide and then drop a body.

"Oh my God," Sanjay whispered, picking up an especially complex drawing.

"These aren't what they look like. He was working on trying to figure out how someone outside of the séance could have hidden Corbin's body to drop during the séance."

Sanjay glared at her. "You never tell me anything."

"I'm telling you now." She snatched the paper. "Don't wrinkle that. We don't want him to know we were here."

"This room is a mess. How would he know if we moved anything?" He spun a wooden model of an airplane between his hands, the same motion he used to spin his bowler hat. The plane's wings spanned the same width as his hat, so Tempest wasn't worried he'd break it. His gentle and adept fingers worked mechanically without him needing to think about what he was doing.

"I don't know him well enough to know how his mind works. He's smart. He could be a genius who knows the exact placement of everything."

"A method to his madness . . ."

"I hope you remember where you found that airplane."

Sanjay put it back and switched to spinning his bowler hat between his fingers. "I don't know what I'm looking for here. We also don't know when he'll be back. You stay in here and I'll search the rest of the house."

Tempest spent the next ten minutes looking through Victor's office. She learned more about his love of Gothic Revival houses, but nothing that screamed that he was guilty of anything beyond being bad at taking care of house plants.

A feeling of dread came over her as she came down the stairs and heard voices. How would Sanjay explain himself to Victor?

She decided instantly what she had to do. She'd take the blame, just like Gideon had done for her earlier that week. No question. She'd first try to talk them out of the situation. Would Victor believe she'd forgotten something at his house when she'd been there a month before, and that his door happened to be open?

Probably not.

She took a deep breath and stepped into the living room.

Sanjay was alone. His phone was set on speaker, and the voice of the person on the phone came through loud and clear.

"Now really isn't a good time," Sanjay answered. "I'll call you back later this afternoon." He clicked off and slid the phone back into his pocket. "Sorry about that. I don't have my headphones with me. Why do you look so upset? I doubt he has his own house bugged. We've already been talking to each other anyway—"

Tempest stopped his words with her lips. The quick, intense kiss came out of nowhere. She hadn't planned on that, but her whole body was buzzing with excitement she couldn't contain. Sanjay just happened to be the closest thing for her to quiet her overloading brain.

"Sanjay," she said to the shocked man standing before her. "You've solved it. I know how it was done. The whole trick."

"I did?" Sanjay blinked at her. "You do?"

"I think so. There's just one thing I need to check to make sure."

She'd been so focused on the pages she found implicating her father, Moriarty getting close to Grannie Mor and helping figure out what happened to her mom and aunt, and now Sylvie's kidnapping, she hadn't stopped to properly think about what she'd missed. She hadn't stopped to realize she'd fallen into a trap, the likes of which magicians set. She'd been misdirected.

Tempest Raj now saw through the spotlight that had guided her field of view to the wrong spot. The Tempest was ready to pull back the curtain.

# Chapter 34

**B**efore telling her idea to Sanjay or anyone else, she had to test if her theory was right.

The best route to Forestville to avoid traffic took Tempest north across the Carquinez Bridge, and then west, skirting wine-country strongholds Sonoma and Napa. The name of the town suited it. In Hidden Creek, you knew you were on the outskirts of a metropolis. Here in Forestville, you knew you were in a different world. The air smelled strongly of pine trees and the faint aroma of wood-burning stoves. The quaint general store was no bigger than Tempest's Secret Fort and looked as if it hadn't been renovated in a century.

Tempest had been a passenger with Ivy driving when she'd come to Forestville earlier in the week, distracted by the task ahead of them. Now she felt as if she was truly seeing it for the first time.

She turned off the two-lane highway onto a single-lane road. After five more minutes of easing around blind turns on the bumpy, winding road, she spotted Hazel on the front porch of the house. She hadn't seen Hazel up close the day she snuck into her house. The internet personality looked so different from the videos and still images Tempest had seen of her online.

The real-life version of Hazel had dark circles under her eyes, lips devoid of maroon lipstick, and a navy blue jumpsuit. No concealer, vibrant makeup, or colorful designer dress. Tempest shouldn't have been surprised. Tempest Raj of Hidden Creek lived in her fitted white T-shirt, jeans, ruby-red sneakers, and no makeup except for red lipstick. She was a far different person than The Tempest's persona on stage.

This rumpled Hazel stood in contrast to her photo-shoot-ready deck with a faux-rustic vibe. She was snapping photos of an artfully composed cocktail placed next to an outdoor fireplace with cozy flames rising from small white rocks.

She looked up from her camera as Tempest stepped out of her car. "This is private property."

"I know you don't want to talk to anyone," Tempest said without coming any closer, "but please, hear me out. I'm so sorry for your loss."

"I'm not doing any interviews about Corbin." Hazel clutched her phone and backed toward the door.

"I'm not a journalist. I was there at the séance. I'm Tempest Raj. My grandfather has been arrested for Corbin's murder."

Hazel kept her eyes on Tempest but grabbed for the doorknob.

"He didn't do it," Tempest added hastily. "I want to help find out who really did."

Hazel didn't let go, but her grip softened and her gaze shifted from Tempest to the highest branches of the trees surrounding them. She was still looking upward with an unfocused gaze when she spoke. "I know he didn't do it. Because I know who killed Corbin."

Tempest gaped at her. "You do? Who—?"

222 ※ Gigi Pandian

"You're really here because of your grandfather?" Hazel's gaze snapped back to Tempest.

"I am."

"And you don't think I'm involved?"

"No." It was true. Tempest no longer believed Hazel was *consciously involved* in the trick that led to Corbin's murder. But she had to be sure she was right.

Hazel didn't answer right away. For an excruciating eight seconds, Tempest was certain she was about to be turned away. She was so close to answers.

"Come on," Hazel finally said. "If you really don't know, we have a lot to talk about."

The house looked different than the last time Tempest had been inside. The raven painting still dominated the room. *Nam Fitheach.* Tempest had looked up the words. It meant *of the ravens* in Gaelic and was also the name of a Scottish mountain range. The words painted on its wings in silver paint shimmered in the light. And now, underneath the painting, were even more talismans to ward off evil, from colorful amulets to prayer beads.

"That's who killed him." Hazel turned her gaze from Tempest to the raven painting. "I didn't use to be superstitious. I never took any of this supernatural crap seriously—until Corbin."

"I didn't think he believed in his plots."

"He didn't. Not really. But he messed with some stuff that a lot of people believe in." Hazel shivered. "The messages he got . . . I was careful to keep this place hidden, so his fans couldn't find him here. I own it with my real name. Not 'Hazel.' How did you find—"

"From Lavinia. And I won't share it." It was plausible. She didn't say how easy it was to find information about Hazel online. She didn't want to derail this conversation before it even began.

Hazel waved her concern aside. "Cat's out of the bag. One of his fans broke in earlier this week to get something of Corbin's."

So Rinehart hadn't told her who was responsible. "I'm sure it won't be a usual occurrence. I hope you're not too worried."

"Not about that." Hazel grabbed a black shawl from the back of the couch and wrapped it around her shoulders.

"I wanted to ask you about how you film your show."

Hazel raised an eyebrow. "You trying to tell me you're a fan and that's why I should trust you?"

"No. I'm not going to lie to you. I had never heard of your show until this week. I don't use social media."

Hazel snorted.

"Look me up," Tempest said. "I quit it all last year after . . . the details don't matter. I'm really not on social media. I don't care about your show. I do care about getting justice for my grandfather—and for Corbin."

Hazel reached for her phone. "Oh, honey," she murmured a few seconds later. "You're *that* girl? Now I understand why you hate social media." She let out a laugh that sounded more like a cackle as she stood there, wrapped tightly in a black shawl underneath what was essentially an altar to a creepy raven.

When she was done cackling, Hazel stood up abruptly and tossed the shawl aside. "If your life is half as messed up as my little phone screen says, you need a drink before we get into it. Name your poison."

"What are my choices?"

"Caffeine or booze. Even though I make an absolutely

gorgeous green smoothie with the cutest broccoli sprouts on top, you don't get to pick wheatgrass."

Ten minutes later, they were seated on bar stools at Hazel's kitchen island, sipping frothy coffee drinks with plenty of sugar but none of the fancy toppings that would have made the drinks pop in a social media photo, laughing about the most ridiculous things that had been said about them both online before they'd stopped reading comments for their mental health.

"I apparently had plastic surgery done on my thumbs," said Hazel, "because I used to have fat thumbs but now they're beautiful."

"I didn't even realize thumbs could be beautiful. And if so, why can't fat thumbs be beautiful?"

"Good point. I hadn't even thought of that. I won't even tell you about the really icky stuff. As a woman of color in show business, you already know how bad it can be."

Hazel wasn't the husband-stealing monster Tempest had imagined. She claimed that Corbin said his marriage had been over for a long time but he hadn't gotten divorced for publicity reasons, until he met Hazel and knew he could no longer live a lie. Hazel could have been a good actress, but Tempest was inclined to believe her. Corbin Colt was a man who'd already proven himself to be ruthless and have plenty of secrets.

"What do you think happened?" Tempest asked. She had her own theory now, which is why she'd come, but she was curious to see if what Hazel had hinted at was what she really believed.

Hazel stood up and walked to the window overlooking a copse of trees. "It's just like a plot from one of his books. Especially *The Raven*, but he did all sorts of research. He made a homunculus once. Just to talk about the experience in interviews. Not that he really thought he could bring an inanimate object to life. But some of the things he learned about . . . He should never have dabbled in the occult."

"You believe a supernatural entity killed him?"

"There's no way he could have showed up fifteen minutes later at *her* house—"

"About that," said Tempest. "I know how he did it."

# Chapter 35

t's not a supernatural explanation," said Tempest.

A strong emotion flashed in Hazel's eyes. "Anything else is impossible. It had to be Lavinia, channeling something she learned about from Corbin's research."

"You told the police you saw him right before he showed up dead at the séance." She had to tread carefully here. She didn't want to muddle Hazel's memories any more than they already were.

"I did. Because I did. I wasn't lying. That beady-eyed detective asked me the same questions again and again, trying to get me to trip myself up. But he couldn't find any holes in my story. Because I wasn't lying. I saw him. My fans did, too. The only explanation—"

"Corbin wasn't killed through a supernatural force, Hazel. Lavinia didn't summon an evil spirit to kill your boyfriend."

"She held a *séance*." Hazel glared at her. "Séances call spirits from that realm into this one. She hired a medium. What the hell did Lavinia think would happen? Corbin knew she was doing it, you know. That's why he was upset that day and wanted to spend all afternoon in his office writing. I'm sorry your grandfather has been blamed. I already told the police to look at Lavinia. She hired that medium—"

"Sanjay isn't a medium," Tempest explained. This conversation wasn't going as she'd hoped. She needed to rein it in. "He's a stage magician."

Hazel blinked at her, truly surprised. "What, like pulling a rabbit out of a hat?"

Tempest wanted to say he'd never use a live animal in his act. But that wouldn't help things at all. "He does large illusions on the stage. He's performed all over the world. He's good at creating illusions. Nothing supernatural involved. The séance was a trick. A show. Something to help Lavinia move on. What you saw that night was also a trick. Corbin's trick."

"Corbin isn't—wasn't—a magician." Tears welled in Hazel's eyes.

Tempest gave her a moment to compose herself. "You were filming in the room you always use for your livestreamed happy hours, right?"

When Tempest had previously visited Hazel's house, her one mission had been to find the book that Ash wanted to get back. She hadn't been paying attention to the layout of the house for its own sake, but she'd done it automatically. Paying attention to the layout of her surroundings was so important both to her stage shows and to her dad's business.

They knew Hazel hadn't been mistaken about the time, because she was livestreaming her happy-hour show when she saw Corbin. She couldn't have recorded it ahead of time. Even if she had done so but hadn't wanted to admit to it, she was interacting with her fans' comments in real time. Tempest had previously speculated that it could have been a complicated trick. *But it wasn't.* Hazel's fans had heard

Corbin leaving off camera. What they had seen was Hazel's reaction. They had *seen* Hazel acting like she was talking to someone directly off camera, but they'd only *heard* Corbin. Just like Tempest had heard Sanjay on the phone. They didn't see him. Nobody did.

Hazel *said* she'd seen him—but had she?

Hazel couldn't have seen him. In the video, fans reported that she looked over her shoulder, as if she was looking at someone. But it's natural to look in the direction from which you hear a voice. From the space where she filmed her show, *there was no way for her to see the door to his office or the front door of the house.* Unless he'd paused in the doorway of her filming room, she couldn't have seen him.

"Yeah," Hazel said. "I was filming in the same place I always do. That's where I saw him."

"Are you sure?"

"You think I don't know what I saw? I know you're trying to help clear your grandpa, but think it's time for you to leave."

"I'll leave in just a minute. If you can show me your filming studio first. One minute."

"Fine." Hazel led Tempest to the room.

"Show me where you were filming," Tempest said.

Hazel complied, stepping to a spot in front of a standing desk which had been covered with a farmhouse-style tabletop of mismatched wooden planks.

"You didn't move from here while filming, right?"

Hazel pointed at a blue tape "X" on the floor at her feet. "I'm a professional."

"Your door was open?"

"Yeah. The light is better. I didn't expect Corbin to interrupt. He was working on a new book and often disappeared for hours. I thought he'd be a while."

"Did Corbin stop in your doorway when he spoke to you?"

She hesitated. "Well, he knocked and looked in, but then didn't want to disturb me when he saw I was filming, so he kept walking."

"What was he wearing?"

She pressed her palms to her eyes. "I don't know! He was interrupting. I wasn't paying attention."

"But did you actually *see* him?"

She didn't answer.

"You can't see the door to Corbin's study, or the front door of your house, from where you're standing here," Tempest continued. "For you to see him, he would have needed to be standing directly in the doorway itself."

Hazel swore under her breath.

Corbin's new girlfriend wasn't in on the trick, but like all humans, she was an unreliable eyewitness narrator. She'd been so convinced he was there with her, first writing in his study alone and then leaving on a walk, that it never occurred to her there was a trick. She wasn't expecting a deception, so therefore she didn't see one.

It was in character for Corbin to work without being disturbed. When questioned by the police, her statements were unreliable because she told them what she *perceived*, which was reasonable and what most people would have done, but not what had truly transpired. The livestreamed video backed that up, because she turned toward the sound of Corbin's voice and the sound of a knock. Her reaction was genuine, not acting, because she truly believed she'd seen him. She was so convincing that even those who'd watched the video and heard his voice imagined he was really there.

The fact that she later said how thoughtful it was of him to reactivate the Stay setting on the home alarm should have been a red flag. He wasn't usually that considerate. He wasn't that day, either. He wasn't physically there to disarm and rearm the security system.

Tempest had seen smart speakers in the house. He could have easily used one to play a recording, knowing a time when Hazel wouldn't get up to see him in person. He knew he'd upset her, but he knew it would be worse if she knew he was going to see Lavinia.

It was reasonable that he wouldn't have wanted his new girlfriend to know he was going to see his ex-wife, but was there more to it than that?

Tempest had debunked the supernatural theory for good. Corbin Colt had left Forestville for Hidden Creek long before Hazel's livestream. But she couldn't trust the detective assigned to the case as someone to turn to with this information.

Tempest thanked Hazel for her honesty and time.

"Here's your last dose of honesty," Hazel said from the front door as she showed Tempest out. "I bet we would have been friends in another life, but in this messy one with so much death and deception, I hope I don't see you again. All I can do is wish you the best of luck clearing your grandpa and getting answers for all of us."

Tempest's hands shook as she started the engine. She was so close to solving this. The trick of Corbin getting himself to Hidden Creek on his own was the biggest piece of the puzzle. It was the one part of the trick that would cause the rest of the pieces to fall into place. She could almost see it. *Almost*.

☠☠☠

On her drive home through the bewitching ancient trees that made this region both so special and so susceptible to burning down every so often, Tempest left the windows down, listening to the sounds of nature and breathing in its rich scents. Birds she couldn't identify spoke to each other. Water trickled over smooth rocks in the nearby river. Branches of Douglas firs swayed in the wind.

Her phone rang from the passenger seat, startling her from forming her next steps. She'd set it to silent mode so that only emergency calls would come through while she met with Hazel and had forgotten to set it back. A photo of her grandfather flashed on the screen. His favorite fedora filled half the screen, and his joyful smile reminded Tempest of the day she'd taken the photo on the tree house deck while Grannie Mor was playing her fiddle during a small dinner party.

"I thought we'd have more time," Ash said when Tempest answered. "I suppose it was narrow-minded to think that the police wouldn't be big readers."

"They found Corbin Colt's manuscript?" She'd thought they'd have more time as well.

"A young policewoman cataloging the Agatha Christie book into evidence found the pages in the hollowed-out hiding spot and read them. The detective is talking with your father now. In light of the true facts twisted into that damn fool's manuscript, Detective Rinehart wants to reopen your mother's disappearance."

# Chapter 36

Tempest was so close to the truth she could feel it but not quite grasp it. Like it was hovering in her peripheral vision but her eyes refused to focus.

Corbin Colt's old manuscript was so damning that her dad was now being interrogated for her mom's disappearance five years ago, even though the manuscript was supposedly a work of fiction.

Corbin had tricked his girlfriend in order to visit his ex, but that only answered *one* of the four impossibilities.

Sylvie had been investigating something before she was attacked at Lavinia's house, but what did she know that made her a threat?

Lavinia supposedly had an alibi for the kidnapping, but was that a trick, too?

*What was she missing?*

Tempest slowed down in a spot of traffic on the freeway. Instead of heading home to Hidden Creek, she was on her way to the airport. Her dad was supposed to pick up Grannie Mor at the airport, but since his presence was now requested at the police station, Tempest was on her way to SFO to pick up her grandmother.

Morag enveloped Tempest in a warm hug as soon as she reached her granddaughter in the arrivals area of the international terminal. Small-boned but the opposite of frail (Morag's nickname Mor, meaning "large" in Gaelic, was also appropriate for its irony), she wrapped her arms around her granddaughter in an embrace so strong that Tempest wouldn't have been able to break even if she'd wanted to. Morag's head barely reached Tempest's chin.

Even after a day of air travel, Morag Ferguson-Raj looked photo-shoot ready. Her white hair was tied back with a midnight-blue silk scarf, and a matching silk scarf was lazily draped around her neck and over her shoulder. A pop of mauve on her lips and cheeks lit up her face.

The only difference today was that her forehead was creased with worry.

"What a lovely surprise that you're the one to come and get me," she said as Tempest took her rolling suitcase and led them away from the crowd. "I thought Darius was coming."

"You're stuck with me."

Her gran gave her another squeeze. "How is Ashok? Tell me the truth."

"He's having a grand time holding court, bringing the world to him to keep his mind off what he's been accused of."

Morag clasped her hands together. They were bare except for her gold wedding band of interwoven Celtic knots. She also wore a gold Thaali necklace, a Tamil marriage symbol. "He doesn't want to worry you."

"You'll be with him in about an hour to see for yourself, but really, he's in good spirits. He has faith he'll be cleared."

"What do you think?"

"That Corbin's real killer will be caught." Even if she was the one who had to do it. . . .

"Then why do you look so worried?"

"We're both worried about something else."

Her gran raised an elegant eyebrow. "Nothing else can have happened while I've been in the air, can it?"

"You haven't checked your phone for email or voicemail messages?"

"I've been more than thirty thousand feet in the air, dear." Morag Ferguson-Raj wasn't someone who kept up with the latest technology. She'd turned off her phone when she got on an airplane and apparently hadn't yet turned it back on.

"Let's get to the car." Tempest yanked on the silver suitcase in a futile attempt to get its sticking wheel to cooperate.

"Tempest. What's going on?" Morag stood with her chic black boots, dotted with a few nearly undetectable splatters of paint, firmly on the floor.

"Do you want a coffee? Or food of any kind?" SFO was like a sanitized reproduction of an international boulevard.

"Tempest."

"How much did Ash tell you when you spoke on the phone?"

"He doesn't keep secrets from me."

Tempest sighed. "You know about Corbin Colt's manuscript?"

"Page of lies about our Emma and your da."

"And what it suggests about what my dad did?"

Morag grabbed Tempest's hand. "That's why Darius isn't here?"

"The police have read the manuscript. They're reopening my mom's disappearance. Papa is talking to them now."

Morag swore. "Those two should never have threatened that man all those years ago. And they shouldn't have kept it from you. This family has too many secrets."

In spite of her grandmother's concern, Tempest couldn't keep her anger in check. "If that's true, do you want to tell me what you were really doing in Scotland?" she spat out.

Morag's eyes widened. "I don't know what you mean."

"Gran. I know you want to find out what happened to your daughters as much as I do."

"Car. Now."

They walked in silence, the cacophony of airport sounds around them enough to fill what could have easily been an awkward silence. Only when they were out of the parking structure and driving north on the 101 did Morag speak.

"I didn't even tell Nicodemus." Morag spoke uncharacteristically softly as she looked out at the vast water of the bay. "How did you find out?"

"From the man who took you to the airport."

"The professor?" Morag turned from the sea and stared at Tempest.

"He's not really . . . Never mind. This isn't the conversation we're having right now. Why did you lie to us?"

"I *didnae* lie. Not exactly. I really did travel to the Hebrides for an artist's retreat."

"But that's not all you did."

"No."

It was a full minute before Morag spoke again.

"The curse hasn't been laid to rest," Morag whispered. "Until we know what really happened to them, we can't be at peace."

"There isn't a curse."

"You haven't seen the things I've seen in my life, Tempest. I don't expect you to believe, but I hope you'll understand my actions."

"I've been trying to find out as well," Tempest admitted.

"I know."

"You do?" Tempest took her eyes off the road to steal a glance at her grandmother.

"That's why I had to do what I did. To omit facts about certain things. *To protect you.*"

"What did you do?" Tempest's throat was tight.

"You know I stayed with Nicodemus in Leith for two nights before traveling to the artist's retreat. I told him I wanted to go on one of my favorite hikes, up to Arthur's Seat. His health isn't what it used to be, so I knew he wouldn't come with me."

"You didn't go on a hike."

"No. I visited the police station."

"What did you find?"

"Watch out for that lorry, dear."

Tempest swerved around a truck that had slowed down unexpectedly.

"Maybe we should pull over to finish this discussion?" Morag suggested.

It wasn't a bad idea. Tempest took the exit leading to Candlestick Point, overlooking the bay. "You were about to tell me what you found out."

"That the world has moved on. The detective inspector who declared her death an accident has retired. Nobody could find his notes on the case."

As soon as the car came to a stop, Morag jumped out. For a terrifying second, Tempest was afraid her gran was about to jump into the bay, like a selkie returning to sea. Instead, she opened the back and unzipped her suitcase. Tempest joined her in time to see her pulling out a hard case containing artwork.

Morag held up a mounted canvas in one hand and what looked like a greeting card in the other.

The color palette of the underwater scene was restricted to

blues and greens, with perhaps a hint of gold. Two selkies, in the process of shedding their seal skins, swirled in the frothy ocean waves. No, that wasn't right. It wasn't only two selkies. Two more half-women, half-seals could be seen further back in the dark waters.

Morag handed Tempest the smaller card. The haunting image of a selkie emerging from the sea dominated the front of the 5 x 7 folded notecard. The back of the card was a wash of turquoise with the text:

*Selkie: A mythical creature from Scottish, Irish, and Scandinavian mythology. A seal who is able to shed her seal skin and take human form, but only for a brief time.*

*To be free, a selkie is always pulled back to the sea.*

*Always.*

"I had a silly thought when you jumped out of the car," said Tempest.

"That I'd return to the sea?" Morag gave a wicked smile.

Tempest's heart thumped furiously as she saw so much of her mom in her gran's smile.

"Legends of selkies run through your blood as much as the Raj family curse." Morag's eyes twinkled. "But I wasn't at the police station to plead the case of a curse killing my daughter. I was trying to find out more about how they covered up the true cause of her death."

"We know why. Because it was the start of the huge Edinburgh Fringe Festival. They didn't want a murder ruining the festivities. An 'accident' was much more convenient."

"That's *why*. But not *how* they did it."

"You didn't find anything?" Tempest asked.

"Not on my own. Not yet." Conflicted emotions flashed across Morag's face.

"I'll help you," Tempest said. "But I need your help, too."

With the mythical selkies packed away safely in the back, Tempest explained her idea to her grandmother on the drive home.

"Don't do this on your own," Morag said as they drove up the street approaching Fiddler's Folly. "At least go see Blackburn before you accuse anyone."

"He's retired."

"He's still a good man. And one who wants to solve the one case he never did."

Tempest pulled into the driveway but idled the engine.

"You're not coming in?" her grandmother asked.

"I want to give you two time to catch up privately."

Morag hesitated with her hand on the door handle. "It *woudnae* do any good to tell Ashok and Darius about my failed excursion."

*What about not keeping secrets?* "As soon as we find anything, we tell them."

"For now, we make sure my husband and your Da are safe."

Tempest nodded. "Your secret's safe."

# Chapter 37

A solitary raven and a handful of other birds were circling when Tempest pulled up in front of Lavinia's house.

"I know what's going on," Tempest said as the front door swung open. "*Nearly* all of it. I need to borrow the Oxford Comma tonight, and to bring everyone back."

"I knew it." The voice wasn't Lavinia's. Kumiko appeared at the side of her shocked daughter. "She thinks she's Nancy Drew."

"More like Hercule Poirot," Lavinia said.

"We don't need either of them," Kumiko bemoaned. "We need Kindaichi. You're too competent, Tempest. The killer won't let their guard down around you. Kosuke Kindaichi is the Japanese equivalent of Columbo. Created decades before, but every bit as self-effacing."

At the sound of a loud *caw*, the three of them looked up.

Lavinia stepped out onto the porch and pulled her sweater more tightly around her. "I don't know what's going on, but more and more birds are appearing each day."

"It's your imagination," Kumiko snapped. "You live in the hills surrounded by trees. There are birds."

"I don't think it's your imagination." Tempest shielded her eyes from the sun and squinted at the circling birds. "If they were buzzards I'd be even more uneasy, but they're definitely interested in something."

A voice cried out in the distance. This one wasn't a bird. *Tempest could have sworn it was human.*

Lavinia glowered at Tempest. "Is this a trick?"

Tempest held up her hands. "If it is, it has nothing to do with me."

"Help!" The muffled voice sounded far away, but urgent. "This is probably a wasted effort. . . ."

Tempest and Lavinia locked eyes. The voice was familiar. Affected. "Sylvie?" Tempest whispered.

"What are you two waiting for?" Kumiko snapped. "It's not that frightful woman's ghost. She's woken up from wherever the person who knocked her out stashed her."

"Help!"

Kumiko pointed at the stairs. "That came from inside the house. I'll be much slower than you two, but if you insist on just standing there . . ."

Tempest bounded up the stairs, followed a second later by Lavinia.

"Sylvie?" Tempest called.

"Where are you?" Lavinia said at the same time.

"How would I know where I am?" Sylvie's annoyed voice called. "I can't see with this blasted blindfold on."

"Closet." Lavinia ran through a bedroom and flung open the door of a walk-in closet.

"Well," said Sylvie's tied up and prone form, "get these damn things off me."

# Chapter 38

Two hours later, Tempest found Sylvie at the hospital after they were both done giving statements to the police.

In an opinion she knew was the opposite of the norm, Tempest loved hospitals. Probably because her grandfather had always told her stories of caring doctors, loving families, and the miracle of modern medicine that made people whole again in the hospital. Sickness, injury, and death were present, but so was love and compassion, with so many people packed inside each hospital's walls who cared and fought to heal patients. Ash still received honest-to-goodness printed Christmas cards from dozens of his former patients in the U.K.

There was no immediate evidence of who attacked Sylvie. Kumiko said she had turned off the motion-sensor video camera outside the front door because so many birds were around that kept triggering it, distressing both her and Lavinia since at least one of them was a raven.

"Getting attacked by a maniac gets one a private room," Sylvie said as she adjusted her solitary and tiny pillow. "I wish I'd known that when I fell off my bicycle. I would have made up a better story of why I fell."

"I heard we're both investigating."

"Thanks for your concern for my well-being." Sylvie's look could only be described as a sneer. How did she even manage to look down her nose at Tempest from her vantage point in the bed?

"I didn't think you were one for false pleasantries."

"Finally sticking up for yourself? Glad to see it." Sylvie rubbed her bandaged wrists. A bandage also poked out from the side of her hair. A spot of blood showed through the bandage on her head.

"If you're not well enough to talk—"

"Oh, I'm ready. I'm ready to do anything that helps catch the wretch who dared kidnap me."

"You really don't know who it was?"

"I didn't see—"

"I know. You already said that. I meant your investigation. I talked to your neighbor. I know you found out something about Corbin's killer. That's why they had to get you out of the way."

"I didn't take you for such a stupid girl. If I knew anything concrete, I'd be dead."

"And I didn't think you were so shortsighted. This isn't a cold-blooded killer. It's someone who hated Corbin Colt. They don't want to kill again if they don't have to."

"You're naïve to think I wasn't in danger."

"I didn't say that." Tempest was tempted to throttle Sylvie herself. "I'm saying it makes sense that they'd try alternatives at first."

"I'm not working with you to catch a killer," Sylvie said.

"That's good, because I wasn't asking you to. I want to know what happened to you."

"Pool our information?" Sylvie clasped her hands together

in a mocking gesture, realizing a second too late that it would hurt her injured wrists. She swore and turned away. "I'm not working with Nancy Drew."

"That's not the insult you think it is. I don't want to work with you any more than you want to work with me. I just want to know—"

"Haven't I been through enough? Read the police report."

"I'm betting you didn't tell them what you were up to. I don't think you told your neighbor everything, either."

A thin-lipped smile formed on Sylvie's face. "Maybe you're not so stupid after all. I'm tired. You have ten minutes. What do you want to know?"

"You really didn't see who did this to you?"

"And not tell the police so I can capture them myself? No. I didn't see who did this to me, I lost consciousness. I woke up in a dark room, managed to pull off my gag by tugging on something that was probably completely unsanitary and is going to give me tetanus. Then I started shouting."

"Why were you there in the first place?"

"I was woken up early by a phone call. Around five o'clock in the morning. This morning?" Sylvie sat up straighter and looked around the room. "How long was I out for? Was it only this morning?"

"It was," Tempest assured her.

"That's a relief. You hear about those people who wake up in the hospital and it's been six months. You look the same, though. Don't you ever wear anything besides a bland T-shirt and jeans?"

"You were talking about your five a.m. wake-up call." With dozens of racks of exquisite clothes meant to pop on stage and allow for seamless illusions, many of which she'd donned nearly every night for two years, T-shirts, jeans, and her favorite ruby-red sneakers were a welcome change.

"I thought," Sylvie said, "that it was Lavinia calling."

"You *thought*?"

"The voice said she'd figured out what happened to her ex-husband and she needed my help. A woman was whispering. Because she referred to her ex-husband, I knew it was Lavinia—at least that's what I thought. But the detective told me it can't have been her who attacked me. Which is a relief. She and Victor were together at his house in San Francisco and were also seen at a café where they were getting take-out coffee at dawn."

"You didn't think it was suspicious that someone called you in the middle of the night?"

"It wasn't the middle of the night. It was around five o'clock in the morning. We all know your grandfather didn't kill Corbin Colt, so I wanted to help."

"I know."

"Right. You said you heard I was investigating. I don't know that I'd call it *investigating*. . . . Laura isn't the brightest bulb in the box. But I have learned a thing or two from my Dorothy Sayers novels that gave me some ideas—Oh! Lord Peter!" She tried to stand, but her arm was a jumble of IV tubes rehydrating her. "My dog. I need to check on him—"

"Your neighbor is looking after Lord Peter."

Sylvie gave her an appreciative nod and after one last tug on a tangled cord, lay back onto the bed.

"You don't know what you uncovered that made someone attack you?"

"I wasn't even properly investigating. Simply going over mental exercises."

"Mental exercises?"

Sylvie glowered at Tempest. "Do you want to hear the story or not."

Tempest raised an eyebrow but held her tongue.

"You probably won't understand this, Tempest, but I'm convinced that the answer to Corbin's murder lies in the pages of a book."

Tempest froze. Did Sylvie know about the hidden manuscript?

"Ah," said Sylvie. "You know more than I thought. How did you know Corbin was spying on us?"

"What?"

"Oh. So you *don't* know? I'm surprised Lavinia didn't tell you. He was spying on the book club discussions to get ideas for his books. I haven't figured out how it's related, but we talk about all sorts of things at the book club. Ivy, in particular, shares a lot—"

"Ivy isn't involved. She wasn't even at the séance."

Sylvie appraised her. "You're loyal. I'll give you that. I'm not accusing Ivy of anything. I'm merely pointing out that we talked freely, not realizing anyone was spying on us. Especially a writer."

"If any of you revealed something terrible enough to kill someone who overheard it, then why only kill Corbin?"

"People," Sylvie said, "don't like being betrayed. I'm sorry. I'm not feeling so well."

"I'll leave you to get some rest. If they release you tonight, meet us at the Oxford Comma pub at Lavinia's Lair at midnight."

"Why on earth would I do that?"

"Because I know what happened to Corbin Colt."

# Chapter 39

Retired Detective Blackburn lived high in the hills of Hidden Creek. Tempest had never visited his house, and she didn't know the exact address, but she knew how to find it. She'd heard stories about the house. Unlike most homes in Hidden Creek, his was far away from all the others and only accessible by a one-lane road.

Tempest turned off onto the narrow road she suspected was right, and kept going until she found the house she knew must be it. Blackburn's blackberry bushes created a wild hedge in front of the house near the top of the hill.

"Anyone ever tell you this looks more like a serial killer's house than a detective's house?" she asked when he opened the front door.

That got her half a smile. "Come with me."

Blackburn's white hair was slightly longer than the last time she'd seen him. Not *actually* long, but gone was the precision that had mirrored his investigative meticulousness. Also gone was his suit, though he still wore a crisp, gray dress shirt. Tempest wasn't sure how old he was, but he was too young to be retired. His hair had turned prematurely white, a process that had sped up after Emma Raj vanished.

Tempest had promised her gran she'd see him before moving forward with her plan. She was so close to getting at the truth, but she wasn't going to put herself in unreasonable danger to get it.

She followed him through an open-floor-plan living and dining room to a high deck with the most breathtaking views of the San Francisco Bay, completely unencumbered by utility wires or other houses.

"Wow," she whispered.

"This is where my wife and I would always come after I'd had a hard day at work."

"Wife?"

She'd never known he had a wife. They'd spent so much time together when her mom vanished, but she realized now how little he'd said about himself. And he never wore a wedding ring.

"I was allergic to the first two rings we tried," he said with a smile, following her gaze to his left hand. "I wear this instead." He rolled up his sleeve to reveal a tattoo of a date twenty-three years before, with the word "Always" in a distinctive cursive script that looked more like a real person's handwriting than a font. "I'd introduce you if she was here, but she's out. Are you going to tell me why you tracked me down? Don't tell me Ash sent you."

"You know about his arrest this week."

"I do. And I'm sorry."

"Why did you think he sent me?"

"Even before Corbin Colt's murder, your grandfather was trying to convince me to become a private investigator."

"Really?" she said, though it didn't really surprise her. Her grandfather thought he knew what was best for everyone. He usually did, which was a bit infuriating.

"He thinks I'm like him. He didn't really retire. He cooks

and rides that old bike of his all over the place to deliver the food. He warned me I'd feel aimless after retiring and would need something to focus on, like he does." He paused and ran a hand through his white hair. "He also called me after he was home with his ankle monitor."

"Yeah, he's been holding court."

Blackburn chuckled. "That's a great way to put it."

"I didn't know you were one of his guests."

"I declined the invitation."

"Even though you believe he's innocent?"

"I didn't want it to look like I was getting involved. The investigating officers will surely be watching who he contacts. That's what I'd do. I told your grandfather as much. When he hinted that's why he might need help, I pointed out that I don't have a PI license yet. I'm simply a man who's recently retired and is enjoying tending my garden."

"It's winter."

"In California."

Tempest didn't believe for a minute he loved his garden. Not because it had more weeds than well-tended plants. Not because of any stereotypes about what a middle-age, retired detective might enjoy. But because of her grandfather's insight. And because of how much Blackburn fidgeted when he talked about his garden.

"I've figured it out," she said quietly.

His jittery leg stopped tapping. "You figured *what* out?"

She took a deep breath. "What happened to Corbin Colt."

"Who—"

"I know the *how*. I *think* I know who, but first I need to—"

"What you need to do is go to Detective Rinehart—"

"He has it in for my dad and grandfather."

"You're not a detective, Tempest. Leave it to us. *Damn.* I

mean them." Blackburn flushed. "Still getting used to being retired. Maybe I'll try writing a book."

"I thought you were gardening."

He shrugged. "A man can have more than one hobby."

Tempest nodded. "Neither of us is currently a detective, but since I'm here, do you want to hear how I solved Corbin Colt's impossible murder?"

"You really should go see Rinehart."

"That's the least convincing thing I've ever heard come out of your mouth. You weren't even pretending you meant it. If you can say those words once more with feeling, then I'll go talk to him." She held her breath, hoping he wouldn't call her bluff.

Blackburn ran a hand through his white mane and laughed. "Let me go grab the pot of coffee from the kitchen."

With her hands warming around an HCPD mug filled with rocket-fuel coffee, Tempest told him what she'd discovered, and what she had planned.

"It's all still just a theory," Blackburn said when she'd finished. "Not solid evidence. Not enough for Rinehart to act on, because it still doesn't tell us what happened. Only that it wasn't impossible."

"If I go to him with this information, it won't force him to help me get my grandfather cleared."

"Tempest. The overwhelming physical evidence—"

"Points to my grandfather. I know."

"Plus his motive."

"Thanks."

He gave her an exasperated sigh. "I'm not your friend, Tempest. I'm not your father."

Tempest stood and slammed the empty mug down. "You made that clear. I'm sorry I disturbed you—"

"Sit down, Tempest. I do care. I did my best to find out what happened to your mom when she vanished. My wife says it's why my prematurely graying hair went totally white. I think she's right, but you know what? I don't regret it. Not for one second. I only regret that we couldn't figure out what exactly happened."

"You think she died by suicide in the bay."

"I think that's where the evidence led us. Even so, I kept looking elsewhere."

Tempest's breath caught. "You did?"

"Why do you think I did all those follow-up meetings with your family?"

"Because the PR department told you to?"

"You really think that about me?"

Tempest stood again, but not to leave. She stood at the railing of the deck and looked out at the distant city across the bay. "I don't know what to think about anything anymore."

Blackburn joined her at the railing. "I hate gardening. Why do people think it's relaxing?"

She turned around and faced Blackburn. "Midnight. Here's the address where you should be." She handed him a piece of paper with Lavinia's address.

"Midnight? Very theatrical of you. You're never going to stop being The Tempest."

Tempest looked out over the expansive bay. The sights and smells she'd grown up with. The wonderful memories of times spent with her family in their quirky house on this hillside. The magic she'd created in the sprawling house unlike any other. *She could do this.* "Why would I try to be anyone else?"

# Chapter 40

I t wasn't like a book. Nobody resisted the invitation. If anything, each invitee was overly eager. They were curious, too. Except for one of them who was pretending. One of them was a killer who would try to misdirect the conversation. But Tempest was ready for them.

She hoped.

Sylvie wasn't sure if she'd be kept overnight at the hospital, and Ash couldn't leave the tree house, so Tempest brought in two stand-ins she could trust to play their roles: her partners in crime Ivy and Gideon.

There were too many secrets swirling around, so she'd told everyone in her family that she was recreating the séance. She'd already told Grannie Mor, whose idea it had been to involve Blackburn. Her dad and grandfather objected until she told them the former detective had agreed to help. Blackburn was still wary of endorsing the ploy, but he knew Tempest would go through with it without him, so he at least wanted to be there for her. Darius insisted on being there as muscle, but Morag stayed behind with her husband.

Before heading from Fiddler's Folly to Lavinia's Lair, Tempest climbed her secret staircase to clarify her thoughts in a notebook. She had dozens of paper notebooks in which she'd created various illusions. This time, she was *solving* one.

She scribbled furiously, making sure she had her thoughts organized. Had she missed anything? No. Her ideas were solid. She was right.

Each time she paused to think, her fingers kept moving. Perhaps it was the year she'd spent practicing cardistry, something she'd never kept up, but her fingers often felt like they took on a life of their own. Tonight, they sketched ravens.

Dozens of ravens filled the margins of the paper notebook. They started small, but as the muscles of her hand grew tired, the beaked figures became larger and looser. On the last page where she completed her thoughts about the trick she was unraveling, the last raven appeared. She hadn't meant to draw what she did, but there he was, staring back at her from the page.

A long-beaked raven mask formed a plague-era doctor's mask.

The costume worn by medieval doctors during the plague was meant not to conceal their faces but to keep bad air from reaching those attending to plague victims. Yet it also served the purpose of disguising the person wearing it. That was the trickiest piece of the puzzle. Who was hiding behind a mask?

The killer of Corbin Colt—the Raven—had disguised themselves as one of the innocent spectators at the séance. It was time to pull back the mask.

She traced her fingers over the lines of the raven mask. Her fingers slid off the page and toward her phone. Before she realized what she was doing, she hit the button to call someone she didn't think she'd be calling again.

*What was she thinking?* Before the phone could complete

its first full ring, she hung up. She had her dad and Blackburn as backup that night. She didn't need a morally ques-
tionable person helping. She believed Moriarty when he said
he wanted to help. She wasn't that desperate. Not yet.

Tempest slammed shut the notebook and gripped it as she
ran down her secret staircase.

☠☠☠

At twenty-seven minutes to midnight, Tempest pulled up in
front of Lavinia's house. Her dad was right behind her.

The police had finished with the crime scene at Lavinia's
Lair and a cleaning crew had cleaned the space. The ceiling
had been damaged by the authorities while they searched for
a spot from which they thought a body could have dropped,
and the sliding bookcase had been taken off its slider, but
otherwise the space was much as it had been before.

Two minutes before midnight, Tempest seated her guests
around the séance table in the same arrangement as they'd
been on the night of the murder.

Seven chairs were again set around the table, with room
for Kumiko's wheelchair. Sanjay sat at the spot facing the
entrance doorway to the Oxford Comma pub. Lavinia and
Kumiko sat to his left and right. Tempest was next to Lavinia, followed by Ellery, Gideon (originally Ash), Ivy (previously Sylvie), and Victor. Detective Blackburn and her dad
stood in the pub's doorway, just inside the pub. On the other
side of the door, the silent gargoyles kept watch. This time,
everyone kept their cell phones and they left the lights on.

"Good evening," Sanjay began. "If you'll all join hands."

"We're not recreating the séance precisely, are we?"
Kumiko asked as the guests complied.

"I'd *hoped* it wouldn't be necessary," Sanjay said, "but

our host is keeping me in the dark about what exactly is planned."

The lights went out.

Several gasps reverberated around the table.

"Who touched my cheek?" Kumiko snapped.

"Has anyone felt a hand in theirs let go?" Tempest asked. Nobody answered affirmatively.

"It wasn't my imagination," Kumiko muttered.

"Was that a feather?" Ivy whispered.

"Is that what I felt?" Ellery asked. "It was, wasn't it?"

"I felt the same thing." Victor sounded like the words had been dragged out of him. "Feathers."

"Anyone else?" Tempest asked.

"This is really weird," Gideon said. "When you take away one sense, I thought my other senses would be stronger. But really, they're just confused. It's like that Halloween game where you touch peeled grapes and are told they're eyeballs, rice is supposed to be maggots—"

"And we're told spaghetti noodles are brains," Sanjay added. "We get it already. I don't think Tempest wants to hear about Halloween games."

"It's fine," she said. "I want to hear anything people are feeling right now. Anyone have any other sensations?" She waited.

"I thought the noodles were guts," Victor said. "Not brains."

"Really?" Sanjay's voice. "I always thought—"

"Something touched my cheek." Lavinia's voice. "I'm not sure if it was a raven's feather. It felt like silk fabric, but that's more what I'm used to touching my face."

Tempest counted silently to five, making sure everyone who wanted to speak had done so. "Thank you all. Lights, please."

The lights clicked back on. They were all seated exactly as

they had been, with their circle of clasped hands unbroken. She nodded thanks to her dad, standing at the light switch.

"What was the point of that?" Kumiko glared at her.

"Nothing touched your faces." Tempest made an "o" with her lips and blew out her breath.

"Nice," said Sanjay.

Victor scoffed. "You're trying to tell us nothing touched us? Only air from you blowing your breath?"

"In the darkness, you felt *something*, so you all fed on each other's imaginations. By the time everyone spoke, you were convinced a raven's feather was floating around the table. Even though none of you had seen it, or even felt it. I needed you all to understand how easy it is for that to happen."

"Can we let go of each other's hands now?" Kumiko asked. "Victor's hand is sweating."

He grunted, but bit back whatever it was he clearly wanted to say.

"Just one more minute," Tempest said. "I had a purpose for—"

She broke off as loud banging sounded. Hands unclasped. From the Oxford Comma's doorway, Darius frowned and ran into the main section of Lavinia's Lair, where the sound originated. Tempest followed suit as the pounding continued.

When she reached the bamboo forest, her dad and Blackburn had reached the site of the sound. Someone was knocking calmly on the glass.

"Am I too late?" Sylvie asked through the window. "I couldn't stand another minute in the hospital so I forced them to let me out."

# Chapter 41

All eyes were on Sylvie as she stepped past the merry-go-round horse and into the Oxford Comma.

She gave them a thin-lipped smile. "Don't be so shocked. I'm not dead. Only a little worse for wear. I had no idea a head wound could bleed so much."

Sylvie had taken time to go home and clean herself up. If not for the bandages on her wrists barely peeking out from the cuff of her blouse, and the discrete square of gauze on her head that was mostly hidden by her hair, you'd never know she'd been attacked less than twenty-four hours before. In indigo slacks and a white cashmere sweater, she was the most put together of any of the attendees.

"Have they figured out what happened to you yet?" Ellery asked.

"It's a mystery." Sylvie's reply was even more clipped than usual.

"Don't be modest," Tempest said. "Sylvie was getting close to figuring out what happened."

Sylvie glared at her. "It's on your conscience if they try again."

Ivy gasped. "You don't really think—"

"Nobody is getting hurt." Blackburn stepped in front of Sylvie. "Why don't you all take your seats again?"

Two minutes later, they were seated again around the book-club-cum-séance table. They sat in their original seats. Sanjay at the nominal head of the circular table, with Lavinia at his left, followed by Tempest, Ellery, Gideon (as Ash's stand-in), Sylvie, Victor, and Kumiko. With Sylvie's return, Ivy was relegated to the sliding bookcase seat nook. Darius and Blackburn flanked the faux pub's doorway. Nobody was required to join hands. Lavinia asked if people would like tea or coffee—the beer tap still hadn't been installed—but those who wanted drinks opted for water.

"I talked with Hazel Bello earlier today," Tempest began, "and I know how Corbin got here the day he was killed."

Murmurs rippled around the table, but Tempest launched into her explanation before anyone could speak. She went over exactly what she'd learned from speaking with Hazel, concluding with the revelation that led to the rest of the pieces of the puzzle falling into place: "That's how Corbin had left Forestville long before Hazel's livestreamed video. He tricked her so she wouldn't know he was visiting Lavinia. He never thought he'd be killed. It was never meant to be impossible. Only a lie to slip away."

"The biggest impossibility solved," Sanjay whispered.

"He had a *reason* for coming to the séance," Tempest added. "He wanted to get back the book notes he thought he'd left behind when he heard that Lavinia planned on burning them. He didn't want to tell his girlfriend he was coming to see his ex. He came here of his own free will."

"It doesn't matter if he was alive when he arrived," Lavinia said. "Where was his body when we started the séance? I gave you all a tour of the space right before Sanjay started the séance. There was no body hidden. You know the space

258 # Gigi Pandian

as well as I do, Tempest. There wasn't even anyplace big enough for a typewriter to be hidden."

"Because he wasn't yet a body," said Tempest. "It would have been impossible for a body or a person tied up to be hidden—*but not a person hiding from us.*"

Tempest took a breath as a ripple of gasps floated through her audience. It was the easiest thing in the world. Tempest hadn't seen it because it was impossible to see without the timing trick being solved first. When they thought it was impossible for anyone to be hiding in the space, they had been thinking of the impossibility of hiding a *body.*

"If Corbin was both alive *and* came to Hidden Creek of his own free will," said Tempest, "if he wanted to remain hidden, he would have had ample opportunity to move from place to place as people toured the different areas."

Kumiko scoffed. "That wouldn't have been easy."

"It would have been much easier," said Tempest, "if he had someone helping him."

More gasps.

"*Corbin Colt was alive,*" Tempest concluded, "when he managed to evade us as we toured the space. He was also *still alive* when he maneuvered past our unbroken circle and onto the table."

"We all clearly saw him dead." Kumiko crossed her arms and gave Tempest a glare that rivaled her own famous glare.

"Did we?" Tempest let the words hang in the air. For six seconds, nobody spoke.

Sanjay broke the silence with a groan.

"You understand?" she asked Sanjay.

He nodded and looked chagrinned.

"I don't get it," Lavinia said. "I have perfect vision. And great attention to detail. He was right in front of me. I saw his blood—"

"You saw what he wanted you to see," Tempest said. "With the shock of seeing him there on the table, with only a couple of seconds to process what we were seeing, he manipulated the situation exactly as I would have done it for an illusion. *That's why he needed to use a fake knife.* It was never meant to be perceived as real for more than a few seconds. That's all he needed. He and his accomplice controlled the situation. Until his accomplice betrayed him."

Ellery gasped. "His accomplice?"

"Yes. He wasn't dead when we saw him with the knife sticking out of his chest—or rather, the fake knife. We had all assumed Corbin was the one to ruin and hide Lavinia's beloved typewriter because it was in line with his sick sense of humor. He couldn't have been the one to break the typewriter."

"He was on the other side of the country," Sanjay said, "when the typewriter went missing."

"It was so easy to think it was him," said Tempest, "because he would do something like that. So it's not a stretch that when he came here to get back what he thought were additional handwritten book notes he'd left behind, he'd also play a trick on you. Since Lavinia was essentially mocking him by having a séance to cleanse his old office of his spirit, he'd mock her by showing up 'dead' at the séance, then get up and have a good laugh. Except his accomplice had other ideas. His conspirator made a light flicker on—just long enough for us to see Corbin's staged body. Staged with the fake knife to look like he was dead. A red silk scarf around the knife is what we took to be blood in the brief flicker of light. But he wasn't dead. His accomplice killed him when the room plunged into darkness again."

"When there was chaos," Sanjay murmured. "Very smart."

"Why didn't he cry out if someone was stabbing him to

death?" asked Ellery. "You think he'd just lay there while someone plunged a real knife—"

"I'm going to be sick." Lavinia held her hands to her mouth and ran from the room. Victor was on her heels and followed her out.

Darius caught Tempest's eye. "I'll go after them—"

"Just make sure she uses the bathroom in here to be sick. Not the main house. Nobody leaves yet."

Her dad ran after them.

Blackburn hesitated, unsure whether to stay or go. "You mean she—"

"She didn't kill him," said Tempest. She was nearly certain she was right that Lavinia didn't kill her ex-husband. "And neither did Victor. They don't need to hear the rest."

"Hear the rest of what?" Ellery asked. "It's ridiculous. He'd cry out if he was being killed. He was so close to us. He was—" she broke off and shivered.

"Remember," Tempest cut in, "it was pandemonium after we saw the flicker of light came on and we saw what we assumed to be a dead body. We *did* hear screaming. We assumed it was our own voices. Both male and female voices were screaming. *It never occurred to us that a dead man would cry out.*"

Another gasp.

"Corbin Colt wasn't a raven like the character of his most famous novel," Tempest continued, "and there's a rational explanation for everything that initially seemed impossible. He didn't want his girlfriend to know he was going to see his soon-to-be ex-wife so he tricked her into thinking he was writing in his office and then left for a walk when he knew she couldn't chase after him; there was no invisible hidden body, simply a man who moved from place to place as we moved around; Corbin jumped onto the séance table himself to play a nasty joke on Lavinia by making her think he was dead, no mechanisms to drop his body required or fake hands for anyone to hold onto at the séance table; and the fake knife was the pièce de résistance to make sure we'd think he was dead. His accomplice created even more misdirection to make sure it wouldn't even occur to us he wasn't dead."

"The tape residue." Sanjay grimaced.

"An added layer to the trick. If they put on tape and immediately ripped it off, the police wouldn't know how long the tape had been there and assume he'd been bound for a longer period of time, confusing things further. Maybe the killer even applied the tape to stifle any scream."

"Four impossibilities solved," said Sanjay. "Brilliant. That was brilliant, Tempest."

Gideon groaned. "I don't understand any of you. You're treating this like it's a *game*."

"Because that's exactly what it is." Kumiko wheeled up to him. "We didn't make this a game. The person who killed my ex-son-in-law did. Treating it like a game is the only way to beat them at the game they've created. Getting emotional won't help anything. Someone is playing a sick game. I applaud Tempest for assuming the role of sleuth."

Sanjay cleared his throat.

Kumiko glared at him. "You're her sidekick at best."

Sanjay sputtered. Tempest put her hand over his mouth before he could speak. "My grandfather wasn't supposed to be here that night. He was a last-minute addition. His medical-doctor instincts kicked in. He wanted to check in case he was still alive and could be saved. His presence is what muddled everything."

"I was following you up until now," Sanjay said, removing Tempest's hand and glaring at her. "Wasn't it in the killer's interest for someone else to take the blame?"

"It was," said Tempest. "But if Ash hadn't been there, there was one other person who would have rushed forward and gotten blood on themselves."

"Lavinia," Ivy said. It was the first time she'd entered the conversation. "It would have been his wife. Lavinia. Even if someone has come to hate someone they once loved . . . She would have gone to him."

"None of us were thinking rationally yet," Tempest said softly. "Just reacting."

"Why didn't the killer get blood on them when they stabbed him in the darkness?" Ivy asked.

"The police never searched us for gloves, which can easily be hidden. They searched us for the murder weapon. Because they didn't yet know the blade was inside his body. Only that a fake knife was sticking out."

Sanjay groaned. "Misdirection to the nth degree."

"Exactly as the killer wanted." Tempest spun on the heel of her ruby-red sneakers and came face to face with Corbin Colt's killer.

# Chapter 42

E xactly," Tempest said, "like you wanted, Ellery."
Ellery gaped at her. "You can't be serious. Why? Why
would I kill Corbin?"

"You didn't know Corbin revealed your secret in a manuscript he was writing, did you? That's what gave it away."

Ellery narrowed her eyes as all eyes turned to her. "What
secret? I suppose in a twisted way it's flattering you think I
could stage such a baffling crime. I didn't, you know. Is your
suspicion because I love puzzling mysteries?"

"No," said Tempest. "Corbin was writing a book loosely
based on my mom's disappearance. In it, he features a book
club. A character based on you is having an affair with the
spouse of another member of the book club. Don't bother
denying your affair. A private investigator is already working
on finding evidence. It's only a matter of time."

"I'm almost disappointed," said Ellery, "that I don't get to
remain a suspect for longer. If that's your reasoning, I have
to disappoint you. I wasn't having an affair with Corbin.
More importantly, I'm a caregiver for my father. He had a
turn for the worse last night. I spent the entire night, until
about ten o'clock this morning, at the hospital. I couldn't

have harmed Sylvie. You think the two crimes were committed by the same person, right? At least half a dozen people
can verify where I was when someone kidnapped Sylvie."

Tempest had been so sure. She'd eliminated everyone else.
Hadn't she? She would stake her life on the innocence of
Sanjay and her grandfather. Lavinia and Victor had alibis for
Sylvie's disappearance, and Tempest was pretty sure the police had interviewed additional witnesses. *That just left Kumiko*, the woman who'd come to her for help. Which didn't
make any sense . . . Did it? How could she have gotten Sylvie
upstairs? Even if her arms were that strong, surely Sylvie's
body would be covered in bruises from being dragged upstairs. And what about the blood?

Was Lavinia and Victor's alibi a trick? Ellery's couldn't be.
Not if she was telling the truth, which could be easily verified.
The trick wasn't completely solved. Yet.

☠☠☠

"Nice try, kiddo," Blackburn said as he escorted her to her
jeep.

"You weren't just being polite to insist you walk everyone
to their cars."

"Something strange is going on. Until we know what it
is, I don't like thinking about any of you out there on your
own. Especially not after midnight."

Tempest raised an eyebrow. It was too dark to make out
much of Blackburn's expression, but she heard the worry in
his voice. "You think one of them is a killer."

"Of course."

"Not my grandfather."

"Rinehart doesn't, either. He must know something isn't
right. That's why he's still investigating."

"He won't figure it out."

In the shadows, Blackburn's face would have looked menacing if she hadn't known him for so long. He took his time reading her face before speaking. "Rinehart is a good man, from what I've seen. I admit I wouldn't have made the same decision to arrest your grandfather, but the evidence was there and I don't know what kind of pressure he was under. In spite of that, he's still investigating. Why won't you trust him?"

"He didn't exist until ten years ago."

Blackburn stared at her. Then he broke into a whoop of laughter. "That's why you don't trust him? Because you think he's a con artist? You don't think a police department would do a little research—

"He. Didn't. Exist."

"I know."

"You *know*?"

"I'm still friends with people in the department. Not Rinehart, but I hear things. He's from a family that shares a surname with a serial killer. It was wrecking people's perception of him—both on and off the force. He had some distant familial connection to a mystery novelist by the name of Robert Rinehart. He wrote a book about a staircase."

Tempest groaned. "Not Robert Rinehart. *Mary* Roberts Rinehart. *The Circular Staircase* is her most famous novel. She was known as the American Agatha Christie."

"That's it. When Austin was getting grief for his family connection, he changed his name to that more distant relation. All above board."

"Oh."

"You make things too hard sometimes, Tempest. Be safe." He knocked on the top of the jeep. Why did men so often do that?

The sound must have startled a bird in a nearby nest. After a gentle rustling in a tree, a large bird swooped so low overhead and onto the roof of Lavinia's house that they ducked.

"That's all I can take." Tempest nearly screamed the words. "I'm solving at least one mystery right now. Do you have a ladder?"

"In my sedan? No."

Tempest marched up to Lavinia's front door and knocked. "Can I borrow your ladder?"

Lavinia was too shocked to object. She opened the garage. Tempest hauled out the ladder and rested it against the roof. They were at the back of the house, where the roof was closest to the ground on the sloping hillside.

"Hold this," she said to both Lavinia and Blackburn, then climbed the rungs. When she reached the top, she shone the light of her phone toward the area where they'd seen birds. She climbed down. Two rungs from the bottom, she jumped to the ground.

"I don't suppose you placed a bird feeder on your roof and filled it with a colossal bag of birdseed?"

Lavinia stared at her like she'd gone mad. "Why would I do that?"

"Someone," Tempest said, "installed a bird feeder sure to attract a lot of birds."

"Why?"

"My guess? Because they knew it would make you turn off your video camera. The person who kidnapped Sylvie wanted to make sure they weren't captured on camera when they came to the house this morning."

# Chapter 43

Tempest stepped through the archway with the stone face of a Janus above. The profiles were based on traditional Roman images, but at this house, the faces were those of two red-headed sisters. Their enigmatic profiles were unpainted, but their hair had been painted copper.

She passed the unusual garden gnomes—a red-headed gnome with a magnifying glass, a dark-haired gnome with a courthouse gavel, and a laughing baby gnome—and reached the locked gate at the base of the circular staircase. She knew the trick to open the gate. You stuck your hand inside a humorously oversize keyhole and twisted the carved key.

The gate swung open and Tempest hurried up Ivy's steps. She lived in the upper half of a rented duplex, with her sister Dahlia and Dahlia's family below.

"Thanks for inviting me over," Tempest said when Ivy opened the door and ushered her inside.

"After that tense drawing-room gathering of suspects, there was no way I'll get to sleep for hours anyway. Like Sanjay said, it was brilliant. *You* were brilliant."

"I still failed. I missed something."

Ivy closed the door behind Tempest and leaned against it.

"Only because you've forgotten your roots. Remember the master of impossible crime stories. What would John Dickson Carr's Dr. Fell do?"

"Don't forget Clayton Rawson's magician detective Merlini. They'd both unravel the misdirection, of course."

"I feel like we should be in the Locked Room Library for this conversation."

"It's after midnight, so traffic across the bridge would be pretty minimal."

"I have a key, but that would totally freak out Enid. She lives above the library. I'm afraid you're stuck with my cozy house. Want popcorn?"

"Definitely. And I love your cozy house. You have your own space. Your own popcorn. That's huge."

Ivy headed for the kitchen. "I didn't turn on the overhead light when you came in because the place is a wreck. I don't even know how that's possible, since most of my reading for school is electronic so I shouldn't have papers strewn everywhere, and most of my clothes are a shade of pink so I don't need to separate my loads." Ivy heated oil a large saucepan on a gas burner and grabbed a half-empty jar of popcorn kernels from a cabinet. "What mystery movie should we put on for inspiration to figure this out?"

"*Dangerous Crossing.*"

"That was quick. And perfect. Based on John Dickson Carr's *Cabin B-13* radio play."

"The answer is in plain sight the whole time, only they can't see it. It's the same for us. I know it is. If only I could see it."

They fell into a companionable silence listening to the popcorn crackle on the stovetop as Ivy shook the pot. The popping slowed and Ivy filled and salted two heaping bowls. Tempest carried them to the couch while Ivy set up the movie. She moved a potted snake plant in a pink ceramic pot to one side, opened her laptop computer, and turned on a projector. Ivy didn't have a TV screen larger than her laptop, but she kept one white wall clear for projecting movies.

"Do we need to keep the movie volume down?"

Ivy shook her head. "We added extra insulation between the units to avoid strangling each other. It's not just my late-night movie habits. Natalie is the most enthusiastic six-year-old squealer you'll ever meet. *Shhh*. It's starting."

"You're the one talking."

"Your impeccable logic is one of my least favorite things about you."

Tempest tossed a popcorn kernel at Ivy and stuck out her tongue. An hour and fifteen minutes later they were giggling like they used to when they were teenagers.

"I'd forgotten how the movie buries one of the biggest clues from the original radio play," Ivy said, shutting off the projector. "Shake loose any ideas?"

"Only strengthened my conviction that I should trust myself instead of the simple facts on the surface. You need to give me your locked-room mystery lecture again. Since clearly I failed at my methods."

"Oh! Did I tell you I'm giving my lecture on locked-room mysteries at the library now? Once a week on Saturdays."

"That's fantastic."

"My biggest audience has been four people so far." Ivy bit her lip. "And one of them was only there because her boyfriend dragged her along."

"That's a good way to begin. You'll have it perfected by the time you have a big audience. Are you doing your Ivy Young-blood version of Dr. Fell's famous lecture about different ways impossible crimes can be pulled off?"

"Enid asked me to be more general and talk about the

history of locked-room mysteries, historical authors to modern ones, from Poe to Halter."

"As soon as I clear my grandfather and papa, I'll come to your talk."

Ivy pulled her knees up under her chin. "Those trick explanations you came up with earlier . . . I was thinking about them more while we watched the movie. You weren't wrong, Tempest. Those solutions you came up with explain the only plausible way Corbin Colt ended up on that table in front of you."

"Which led me to Ellery. Which is impossible. I've solved the impossible trick, but it's *still* impossible."

"It's not," Ivy declared. "Because I know who did it."

# Chapter 44

There's only one explanation that ticks all the boxes," Ivy said.

"Which I thought I figured out." Tempest tossed the bowl of cold popcorn remnants aside. "But I was wrong."

"You were right about everything except the killer," Ivy insisted. "You just didn't follow your tour explanations through to their rational conclusion."

"I'm pretty sure I did. Which led me back to it being impossible for anyone at the séance to have killed Corbin."

"Because none of them did." Ivy leapt off the couch with a dramatic flourish, scattering puffed kernels of popcorn everywhere. "Corbin Colt *killed himself.*"

Tempest brushed popcorn from her jeans. "I don't see how."

"It fits, Tempest. It was a stressful time in his life, and this would be a grand finale. Can't you see—"

"You're saying Corbin came back from the grave to temporarily get Sylvie out of the way? And he was so stealthy that he acted alone yet nobody saw him when he moved around Lavinia's Lair during our tour? Neither works. He's only guilty of trying to play a joke on Lavinia when he came to get his papers back. He was there, but he had an accomplice."

Ivy deflated and began picking up popcorn. "Since he's dead, I guess their secret died with him."

"There has to be evidence of who it was." Tempest joined Ivy on the floor to pick up popcorn but stopped after grabbing only two puffed kernels. "I can't let go of thinking we can get the answer from Corbin himself. He wove so many elements of real life into his fiction, I keep thinking he must have left a clue. Not on purpose, like foreseeing his own death, but something hidden. He loved symbolism and playing with words. Like how he called my dad 'Angel Diablo' in *The Vanishing of Ella Patel*. Why the specificity of a character named Alice having an affair with one of her book club member's spouses, making the point that she was named after Alice from Lewis Carrol's *Alice's Adventures in Wonderland*?

"It could be a coincidence," Ivy suggested. "They do happen."

"What's more likely is that Ellery was lying about not having an affair with him, but it doesn't actually relate to who killed him. Ugh. I think I just sat on popcorn."

"Sorry. I was excited about my suicide theory. Your affair motive doesn't make much sense, either. Ellery is decades younger than Corbin."

"So is Hazel."

"Fair point."

"Why did someone need to get Sylvie out of the way today?" Tempest could understand wanting to permanently get rid of someone who saw something they shouldn't have, but they hadn't killed Sylvie.

"It's after two a.m., so technically she was kidnapped yesterday. Oh! Evidence the killer needed to dispose of."

"At Sylvie's apartment? Why not just wait until she left? That's far less of a risk. The *timing* has to be important. But why?"

"Misdirection?" Ivy suggested.

"I'm beginning to hate that word."

"Blasphemy."

☠☠☠

Tempest crept into her house, trying not to wake her dad. She knew she'd never sleep, so she needed a book to wind down with.

The hearth in the living room looked like a real fireplace. But like so many architectural details from Secret Staircase Construction, this one wasn't what it seemed. Through the fire screen, you'd see logs and a brick backdrop. When you pulled the screen aside, you might notice the logs and bricks weren't quite right. The bricks were a painting on plywood and the logs were bolted into place. All but one of them.

Tempest lifted the log on the back of the stack. The painting of bricks slid to the side, revealing a secret room. The small-but-mighty library.

Stepping through the hearth, Tempest emerged into a room that was only six feet in each direction, but it stretched two stories high. Two walls were lined with built-in bookshelves that climbed to the skylight ceiling. A sliding ladder kept the shelves functional.

Two narrow-yet-comfy armchairs had been wedged into the space along with a small end table large enough for each reader to set a cup of tea or coffee or a cocktail.

Most of the books still on the shelves had been there since Tempest's childhood. They'd never moved houses, instead expanding this one, so the only books that had left the house were ones that had been given away. Books were never sold or thrown away. This was nothing like Ivy's collection of classic mysteries. Kids' picture books with teeth marks (Tempest suspected the teeth marks were why these hadn't been given to friends), chapter-book mysteries (the largest section), books on the craft of magic and the history of magic, other history books, travel memoirs, the Gothic novels her mom had loved, and books on an assortment of other topics. Her dad's carpentry books and magazines were in his workshop. The books in the library weren't especially well organized, since with the tall bookcases it was difficult to move more than a couple of books at a time. It might take a while to find what she was after.

Tempest climbed a few steps of the ladder. Henning Nelms's *Magic and Showmanship* was next to Barbara Michaels's *The Sea King's Daughter*. Children's classic *From the Mixed-Up Files of Mrs. Basil E. Frankweiler* was next to two books on Cambodian folklore. The books were even less well organized than she thought.

She held the sides of the ladder and stepped higher and higher. Until she found them. Corbin Colt's books. Only five of them. His most recent release wasn't there, but *The Raven* was. She lifted it off the shelf and climbed down.

She opened the jacket flap and ran her finger over Corbin's headshot. She wished she could remember him like this, the handsome face with a mysteriously veiled expression she'd found intriguing as a teenager, not the angry man who'd given up on his wife and played a cruel joke that ended up with him dead.

She turned to the cover of *The Raven*. A man with a hidden face is walking away from the reader on an urban street. Ominous shadows surround him. Two of the shadows on the asphalt street are the wings of a raven. It's up to the viewer to decide whether the wings have come from the man himself.

With the book in hand, Tempest climbed both of her secret staircases. High in her turret, surrounded by posters that should have made her feel a part of something, she felt utterly alone.

"I'm a terrible magician," she said to her wall of heroes. "Why can't I figure out this trick?"

She tossed the book aside and spun and spun, coming to a stop in front of the poster of her mom and aunt performing as the Selkie Sisters. "Corbin Colt knew more about my mom than I ever thought. I don't know what to believe."

# Chapter 45

At dawn, Tempest woke up with her heart racing after roughly two hours of sleep. She'd skimmed the entirety of *The Raven* and downloaded and began reading his most recent book. In her past life she would have only just gone to bed as the sun rose. Now, she knew she'd never get back to sleep.

After reading more by the man who was haunting her family's life, she was more convinced than ever that his hand-written manuscript revealed more than the words themselves. Corbin Colt loved weaving together layers of meaning. What did his manuscript mean? It certainly wasn't that her father had killed her mother. She didn't know what was going on, but she knew that much.

It was still mostly dark outside, but the stars on her bedroom ceiling glowed faintly, showing her the image of a skeleton key. Reminding her she was a key that could open any lock. She tossed off the covers and checked on her grandparents, telling them what she'd learned. She felt terrible that they looked even more dejected than she felt.

The sun had fully risen by the time she slunk down the tree house stairs after talking with them. She grabbed her keys. She needed to do something she should have done earlier if she hadn't been so shortsighted.

"What do you think?" Tempest asked Detective Rinehart after she finished her story.

"I think," he said, "that you're playing the role of sleuth like Ms. Sinclair and Ms. Kingsley. Blackburn told me everything, you know. About your little game."

"It wasn't a game. I already know he told you. That was the plan." It was the only reason Blackburn had agreed to help her.

"To ask forgiveness after the fact?"

"You don't really think my grandfather is guilty, either, do you? And going after my father for my mother's vanish—"

"I'm not *going after* anyone. I have some unanswered questions. About both cases. I agree with you there's more to both cases than the physical evidence indicates. Happy now?"

"You mean motive?" Which still pointed to both her dad and grandfather.

He didn't answer.

"That's why you went ahead and arrested my grandfather and are looking at my dad for my mom's disappearance."

"This isn't a game, Ms. Raj."

"Don't you think I know that?" she shouted. "This is *my* life. Not yours. You get to go home after doing your due diligence—"

"Why do you think I didn't arrest you and your boyfriend for breaking and entering at Miss Bello's house? Don't—" he held up a finger, "make me regret that decision."

"Will you tell me what you've learned?"

"It's an ongoing investigation." He must have been able to tell her head was about to pop off like a cartoon character's, because he continued, "But I can say this much. You have good instincts. I don't condone your methods, but figuring out how Mr. Colt got himself to Hidden Creek and landed on that table helps answer a lot of our questions, which helps us make better use of our resources."

She hadn't been wrong about the mechanisms that made Corbin Colt's murder possible. There was no doubt someone at the séance was responsible for both Corbin's death and Sylvie's kidnapping. Someone's alibi for Sylvie's kidnapping wasn't real.

# Chapter 46

Tempest tugged on the door once more. It didn't budge. With a killer at large, plus Moriarty's surprise visit (not to mention her rabbit's divided loyalties), Tempest was determined to finish installing the door to the Secret Fort with Abra's hutch.

The problem was, she didn't know how to install a door. Her dad had helped her with the initial measurements and picking out the door itself, but he'd had to go to a job site. Luckily, Sanjay was being overprotective and jumped at the chance to come help her. She dearly hoped it wasn't the kiss, which hadn't really been a kiss but more of a brain-explosion-preventer.

Unfortunately, Sanjay knew even less about installing a door than she did.

"I think it's sticking at the top." Using her body as she did so well on the stage, Tempest used the strength of her quads to push herself up and her biceps to pull, rock climbing to reach the top of the stone doorframe.

"Are you sure that's a good idea?"

"I'll only fall a few feet if I lose my grip." She made the mistake of looking down. Abra was directly beneath her. She wouldn't hurt herself if she fell, but she'd crush her beloved bunny. She swung the other way and lost her grip, crashing onto the ground and scraping her palm.

She breathed a sigh of relief that a fifteen-pound lop-eared rabbit hadn't broken her fall. She brushed a lock of her thick black hair out of her eyes. The bunny was safely above her, held in the arms of her human companion.

"See how selfless I am?" Sanjay said. "I rescued Abra even though he bit me."

"He must've had a good reason for biting you."

"I did nothing except rescue him. I swear."

Tempest studied his face. "You're keeping something from me. *Again.*"

Sanjay stared down his nose at the rabbit, who had just chomped his finger a second time.

"What has Abra got against me?" he asked. "He used to like me."

"He's a wonderful judge of character," said Tempest. "He knows you're hiding something."

Sanjay straightened. "He can't possibly know that."

"No. He was just scared. But now you've admitted it to me."

Aside from petting Abra as he'd been doing already, Sanjay didn't move. The only change on his face was an almost imperceptible lowering of the hoods of his eyes.

"You have the world's worst poker face," Tempest continued.

"That is patently untrue."

"You're right. I should clarify, *when you're not on stage,* you have the worst poker face. Only The Hindi Houdini has a good poker face. Not the real you."

Sanjay considered the statement, then using his free hand he tossed his bowler hat onto the hook on the other side of the fort. It landed exactly where he intended. Still holding

Abra, he took a bow. He had long ago perfected the balance of confidence and graciousness in a stage bow.

"Misdirection," said Tempest, "will do you no good."

He took a step closer and reached for her hand. "Won't it?"

In one sweeping motion, Tempest stepped aside and dodged his hand, instead taking Abra into her arms.

"Good bunny." She scratched the rabbit's floppy, oversize ears. "Now, what do you say we get Sanjay to tell us what he's up to this time."

Abra wriggled his nose at Sanjay.

"It wasn't my idea," Sanjay insisted. Tempest could have sworn he was speaking to the bunny instead of her. "And I'm not supposed to tell."

"I don't like the sound of that."

"Your grandfather wants me to hold one more séance at Lavinia's house."

"*What?*"

"He's on trial for his life. How can I refuse?" He groaned. "I'm supposed to bring my Cabinet of Curiosities trunk with me."

"The one with those creepy relics?"

"They're plastic and metal, not real bone, but yes. Relic-hunting gear is in there as well, like faux-aged rope and antique silver bullets." He groaned. "Why does this keep happening to me?"

The siren from an ambulance made it impossible to keep talking. Whatever emergency it was heading toward, it was close.

The siren cut off abruptly.

"Did that just stop at your house?" asked Sanjay.

*It had.*

Without another thought, Tempest set Abra back in his cage and ran toward the tree house. Sanjay followed, but fell a few paces behind because he wasn't as familiar with the sloping hillside terrain. When Tempest reached the tree house, her grandfather was already on a stretcher, being looked after by two paramedics.

"What's happened?" Tempest asked her grandmother, who stood nearby with a pale hand clasped over her mouth.

"I need to go with him," Morag whispered as one of the paramedics wheeled the stretcher down the path toward the driveway.

Ash's eyes lit up with horror. At first, Tempest thought it was pain from whatever had happened to his leg, now aggravated by being jostled. His trousers had ripped below the knee, revealing blood beneath.

No. He wasn't reacting to pain. His horrified expression was directed at something. No, *someone*. Ash was staring at Sanjay.

One of the paramedics told Tempest which hospital they were headed to. As Morag climbed into the ambulance to accompany Ash to the hospital, she told Tempest that Ash had fallen down the stairs. Before Tempest could ask anything more, the ambulance doors shut.

"What the hell was that look he gave me?" Sanjay asked as he and Tempest piled into her jeep. "If those EMTs saw Ash looking at me like that, they'll assume his fall wasn't an accident and I'm the person who pushed him down the stairs."

"Ash is steadier on his feet than I am." Tempest rubbed the smooth silver of her charm bracelet to calm herself before starting the engine. "Something isn't right."

"You'll be my alibi, right?"

"What?" Tempest peeled out of the driveway. "Oh. Of

course. Nobody pushed him down the stairs. Stop catastro-phizing."

"I'm the most optimistic person I know. If I think some-thing is bad, it's bad." Sanjay tugged at his collar. "Why was he looking at me like I was the Devil himself?"

"He wasn't. Put on your seat belt."

Sanjay braced his hands against the dashboard. "Try not to kill us on the way to the hospital."

"He wasn't afraid of you. The look on his face was some-thing else."

"What?"

Tempest shook her head. "I don't know yet."

When they arrived at the hospital, it took them a few min-utes to find parking and an even longer amount of time to find Morag. When they finally tracked down someone who could give them information, they found her sitting in a nearly empty waiting room, a tissue in her hand.

"Your grandfather is gone," Morag said.

"Gone?" Tempest stared at her grandmother, barely aware that her legs were turning to jelly.

"*Auch!*" Morag cried, jumping up and grabbing Tempest's arm to steady her. "That's not what it was meant to sound like. He's alive. Ashok Raj is alive and healthier than ever. That's how he's evaded them."

"Evaded them?"

"Your grandfather has escaped."

# Chapter 47

Tempest knew what Ash was doing. And why he'd been horrified to see Sanjay. He didn't want Sanjay to change the plans they'd made.

This was why he'd asked Sanjay to go to Lavinia's house with his Cabinet of Curiosities trunk, which contained a never-ending rope. A rope that Sanjay had used to tie an inescapable knot that only he knew how to get out of.

Tempest banged on the front door of Lavinia's Lair, with Sanjay beside her, holding the antique travel case.

Sylvie was the one to open the door. "We can't keep meeting like this."

Lavinia, Ivy, and Ellery came up behind Sylvie.

Had Tempest gotten things wrong? "The book club is meeting?"

"Not exactly," Lavinia said. "You two should come inside."

"Is . . . anyone else here?" Sanjay asked.

"My mom is in the Oxford Comma."

So Kumiko was there along with the members of the book club. Not Ash. *Where was he?*

"We each received a text message," Ivy explained as they followed her inside, "saying the book club should meet. We were all cleared of suspicion, so we should get back to normality. The texts came from an unknown number, but the person said they were Sylvie, explaining that she'd had to get a new phone since hers was broken during her kidnapping."

"Which doesn't mean I'd need a new number," Sylvie snapped. "If they'd stopped for one moment to use their brains and think rationally, they'd have known it wasn't me."

"Sylvie was fooled as well," Kumiko said from the Oxford Comma doorway. In a black wrap and with angry eyes, she looked far fiercer than the gargoyles looming above her.

"I was only fooled because I received a phone call from someone claiming to be from the police department," Sylvie said. "Not a text message that would have been easy to see through. They said they needed to go over some more details about my kidnapping here on site. When I arrived, the members of the Detection Keys were the only people here."

"Was it a man's voice?" Tempest asked.

Sylvie nodded.

"Was it Houdini here?" Kumiko pointed at Sanjay. "It was you two who set up this ruse to bring us back together, wasn't it?"

"It wasn't them," another voice said. One Tempest knew well. "I'm sorry for the deception, but I had to see you." Ashok Raj stepped into the room. He was wearing a new set of his own clothes, suggesting Morag had helped him.

"Ashok?" Kumiko wheeled up to him.

"Don't, Ma." Lavinia blocked the way.

"Are you ready to confess?" Ash asked Lavinia. "I'd hoped I wouldn't have to plan an escape from my confinement to see you in person. I thought you'd come forward when you saw I wouldn't be freed. I know you didn't mean to frame me."

286 ❅ Gigi Pandian

"You don't really think it was me?"

"I forgive you," he said. "I know your alibi with Victor is fake. I'd hoped I wouldn't have to resort to this, but I needed you all as witnesses."

"I—I really was with Victor," Lavinia sputtered.

"You were," Ash said. "I'm not disputing that. But my granddaughter solving the trick of how Corbin made his way to Hidden Creek gave me the answer for how you both faked your alibi."

"My, my." Sylvie slid away from Lavinia.

"Don't be ridiculous, Ashok," Kumiko said. "My daughter didn't kill Corbin or kidnap Sylvie."

Ash glanced at Sanjay. "If she tries to escape, Sanjay will tie her up with the rope he's got."

"I will?" Sanjay's eyes bulged.

"Why did you think he wanted that specific trunk?" Tempest whispered.

"For the fake bottles of poison," Sanjay whispered back.

"I'm not guilty," Lavinia cried.

"You were 'seen,'" Ash said, "just like Corbin was 'seen' by Hazel. It was a trick using unreliable eyewitness testimony. You ordered take-away coffees at a café that takes online orders through an app. What's to stop someone else from having picked it up? A busy barista isn't a reliable witness."

One of the trickiest things about tricks is that they work in numerous ways. When a magician performs a successful sleight of hand, it's not uncommon for someone to ask them to do it again. The person thinks they know what to look for now. They might. But what a sneaky magician will do is perform the same effect through different means. The deception and the sense of wonder is repeated, but the behind-the-scenes mechanism is different. But Tempest reminded herself this wasn't a magician who had staged this illusion.

Ivy zipped up her pink vest until it covered half her face.

"You were the most likely suspect all along," Ash continued, his eyes full of sadness as he addressed Lavinia. "I don't judge you for killing him. He was a bad man. If you turn yourself in, I believe they'll go easy on you." He turned abruptly. "Don't touch that phone, Sylvie. I see what you're doing. Don't worry. I'll turn myself in as well, as soon as Lavinia confesses. There's no need to call the police."

Tempest stared at Sylvie, her elegant hand poised above her phone.

Sylvie's kidnapping had ruled her out as a suspect, but if not for that, with what they knew now, Sylvie was the person at the séance for whom all of the facts fit. *Almost* all the facts. Corbin's manuscript had alluded to an affair with someone Tempest took to be Ellery, but since the facts about Tempest's family weren't all true, why had she assumed the other plot points were?

When Tempest had spoken to Sylvie in the hospital, Sylvie hadn't accused Lavinia of kidnapping her, *only because the police told her they already knew Lavinia had an alibi*. In making her plan, Sylvie would have assumed that newly single Lavinia would be sleeping alone without an alibi, not with Victor across the bay.

Sylvie was trying to frame Lavinia. *Twice.*

If Tempest hadn't gotten her grandfather a last-minute invitation to the séance, he wouldn't have been the person to get blood on himself—but someone else would have. Again, it was Lavinia who was being set up. Without Ash there, Lavinia would have been the natural person to look at the body of the man she once loved. If she hadn't immediately gone to him, Sylvie could have easily goaded her.

"Grandpa Ash," Tempest said, "we both got it wrong. Sanjay, I need you to get out that rope. For Sylvie."

# Chapter 48

G et away from me!" Sylvie shrieked. With a look of utter disgust directed at Tempest, she stomped toward the exit.

Ash took a step forward. He was limping. He really had hurt his leg as part of his trick to escape. In spite of the injury, he looked as if he was ready to tackle her if necessary, a chance Tempest didn't want to take. She knelt at the hooves of the merry-go-round horse. They'd put casters on his legs to slide him across the floor without damaging it, and instead of removing the wheels had locked them. She unlocked the wheels and shoved.

The wooden horse slid across the floor toward Sylvie. Ash caught it as Sylvie fell across its saddle.

"You're all crazy." Sylvie pushed herself up, causing the horse to teeter for a moment before crashing down across the opening leading to the hallway out.

"Don't try to climb over him," Ash said. "Tempest, you have the floor."

Sylvie glared at him but didn't speak.

"I thought Ellery was having an affair with Corbin because

of what I thought was a clue he left behind," Tempest said. "I thought he was having an affair with someone who both dyed their hair and was *named after* a literary character, just like a character he wrote named Alice. My assumptions were wrong about both. First, I only had the literary allusion half right. Sylvie's neighbor told me she collects records and has them delivered from an 'LP' shop. The packages her neighbor saw weren't of records. They were signed, 'Lord Peter.' She thinks of herself as a literary character who's the love interest of Lord Peter Whimsey. And even though Ellery's hair dye is obvious, Sylvie presents an outward impression that's so put-together that I didn't even think about the fact that she probably dyes her hair. *Sylvie* was the one having an affair with Corbin. Not Ellery."

"Sanjay." Ash pointed at the rope in his hand. "Time to use that."

"Get. Away." Sylvie tried to slip around Sanjay, but Sanjay was faster.

"Are you absolutely sure about this?" Sanjay asked Tempest.

"Ninety-nine percent," she said.

"Great," Sanjay muttered. "I'm not going to tie anyone up, but nobody climbs over the horsey to leave. If you do, I'll change my mind."

"This is kidnapping," Sylvie said.

"Go ahead and tie her up," Ellery said. "Tempest isn't wrong about the clues she found. Not at all. I'm not the only person in this room named after a character. Sylvie is named after *Sylvie and Bruno* by Lewis Carrol, who also wrote *Alice's Adventures in Wonderland*. I know that little tidbit because that's how the two of us first bonded over books, in spite of our other differences."

Tempest groaned inwardly. She'd jumped to the obvious

conclusion about Ellery's name, so she hadn't even stopped to consider more direct possible parallels in Corbin's sly references.

"And yes," Ellery continued, "though she's never admitted it, at one of our meetings I spotted a millimeter of white in just a few strands of Sylvie's hair."

Sylvie narrowed her eyes at Ellery. "I don't have to stay here and listen to these insults."

"I'd like to hear the rest of what Tempest has to say." Kumiko wheeled herself in front of the fallen horse.

"As would I." Lavinia joined her mom in blocking the exit.

"*Why* kill Corbin in such a convoluted way?" Tempest asked. "Impossible in four separate ways. You were all there when we solved the four impossibilities. The fake knife covering a real wound, a person materializing fifty-five miles away in a matter of minutes, a body hidden where there was nowhere to hide one, and a dead body landing on the séance table with nobody breaking hands. I explained the mechanics last night, but that was just one big piece of the puzzle. I was missing the lynchpin." Tempest held her breath and hoped she was right. "Sylvie's kidnapping wasn't real."

"I'm calling the police now." Sylvie felt around inside her purse, getting more frantic by the second.

"Looking for this?" Ash held up her phone. He tossed it from his left hand to his right, disappearing the phone before it hit his right palm.

"I was so focused on the puzzle," Tempest said to a fuming Sylvie, "which was just as shortsighted as the police being so focused on the physical evidence implicating my grandfather. I lost sight of why it was necessary to kill Corbin Colt *at the séance*." She paused. "It was necessary because Sylvie wanted to frame Lavinia for Corbin's murder."

"Sylvie?" Lavinia gasped. "Why?"

Sylvie said nothing.

"Her plan went wrong in several ways," said Tempest. "Having a complex crime come together must have been more difficult than it appears in books. People have their own free will. They don't act like you imagine they would."

"Ashok wasn't supposed to be there," Kumiko said.

"My grandfather jumped up immediately and tried to help Corbin, meaning Sylvie couldn't get Lavinia to be the one to inspect the body; she thought she'd be able to get Lavinia to do so since it was her husband. Sylvie planned to kill Corbin in the second wave of darkness and then say something to the effect of, 'Lavinia, your stupid ex is playing a practical joke on us, you need to smack him and make him stop,' so that Lavinia would get blood on herself.

"Sylvie's plan had started well. She set it up to be believable that Lavinia wanted to kill Corbin. That's why she wrecked Lavinia's beloved typewriter. Sylvie knew Lavinia would be furious and blame Corbin, and we'd all be able to testify about Lavinia's outrage. Things went downhill from there.

"The fake kidnapping was a desperate move. Sylvie even had to take the risk of injuring herself, but a bit of research reveals that superficial head wounds can produce enough blood to look scary. My grandfather remained the one charged. She needed to try again to frame Lavinia. The kidnapping was meant to make it look like *Lavinia* was desperate. She didn't know Lavinia wouldn't be at home at five in the morning. It was a good bet that Lavinia would be, but unfortunately, she was wrong in her assumption.

"I don't know how much she cares about sending an innocent man to prison, but making her rival Lavinia suffer was a huge part of this plan being a success in her mind. Sylvie copied Lavinia's key, which is how she was able to fake the kidnapping. That's why there was putty on Lavinia's key the day after the murder. I didn't realize what it was at the time when she met me at the Whispering Creek Theater, but there was something sticky on her keys then. Because Sylvie had made an impression of her keys."

Sylvie's gaze was unreadable. "Anyone could have done that. Her bag—"

*Snap.*

A movement appeared outside the window of Lavinia's Lair at the same time as the sound.

A raven.

Only this raven wasn't a large bird. It was a full-size person. One wearing the beaked black mask of a medieval plague doctor like the one from Tempest's notebook.

Tempest stared in horror at the living incarnation of her raven sketch.

# Chapter 49

*S*nap.

All eyes were on the horrifying figure as its beak hit the window again.

*How had the raven from Tempest's notebook come to life?*

Ivy's hands flew to her mouth.

"*Ada-kaduvulae*," Ash murmured.

"How . . . ?" Sylvie's voice trembled.

"What the . . . ?" Even Sanjay's voice wasn't steady.

Kumiko's hands gripped the arms of her wheelchair.

Beyond those small gestures and exclamations, nobody moved. It was as if they had been frozen in place. Tempest wasn't immune. She knew, rationally, that she couldn't be seeing what she was. There had to be another explanation. A trick. Had her grandfather planned this? From the shocked look on his face, she seriously doubted it.

The raven's head tilted to one side, as if it was examining the curious specimens through the glass.

Though Tempest couldn't see his face, there was something familiar about the movement. *Her notebook . . .* She'd left it in her car when she'd gathered the suspects together at midnight. That was right after her abandoned call to Moriarty. Even though they hadn't spoken, he'd have seen that she called. Had he broken into her car?

Tempest willed herself to run out the door and find out for certain, but another glance at Sylvie gave her a better idea. She wasn't going to wait and see what Moriarty might do. She could take this distraction and turn it to her advantage.

"The Raven," Tempest stage-whispered loudly enough to command the room. "He's returned." She drew her arm up slowly, until her outstretched hand pointed dramatically at the raven figure. It was an overly dramatic gesture outside of a theater, but her instincts were good. Nobody moved. They all stared in rapt attention at the intimidating figure beyond the window.

"It can't be." Sylvie's voice shook. She lumbered toward the window, as if compelled.

*Snap.*

The beak hit the window so hard the glass shook. Sylvie faltered, then kept moving. With each slow step, it looked as if she dragged an invisible boulder behind her. In a few seconds she'd be close enough to see it was simply a man in a costume.

"Be gone, Raven!" Tempest commanded.

He cocked his head. Though Tempest couldn't see his eyes, she swore she could feel them. Tempest was certain it was Moriarty in a steampunk costume that looked real through the glass. Well . . . *relatively* certain.

"Be gone," Tempest repeated.

The figure wearing the black beak gave Tempest a nearly imperceptible nod. He raised his arms, swooped as if taking flight—then disappeared.

Sylvie screamed and collapsed onto the floor.

"I think you have something to tell us," Tempest said

gently. Sylvie wasn't looking at her, so she allowed herself a glance at the window. Nothing but trees were visible beyond the glass. She knew the figure had neither taken flight nor disappeared. The window didn't reach the ground. All he'd had to do was swoop down theatrically to vanish from their line of sight.

"Lavinia ruined everything," Sylvie sobbed. "Years ago, Corbin stole my heart. I was his muse. Not Lavinia. I was the one who made him feel special. I was the one who kept him going even when his books got less popular. I knew we wouldn't have a real future together, but what we had was enough. There was no expectation he'd leave Lavinia. He was comfortable in his life here. The kind of comfort you get from a ratty bathrobe or a broken-in old shoe."

"An old shoe?" Lavinia repeated in a whisper. "That's what you really think of me?"

"He loved you, in a way," Sylvie said, "but I was the one who inspired him. I accepted that we had no future together. I was the tragic heroine of a great book. A secret love affair that could never see the light of day. My lover died. That's what people inferred when I told them I couldn't be with my beloved in this life."

"But you killed him," Lavinia's voice was stronger now. "The man you claim to have loved—"

"Only when I learned that I wasn't special at all." Sylvie wiped her hands across her tear-stained cheeks. "It was only a few months ago that I learned Corbin was so unhappy with Lavinia that he had been having a string of affairs over the course of his marriage, including this new young inter-net star . . . that was too much. He betrayed me. They both did."

"Sanjay." Kumiko nudged him. "You'd better tie her up now."

"I'm telling you what you want to know," Sylvie seethed. "You don't have to restrain me."

"She's worried about her daughter's safety," Ash said, not unkindly.

"She's not in danger." The fury in Sylvie's voice belied the sentiment. "I don't want Lavinia to die. Only suffer. Corbin was the one who didn't deserve to live. He was clueless as to the effect he had on so many lives. To him, our affair was no big deal. He loved the adoration of women and even expected it. He was beautiful. A Greek god with raven hair. Of course women would throw themselves at his feet. He thought he was good to us because he made us feel special, so no harm done. He never hid the fact that he was married. But as an *artiste*, he couldn't be shackled by monogamy."

Sylvie broke off and laughed without humor. A small smile formed on her lips before she spoke again. "That was also his weakness. He didn't find it suspicious when I called and told him about the séance to burn his papers he left behind. 'I left notes behind?' he said. He hadn't realized he'd done so, but I knew it wouldn't be suspicious because he wrote so much on paper. Plus, he wouldn't put it past Lavinia to steal important notes of his, just to make him suffer. I was also the one who planted the idea in Lavinia's mind to have a cathartic bonfire. Corbin also knew I loved his writing— it's so much better than people gave him credit for—so he didn't find it suspicious that I'd tell him I was offended that Lavinia was going to burn his manuscript notes.

"It was so easy to string him along, making him feel like it was his own idea to use the séance as a dramatic opportunity to play a practical joke on Lavinia. Then Corbin would be able to publicly shame her for stealing his precious words that she had no right to burn, taking back the pages after the 'practical joke' was over, before she could burn his work.

All I had to do was play to his ego, which wasn't difficult at all."

"I understand how you manipulated him," Tempest said. "But killing him in such a short time?"

"I practiced hundreds of times putting latex gloves on and off quickly, and where to stab someone to be sure to get his heart so he'd die quickly, leaving the thin blade inside him so they wouldn't look for my gloves but would instead look for the weapon. You were right about the tape you mentioned, when you thought it was Ellery. I couldn't be certain I got things absolutely right, so I had to confuse things as much as possible, but still make sure everything pointed toward Lavinia. But because Ashok was a doctor who could know how to stab someone in the heart and had blood on his hands, he became the main suspect. Not Lavinia. I didn't know about the restraining order, either.

"People don't always do what you want them to when you manipulate them," Sylvie concluded. "It's not like in one of our book-club books. It's a lot harder to frame someone than you'd think."

# Chapter 50

The rest of the day was a blur. Tempest gave her statement to the police, then she and her grandfather were able to explain to her dad and grandmother everything that had happened with Sylvie's confession.

Well, *almost* everything. Tempest strongly suspected that Moriarty was the raven. She believed that in his own twisted way he wanted to help her. He had time to get back from Scotland. For all Tempest knew, he might have spoken to her from the same flight back as Grannie Mor had been on. He hadn't been in touch since the incident with the person in a creepy beaked plague doctor mask at the window of Lavinia's Lair, but she expected he would be. It was only a question of *when*.

Ash was back in the hospital, where he'd returned on his own. Vanessa was making sure all charges against Ash were dropped as quickly as possible. Since he wasn't the one who'd cut off his ankle monitor, and there was no evidence he hadn't simply accidentally fallen down the stairs and hurt his leg, Vanessa was also arguing he wasn't responsible for breaking the conditions of his bail. He was back at the hospital after just a couple of hours, after all. Perhaps he'd simply gotten lost in the labyrinthine hallways of the hospital, Vanessa suggested. Anything was possible.

Darius had a secret of his own he finally told Tempest. She prepared herself for him to say he was dating someone. Instead, he said, "I've been working on building a pop-up stage for you to do performances whenever and wherever you'd like to do them. I knew that even though you're doing your one last send-off show, performing is still in your blood. I wanted you to have an easy way to perform whenever you wanted to. The stage folds to fit in my truck. I didn't want to work on it at the workshop, since I wanted it to be a surprise."

"I thought you were wearing a strong aftershave when you came home the other night."

"Eau de paintvarnish."

Tempest laughed and threw her arms around her dad's shoulders.

For the first time since Corbin Colt's death, Tempest felt her body relax. She climbed up her secret staircase and lay down on her bed. She told herself it was only for a minute, but when the beep of a text message alerted her that her grandfather was back home, she saw that she'd been asleep for hours.

"I knew Tempest could solve it." Ash rocked back and forth on his heels happily as he stirred a pot of jaggery coffee. "Now, have you eaten?"

Tempest enjoyed a hearty dinner with her family, then headed to a second dinner at Veggie Magic with her friends. One she was late to.

She hadn't expected Lavinia to show up at her café after all that had happened, but she was already sitting with Sanjay, Gideon, and Ivy when Tempest arrived at Veggie Magic, stuffed from the three-course dinner from her grandfather. She was glad to see they'd eaten without her and were already having dessert and coffee.

Lavinia stood and gave Tempest a hug. "Thank you, Tempest. For everything."

"Sorry I had to wreck the merry-go-round horse."

"Are you kidding?" Lavinia pulled up an extra chair for Tempest and they both sat down at the table. "That act of destruction has completed the christening of the space as my own."

"You make a great pie," Sanjay said, "but I don't have a clue what you're talking about."

"I think she means," Tempest said, "that the classic mystery novels that inspired the distinct sections of Lavinia's Lair each factored into solving the mystery."

Lavinia grinned. "Do you want to tell them?"

"No spoilers," Ivy cut in. "In case Sanjay and Gideon haven't read the books."

Tempest moved her empty right hand over her empty left hand. The king of hearts now rested in her palm, the face card with a sword appearing to cut through the king's head. "During the events this week, we encountered a person we believed to be dead but who wasn't."

Tempest smacked her hand on the table. The queen of hearts took the suicide king's place. "We also had a woman who created a very devious plan because she believed she had been in love."

She twirled the queen of hearts between her fingers as she decided which card would best represent the Oxford Comma. When the card stopped spinning, she opened her palm and revealed the jack of clubs. The lowest-ranked face card that also represents knowledge. "And the whole thing began and ended at the Oxford Comma pub, which transported us in our imaginations to the British university town."

"Bravo." Ivy clapped.

"Nice sleights," Sanjay said, "but I still have no idea what you're talking about."

"Guess you'd better read the classics," Ivy said.

Gideon picked up the jack of clubs and inspected the edges. "It's a regular card. How did you—"

"She's not available for private lessons." Sanjay snatched the card from him.

"I wasn't ask—"

"You were totally—"

"I solved the mystery of the raven who likes to watch my house," Lavinia said, silencing them both. "He was Corbin's half-domesticated pet. I was cleaning up the house and found a bag of hidden dog food. We've never had a dog. I visited our local pet store. The manager remembered Corbin. Said he bought it to *feed a crow* in his yard. That's why it was always near the house. Corbin loved the mystery it conveyed, so he never told me there was a rational explanation."

Ivy groaned. "I can't believe I let a cute little bird freak me out."

"Now that I know the truth," Lavinia said, "I rather like the fellow. He's incredibly intelligent."

"I doubt the raven will stick around if you take in Lord Peter," said Tempest.

"Ellery is taking Sylvie's dog. He'll be looked after well. Now I should get back to the kitchen. Can I bring you anything, Tempest?"

"Just coffee." After the week she'd had, she would have taken an IV drip of coffee.

"Then the only mystery that remains," Sanjay said, still eyeing Gideon as the stone-carving carver inspected the playing card, "is what happened to Corbin's car."

It was far from the only mystery Corbin Colt had left Tempest, but this wasn't the time to think about his manuscript.

"They found his car this morning," Lavinia said as she stood. "It was parked in the big parking structure around the corner. Since they didn't end up charging for people to park there, nobody noticed it hadn't been moved in days."

"That's not the only mystery remaining," Ivy pointed out after Lavinia disappeared into the kitchen. "Who was in the raven-beaked plague-doctor costume?"

Sanjay blinked at her. "Ash set that up. Didn't he?"

All eyes turned to Tempest. She held up her hands. "He's not talking. I expect it's to protect the innocent."

"That plague doctor was anything but innocent." Ivy shivered.

"That makes sense," Gideon said. "Ash doesn't want to get his helper involved any more than necessary."

"Do you think Lavinia will be okay?" Ivy asked.

"*I'm* not okay." Sanjay speared a piece of blackberry pie with his fork but didn't eat it. "It's terribly embarrassing that my only role in solving this case was to stand at the sidelines and hold a rope."

"I don't know," said Tempest. "You did a lot more than that. All three of you did. Thank you."

☠☠☠

Tempest lifted the dragon's wing that opened her secret staircase. As the secret door slid open, she stood on the threshold for a moment and appreciated what she'd accomplished. She had solved Corbin Colt's mysterious murder and saved her grandfather.

She stepped forward onto the staircase. Moving forward. Always. She'd helped bring one killer to justice, but there was more to do. Corbin's notes in his duplicitous manuscript might help her solve her aunt's murder and her mom's disappearance. The accusations about Tempest's dad weren't true, but Corbin had noticed other things. Now that she wasn't so angry and scared, she could see it. Tempest could use the clues from Corbin Colt's manuscript to assist her in finding out what had really happened to her family. She was a step closer to figuring out the real answer behind the Raj family curse that had taken her aunt and mom from her.

Tempest's phone alerted her to a missed call. Her manager, Winston, left a message asking her to call him back right away. Tempest's role in solving the murder of Corbin Colt was great publicity, he said. He wanted to talk more about what she was planning for her final televised stage show. Tempest wasn't yet sure what it would look like. But she knew one thing. Whatever it was, it would be magic.

## Cardamom Chocolate Chip Scones

*Under 45 minutes. Makes approximately 15 scones.*

INGREDIENTS
    1 1/4 cups unsweetened almond milk
    2 teaspoons apple cider vinegar
    3 cups all-purpose flour
    1/2 cup powdered jaggery or 1/3 cup brown sugar +
    optional 2 tablespoons for topping
    2 tablespoons baking powder
    1 teaspoon cardamom
    1/4 teaspoon salt
    1/3 cup coconut oil, room temperature (not melted)
    1/4 cup canola oil
    1/2 cup chocolate chips
    Optional blackberry jam topping—*see recipe below.*

Preheat oven to 400 degrees F.

Pour the unsweetened almond milk and apple cider vinegar into a small bowl, stir, and set aside for 10 minutes while you prepare the rest of the ingredients. The mixture will develop a tangy buttermilk-like flavor.

Mix the flour, sugar of choice, cardamom, baking powder, and salt in a large bowl.

Using your fingers or a pastry cutter, mix room-temperature or cold coconut oil into the flour mixture. It will not fully combine but will look lumpy.

Pour the almond milk mixture and canola oil into the bowl and fold until a lumpy dough is formed. Do not overmix or knead.

Stir the chocolate chips into the mixture.

Use a 1/4 cup measuring cup to scoop dough onto two baking trays lined with parchment paper. Depending on the shape of your scooper, you might want to press the scones down so they're a bit flatter than tall. You'll end up with approximately 15 scones.

Optional: dust the tops with sugar of choice before popping the trays into the oven.

Bake for 15 minutes, until the bottoms have lightly browned.

NOTES:
Jaggery is an unprocessed sugar, common in India, that you can find at Indian grocery stores or online. It's a bit less sweet than other sugars, which is why the sugar substitution calls for a different amount.

If you freeze leftover scones, for best results reheat in an oven or toaster oven for approximately 5 minutes at 350 degrees F, not in a microwave.

## Blackberry Jam

*Twenty minutes—make it after you pop your scones into the oven!*

INGREDIENTS
- 1 10-ounce bag of frozen blackberries
- 2 teaspoons freshly squeezed lemon juice
- 1 tablespoon maple syrup
- 1/4 teaspoon cardamom
- 1/4 teaspoon ginger
- 1 tablespoon chia seeds

Stir all ingredients except for the chia seeds in a saucepan. Simmer on medium heat for 10 minutes. Stir in the chia seeds and cook for 5 more minutes. Let rest for 5 minutes to thicken.

Serve over scones (or oatmeal or pancakes).

Keep extra in a sealed glass jar in the fridge for up to a week.

### Turmeric Pizza

*Two hours from start to finish, but less than half of the time is hands-on. Makes one two-person pizza*

SPICED DOUGH INGREDIENTS
- 1 1/2 cups bread flour
- 1 teaspoon instant yeast
- 1 teaspoon turmeric
- 1/2 teaspoon coriander
- 1/2 teaspoon cumin
- 1/2 teaspoon fenugreek seeds
- 1/2 teaspoon chili powder
- Dash of black pepper
- 1 teaspoon salt
- 3/4 cup lukewarm water
- 1 tablespoon olive oil

JACKFRUIT PIZZA TOPPING INGREDIENTS

- 1 14-ounce can green jackfruit
- 1 tablespoon olive oil
- 1 onion, diced
- 4 garlic cloves, minced
- 1/2 teaspoon chili powder
- 1/2 teaspoon turmeric
- 1/4 teaspoon black pepper
- 1/4 teaspoon salt
- 1/4 cup tomato paste
- 1/2 cup water

Prepare the dough: In a large bowl, mix the dry ingredients, then add the water and olive oil. On a clean surface, knead the dough for 5 minutes (or you can use a bread mixer if you have one). Put the dough back in the bowl and let rest for at least one hour, until it has doubled in size.

Half an hour before you want to bake your pizza, preheat a pizza stone in an oven set to 475 degrees F and prepare your toppings.

Drain and rinse the jackfruit, then break it apart with your fingers so it's in small bite-size pieces and set aside. Sauté the onion in the olive oil for 15 minutes until it begins to cara-melize. Add the minced garlic, chili powder, and salt. After 30 seconds, stir in the tomato paste. After everything has come together, add the jackfruit and water. Simmer on medium-low for 15 minutes. When the water has mostly evaporated, the tasty topping is ready to be spread out on top of the pizza.

Once the dough has doubled in size, roll it out until it's 1/4 inch thick. You can do this with a rolling pin or simply use your hands to pull it apart. Spread the topping evenly on top of the pizza dough.

Bake on the preheated pizza stone for 20 minutes.

Serves two people for a hearty dinner, or more as a side dish.

NOTES:
The jackfruit topping is flavorful enough on its own, but you can add mozzarella or any cheese of choice on top. See the recipes page of Gigi's website for a homemade vegan mozzarella.

For ease of transferring the pizza into the oven, a pizza peel dusted with plenty of cornmeal works well, as does oven-safe parchment paper.

Want to serve four people instead of two? Double the recipe, but cut the dough in half to make two pizzas.

# Acknowledgments

Writing a book is far from a solitary pursuit, and I appreciate so many people who've helped on the journey to create this book. My amazing editor, Madeline Houpt, as well as the whole team at St. Martin's and Minotaur Books who worked on the book: Kirsten Aldrich, Rowen Davis, Gabriel Guma, Sarah Haeckel, Sarah Melnyk, Mac Nicholas, and Ken Silver. Jill Marsal, the best agent a writer could ask for. My family, for being my biggest cheerleaders and always encouraging me, even when I know it's not fun to be ignored for hours at a time when I enter my writing cave.

Thanks to critique readers Nancy Adams, James Scott Byrnside, Shelly Dickson Carr, Naomi Hirahara, Jeffrey Marks, Emberly Nesbitt, Sue Parman, and Brian Selfon; my brilliant weekly brainstorm writers group with Ellen Byron, Lisa Mathews, and Diane Vallere; writing-date meet-up pals Mysti Berry and Lynn Coddington; so many other friends whose support I'm grateful for, including Leslie Bacon, Juliet Blackwell, and Kellye Garrett; and the groups that give me so much support, especially Crime Writers of Color, Sisters in Crime, and Mystery Writers of America.

I need to thank the traditional mystery writers who came

before me. The Secret Staircase mysteries were inspired by classic locked-room mysteries, from my favorite Golden Age of detective fiction author John Dickson Carr to the many classic Japanese mystery writers I'm only now discovering thanks to publishers translating their books into English. I've always loved this style of traditional mystery with puzzle plots and without much violence, and I wanted to put my own spin on the genre to bring it into the twenty-first century with Tempest Raj. *The Raven Thief* is the second book in the series, and I have many more mysteries in store for Tempest.

And a heartfelt thanks to my readers for being kindred spirits who love losing themselves in a twisty mystery. I always appreciate hearing from readers. You can get in touch and sign up for my email newsletter at www.gigipandian.com.